Prey on Patmos

Books by Jeffrey Siger

Murder in Mykonos
Assassins of Athens
Prey on Patmos

Prey on Patmos

An Inspector Kaldis Mystery

Jeffrey Siger

Poisoned Pen Press

First Edition 2011

10 9 8 7 6 5 4 3 2 1

Library of Congress Catalog Card Number: 2010932079

ISBN: 9781590587669 Hardcover
9781590587683 Trade Paperback

Poisoned Pen Press
6962 E. First Ave., Ste. 103
Scottsdale, AZ 85251
www.poisonedpenpress.com
info@poisonedpenpress.com

Printed in the United States of America

To my children, Jonathan and Karen,
and my grandchildren. All joy.

Acknowledgments

Antonia Antoniou; Roz and Mihalis Apostolou; Olga Balafa; Heather and Danny Baror; Eleni Bistika; Merrill Bookstein; Nikos Christodoulakis and Jody Duncan; Terry Dempsey; Violetta Ekpe; Omiros Evangelinos; Andreas and Aleca Fiorentinos; Irene Gouras; Nicholas Griblas; Nikos Ipiotis; Nikos Karahalios; Olga Kefalogianni; Panos Kelaidis; Kristina Klivan; Nicholas and Sonia Kotopoulos; Artemis Kousathanas; Lila and Ilias Lalaounis; Linda Marshall; Robert McElroy; Terry Moon; Nikos Nazos; Renee Pappas; Babis Pasaoglou; Barbara G. Peters and Robert Rosenwald; Theodore, Manos, and Irene Rousounelous; Eileen Salzig; Christine Schnitzer-Smith; Beth Schnitzer; Raghu Shivaram; Giora Shpigel; Deppy Sigala; Alan, Patricia, Frederick, Steven, and Carli Siger; Jonathan, Jennifer, Azriel, and Gavriella Siger; Karen Siger; Mihalis Sigounas and Carsten Stehr; Greg and Valerie Kuchulis Simvoulakis; George and Efi Sirinakis; Konstantine Sougkas; Ed Stackler; George and Theodore Stamoulis; Pavlos Tiftikidis; Jessica Tribble; Nikos Touratzidis; Steve Tzolis, Nicola and Angelica S. Kotsoni; Sotiris Varotsis; Miltiadis Varvitziotis; Carolina Wells.

And, of course, Aikaterini Lalaouni.

Author's Note

In antiquity, Greeks were driven to action by their gods. Today, Greece is a land of unwavering faith in God and a unique commitment to the Eastern Orthodox Church as an integral part of its way of life. To write about Greece and ignore the church is as foolhardy as any surgeon seeking to understand his patient without attending to the heart. This, though, is a story, made-up, a fiction. It touches upon faith in a manner intended to compliment and complement, not offend. But if I failed, I apologize.

Patmos

Livadi Kalogiron

Lambi

Kambos

Skala

Chora

N

S

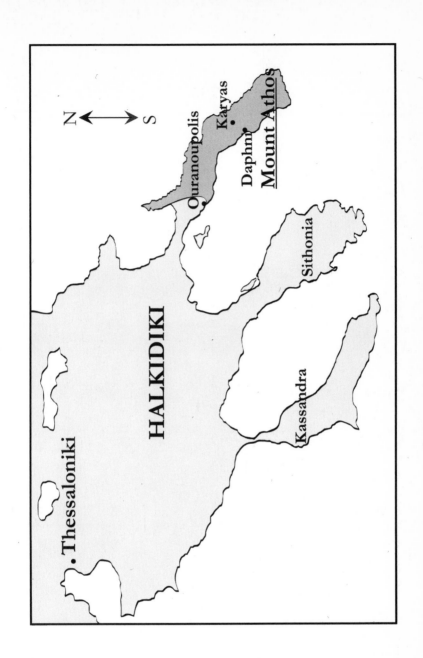

Chapter One

There was an unnatural cadence to the man's walk. Maybe it was the uneven stone lane. But he'd walked this path ten thousand times, though not so soon before first light. Still, he knew it well enough. He paused, as if to listen, then moved five paces and paused again. In the shadows outside the monastery's wall, his black monk's *rasso* was long enough to conceal his body and the short, flat-topped *kalimafki* his hair, but neither hid his snow-white beard. Perhaps he should have been looking as carefully as he listened, but it wouldn't have mattered. The men stood quietly at the bottom of the path, just beyond where it opened into the town square. He could not see them.

Andreas had told Lila he'd be home early. Forget about it. Here he was yelling over the noise of a military helicopter commandeered by his boss, the minister of public order, to get Chief Inspector Andreas Kaldis, head of the Greek Police's Special Crimes Division, and his assistant, detective Yianni Kouros, out of Athens and over to a northern Dodecanese island close to Turkey "before all hell breaks loose."

"There's no reason for him tossing this mess in our laps. No damn reason at all."

Kouros shrugged. "I don't know, Chief, maybe the minister thought a monk turning up murdered the Sunday before Easter in the middle of the town square on the Holy Island of Patmos qualified as a special crime?"

Andreas ignored him. They'd worked together long enough for him to let the younger man tease him, at least when they were alone. Besides, Kouros was right. Throat cut, everything but the monk's crosses taken. Hard to imagine anyone who'd kill a monk being considerate enough to leave them behind.

The two-hundred-mile flight east from Athens took a little more than forty minutes. They landed at a heliport next to a hilltop military installation. There was no airport on Patmos, and lacking permission to land a helicopter, the only way to reach the island was by boat.

Patmos was a nine-mile-long, thirteen-square-mile, dark beige and green ribbon of fertile valleys, rocky hills, eclectic beaches, and crystal blue bays. Slightly more than half the size of New York City's Manhattan, with three thousand permanent residents, it was far less developed for tourism than the better known western Aegean Greek islands of Mykonos and Santorini. Visitors came here for serenity and a slower-paced, spiritual holiday, seeking enrichment for the soul rather than excitement for the body—or so the church liked to think.

The road from the heliport snaked south, down toward the port area known as *skala*, with its ubiquitous one-, two-, and occasional three-story buildings filled with tourist shops, restaurants, hotels, bars, and clubs facing east across the harborside road. The police car made its way through the port, turned right at the first road past the post office, and headed toward the mountain road leading to Patmos' ancient *chora*, perhaps the most desired and beautiful village in all of Greece. During the summer, its quiet lanes and simple but elegant stone houses were home to members of Greece's former royal family, current and past government leaders, and understated wealth and power from around the world.

Andreas sat behind the driver as the police car wound its way up to Chora along a two-mile band of road lined with eucalyptus. It was Andreas' first time on the island, and like every other tourist, he couldn't help but stare down toward the port.

It was an extraordinary view: green fields and olive trees against a sapphire sea laced with muted brown-green islands running off to the horizon, a scene from antiquity.

The driver said, "Locals say this is the same view as he had when he wrote *The Book*." He paused. "And right over there is where he did it."

Andreas didn't have to ask who *he* was. On Patmos there was only one *he*. They were almost halfway up the mountain and tourist buses were parked everywhere.

"The entrance to *The Cave* is over there." The driver gestured with his head to the left. "You should see it if you have the chance."

Andreas thought to remind the young cop that this was a murder investigation, not a sightseeing tour. But he let it pass. After all, this spot was hallowed ground to much of the world: the cave where Saint John wrote the Book of Revelation, the apocalyptic tale of the end of the world—or its beginning, depending on your point of view.

"Take a look at that." It was Kouros pointing up the hill toward a monastery. It dominated the hilltop.

"That's the Monastery of Saint John the Divine. It controls the island. What the monastery wants, it gets. What it doesn't want, doesn't happen," said the driver.

Andreas looked up, wondering not for the first time, why me? Yes, theoretically his unit had jurisdiction over any crime in Greece considered serious enough to warrant special attention, a unique and feared position in a politically sensitive department, but for practical purposes there was no way he could keep up with all the serious, big-time crime threatening Athens, let alone the rest of Greece. Sometimes he wondered if that might have been the plan: give him too much to do to accomplish a single thing. If so, he'd sure as hell surprised more than a few high-profile bad guys now serving time.

I've never been here, Andreas thought. I have no connections here. Why did the minister say I'm "the only one in Greece" qualified to conduct this investigation? The Byzantine thinking of his superiors never ceased to amaze him. If this was just a mugging turned cutthroat, as the Patmos cops had reported to the ministry in Athens, they were far more qualified than he to find the locals responsible. On the other hand, if there were something more, the ministry knew better than to expect political correctness or a coverup from Andreas. Threats and tenders of bribes only pissed him off more. Perhaps this was one of those rare cases where politicians didn't care about scandal as long as the guilty were caught. Yeah, and maybe he should go back to believing in the tooth fairy.

At the crest of the hill, just before the road began twisting down the other side of the mountain, the driver made a sharp right turn. A bus stood a hundred-fifty yards ahead, waiting its turn to discharge a load of tourists and pilgrims to the monastery. There was nothing to do but wait. A man in a black baseball cap marked GO STEELERS in gold lettering stood slowly spinning a rack of postcards outside a souvenir kiosk. From the hat and the camera around his neck, Andreas assumed he was a tourist. On any other island, he'd also assume the man was in the midst of one of those epiphanies overwhelming to so many first-time visitors as they gazed at a host of "Hi from Greece" postcards adorned with nudes and body parts arranged in mind-boggling positions. But here, so close to the monastery, he doubted such commerce was allowed. Then again, this was Greece, and business was business.

Once the bus moved, the car passed through a barrier prohibiting all but authorized vehicles up into a tiny town square overlooking Skala and the sea. They parked beside Patmos' neoclassical town hall of white plaster, beige stone, and pale blue wood trim. Andreas looked across the square. He felt as if he'd stepped back in time, to the eleventh century to be exact. But, today, this was the scene of a twenty-first century murder. Time to get to work.

"Yianni, find who's in charge."

Kouros walked toward three cops on the other side of the square steering the curious and a TV crew away from a lightweight, black plastic tarp surrounded by blaze orange cones of the sort commonly seen guarding potholes.

Andreas was always amazed at how quickly the media got to a crime scene. This crew must be local, or maybe from a neighboring island, probably Kos. No way a crew from Athens could have beaten him here. They'd never get permission to land a helicopter to cover this story. But they'd arrive soon enough. This was too lurid for the press to miss.

The tarp covered an area roughly three times the size of a man and ten feet or so from the entrance to a narrow lane running off between two white buildings. Four more lanes led off the square, all paved in stones of different shapes and sizes.

Kouros waved to Andreas and pointed at one of the cops. Andreas walked to where they were standing.

"Hello, Chief Inspector, my name is Mavros," said the man with Kouros.

From his stripes Andreas could tell he was a sergeant. Andreas nodded. "Where's your captain?"

"He's in a meeting with the mayor and said not to be disturbed. But I can answer your questions."

"How about, 'Where's the body?'"

The sergeant looked surprised. "Back in the monastery. Being prepared for the funeral." In the Greek Orthodox Church, burial occurred as soon as possible after death, absent complicating circumstances such as murder.

The captain in charge of the island's police was too busy making political nice-nice to meet with the chief inspector of special crimes at the murder site. He'd let the body be moved and tampered with before Andreas had the chance to examine it. If someone wanted Andreas to conduct a real investigation, he sure as hell didn't bother to tell the Patmos police.

Andreas drew in and let out a breath. "Any idea of the time of death?"

"Between two-thirty and three in the morning."

Andreas nodded. "Take off the tarp."

The sergeant paused.

Andreas smiled and patted the sergeant on the arm. "I'm sorry, I meant to say, 'Take off the tarp, *please.*'"

"Chief, there's blood everywhere. We can't let the tourists see that."

So that's why the corpse was gone, thought Andreas. "Who told you to move the body?"

The sergeant hesitated. "It's Easter Week. We couldn't leave a holy man lying dead in the middle of the town square."

That's what Easter Week is all about, thought Andreas. A holy man's death in public view. He hoped that wasn't a clue. Some twisted psycho murdering monks was more than he wanted to think about.

Andreas turned to Kouros. "Yianni, do you think he's having trouble with my accent?"

Kouros shrugged.

Andreas turned back to the sergeant. "Please, just tell me, '*Who told you to move the body?*'" Andreas still was smiling, but not in a way meant to calm a sergeant heading toward a pension.

"The abbot thought it disrespectful to the church." The sergeant paused. "But we videotaped and photographed everything."

Great, thought Andreas. Now I've got the police chief, the mayor, and the head of the monastery working together at screwing up this investigation. He shook his head. "Just move everybody back and lift the tarp."

"The captain said not to touch it without his okay." Now he sounded as if he were giving an order.

At six feet two inches tall, Andreas was about a head taller than the sergeant, and Kouros, though an inch or so shorter and at least a foot broader than the sergeant, was built like a bull. Andreas ignored him, looked at Kouros, and nodded toward the tarp.

As much as police sergeants on tourist islands were used to being obeyed, this one must have realized he couldn't win this confrontation on any level. He stepped back to allow Kouros to pass and remove the cones, then helped Andreas and Kouros lift the tarp.

Though only mid-April, it was a bright, sunny day. Perfect for baking blood onto black plastic sheeting. Whatever clues the tarp may once have protected were now part of an ugly, impenetrable mess. They set the tarp off to one side and Andreas studied the ground. There wasn't much left to see except shoe prints. Lots of shoe prints.

"What the hell was going on here, a track meet?"

The sergeant shrugged. "A baker on the way to work found the body, panicked, and ran through the streets screaming, 'Kalogeros Vassilis was murdered in the square.' People came running from everywhere to see if they could help, and when they saw it was too late, they stayed to pray by his body. He was a much loved man, and by the time we got here the square was packed with mourners. We had to pull two hysterical old women off his body."

As if on cue, an old woman dressed head-to-foot in black hobbled into the square from a nearby lane. Chanting loudly, she walked to where Andreas was standing, crossed herself three times, and threw flowers smack-dab into the heart of the blood soaked crime scene. Those gathered at the edge of the square responded in a chorus of *amens*.

Andreas stared at the woman, then looked at Kouros. "Let's get out of here."

Chapter Two

The police station was in Skala. It shared space with the post office in an all-white island landmark on the southern end of the harbor road. The distinctive, three-story tower at one corner of the building looked like a runaway little brother to the massive stone towers guarding the monastery above.

"Everything we found at the scene is in there." The sergeant pointed down a hallway to a door marked CAPTAIN. "It's all inside, on the table."

It was a cave of a room. The only window was shuttered. A dark desk sat on a dark carpet at the far end, with a dark bookcase behind it and two dark chairs in front. A dark table was beside the door. The only color came from a large, gold and crimson poster set in a gilt frame on the opposite wall. It was a reproduction of one of the island's most famous icons, the sixteenth century Vision of Saint John depicting elements of his Revelation. Words wrapped around the poster's edge advertised Patmos' celebration nearly two decades ago of the nineteen-hundredth anniversary of the Book of Revelation.

To its left hung signed and framed photographs of the current archbishop of the Eastern Orthodox Church in Greece and his two predecessors. No politicians shared the walls. Obviously, it was the church that held influence in this office.

Andreas pulled two pairs of latex gloves from the dispenser box on the table and handed one pair to Kouros. Very carefully, they began sorting through the items. Blood seemed everywhere.

"All we found were his robe, hat, sandals, undergarments, and two crosses."

"Do you know what was taken?"

"No, but his pockets were turned inside out."

"Any idea of how many attackers?"

The sergeant did a quick upward jerk of his head, Greek for "no." "No idea, but my guess is more than one. These mugger bastards are cowards when alone."

"A lot of monks get mugged here?"

He gestured no again. "This is the first I know of."

Andreas looked at the crosses. One was heavy, silver, and connected to a long, thick, woven black cord. The other was much smaller and lighter, like tin, and tied to a thin black lanyard. It was the only item without bloodstains. He pointed at the smaller cross. "Why is there no blood on this?"

"We found it clenched in his fist."

Andreas nodded. "Any thoughts on why the crosses were left behind?"

The sergeant shrugged. "No. The captain thinks it's because he was a man of God and the muggers thought it a sacrilege to take them."

Andreas stared deadpan at the sergeant. Kouros started to laugh. "Can't wait to meet your captain," said Andreas. "A monk is butchered in your town square and he thinks the muggers were worried about committing a sacrilege by stealing his crosses?"

The sergeant stammered. "No…no…I…I'm sure what the captain meant was that…uh…they didn't know Vassilis was a monk when they attacked him."

Andreas kept staring. "Show me the photographs of the body."

The sergeant took an envelope off the desk and handed it to Andreas. "These were taken after we removed the body from the square. I'll have to get you copies of the ones we took at the scene, the captain has them."

It contained two dozen eight-by-tens of a very old, very thin, naked man. For an instant, Andreas wondered what passed through that poor soul's mind in his last seconds on earth.

His youth? His parents? His loves? Children perhaps? Regrets? Andreas moved on. He had to be clinical and focus: focus on finding the miserable, damned-to-hell bastards who murdered this old man.

Andreas studied the first few photos very carefully, handing each to Kouros as he finished. Then he quickly shuffled through the rest as if disinterested. "What do you think, Yianni?"

"Only one."

Andreas nodded. "Sergeant. Where's your captain?"

He looked at his shoes, "I don't know."

Andreas took that to mean that he did, and that his captain probably was nearby. "Tell him to get his ass in here now or I'll find him and personally drag him in here *by his balls*."

"Chief, I don't think—"

"*I said now.*"

The sergeant hurried out the door.

Andreas looked at Kouros. "Do you think they're just stupid, or lazy, or is it something else?"

Kouros shrugged.

"Let's hope it's the first two. But watch out for the third. Which reminds me." Andreas spun his hand in the air and pointed to his ear. Listening devices were not unusual in police stations trying to catch suspects talking among themselves.

Kouros nodded. "But do you really think the captain is being blackmailed by his gay lover?"

Andreas rolled his eyes. He'd grown used to that sense of humor. They'd been together since Andreas was chief of police on Mykonos and Kouros was a brash young rookie.

Kouros laughed.

About a minute later the door burst open and a middle-aged man about Andreas' height, but with a noticeable potbelly, stormed into the room. "*Who the fuck do you think you are?*" he screamed, moving his eyes between Andreas and Kouros.

Andreas smiled. "I'm the one you're looking for, Captain. How nice of you to take time out of your busy schedule to drop in for a chat."

The captain pushed himself straight into Andreas' face. "You're an asshole and I don't give a fuck who you think you are, this is my island and no one talks to me that way. No one."

Andreas smiled. "Simple choice. Start cooperating or grab your worry beads and start praying. My job description includes investigating police corruption *anywhere* in Greece. So if you and *your* island want to make it to the top of my shit list, just keep it up," Andreas lifted his hands and patted the captain's cheeks, "*kukla.*" The use of the endearing word for "doll" in Greek did not hide Andreas' message: go ahead, test me, asshole.

The captain drew in and let out a quick breath, then stepped back, so fast that Andreas made a mental note to seriously consider starting an investigation.

Andreas stared at the captain. "I understand you believe the monk was the victim of a random mugging?"

"What else could it be?" His tone was edgy.

"That's what I'm asking you."

"He was a monk. Been here forty years. Everyone loved him. He had no vices, no girlfriends, boyfriends, or enemies. His life was an open book. No one had a motive."

"You think he just happened to be in the wrong place at the wrong time?"

"Yes, he probably was attacked by some of that same scum that drifts in during tourist season to prey on whatever looks easy. We get that sort passing through every once in a while." The captain paused. "Why, do you think some psycho with a grudge against the church decided to take it out on poor Vassilis?" He smiled as if he'd already anticipated and dismissed Andreas' thinking.

"As a matter of fact, no, I don't. But, for the same reason, I don't think it was a mugging." Andreas handed him the photographs. "What jumps out at you from these?"

The captain looked through each one and shrugged. "His throat was cut."

"Anything else?"

"No."

"Exactly. And what does that mean to you?"

The captain bristled. "I don't have time for your bullshit."

Andreas remained calm. "Yianni?"

Kouros answered matter-of-factly. "There are no other marks or stab wounds on the body."

"So?" said the captain.

Kouros continued. "A single cut, administered at precisely the point most likely to cause as quick and painless a death as can be done by a knife."

The captain shrugged.

"Muggers aren't that careful, precise, or trained," said Andreas. "I can't remember ever seeing a mugging-turned-murder victim cut just once. Have you, Captain?"

The captain didn't answer, just glared.

"I'll take that as a no. And if this were a psycho lashing out against a symbol of the church, I can't imagine rage great enough to drive a deadly, random attack on a monk being satisfied by a single, surgical slice."

The captain clenched and unclenched his fists. "So what are you saying?"

"Premeditated murder."

Andreas expected an argument.

"I can't imagine why. But I see your point."

Andreas was surprised. Perhaps this asshole actually had an open mind. Maybe he ought to try mending fences. "I'd like to speak with the abbot. Do you think you possibly could arrange for him to see me now?" Andreas didn't need his help to make the appointment, but he wanted the captain to feel that he did. It was always better to have the head of police on a small island inside your tent pissing out, rather than outside pissing in.

The captain walked over to his desk, picked up the phone, pressed a speed dial button, and after a hushed, thirty-second conversation, hung up. "He'll see you in an hour at the monastery."

"Thank you."

"You're welcome." The captain extended his right hand.

Andreas wasn't sure if that meant they'd made up, or that a farewell sucker punch was on the way. Andreas smiled, reached out and shook the captain's hand, but all the while kept an eye on the man's left, just in case.

Andreas and Kouros parked in the square across from where the monk was murdered. Flowers now covered the bloodstains. A sign pointing to the monastery was posted on the wall of the path that began a few feet from where the body was found. They followed it out of the square. The route soon merged with another path funneling tourists up from the parking area below. They followed the crowd uphill, past a taverna on the left and a few souvenir shops on the right.

Just before the path started downhill, almost everyone made a sharp right up onto a set of terraced steps leading into a small *piazza*. It was packed with tourists. On the far left side, a dozen more steps led up toward the monastery's entrance. Andreas looked at his watch. They were thirty minutes early for their meeting. He suggested they have coffee at the taverna they'd just passed.

It took only a minute to get there, and no sooner did they step inside than a man built like Kouros, but twice his age, yelled out, "Welcome to Dimitri's! Come, let me show you to our best table."

"We just want coffee," said Andreas.

"Does that mean I should not give you our best table? Please do not offend me by suggesting I treat my guests as euros. My duty is to show Patmian hospitality to all pilgrims to our holy island."

Andreas wasn't buying the pitch. "We're not pilgrims."

The man smiled. "I know, you're cops."

He'd caught Andreas off guard. "Are we that obvious?"

The man laughed. "No, I saw you in the square with Mavros."

"Mavros?"

"The sergeant." He patted Andreas on the shoulder. "Hi, I'm Dimitri, and welcome to my place. Follow me, please." He led them out a rear door onto a broad balcony running the length of the building. It literally hung off the edge of the mountain, looking out above Skala and off to the horizon as far as the eye could see.

"This is quite a view," said Kouros.

"Sure is," said Andreas. He wished Lila could be here.

"Thank you. Please, sit down." Dimitri pointed to a large table by the open railing at the edge of the balcony. "I'll bring your coffees. I know you are in a hurry to see the abbot."

Before Andreas could speak, Dimitri added with another smile, "Only a hunch, but I saw you leave for Skala. Now you're back in Chora, and five minutes ago you walked past my place headed in the direction of the entrance." He pointed toward the monastery. "Now you're back again and only want coffee. I assume you're waiting to go inside, but since the monastery is about to close to tourists for today, my guess is you've come back to meet someone inside. And the only one in the monastery who would dare talk to the police about what happened to Vassilis is Abbot Christodoulos." He walked away from the table.

Kouros stared at Andreas. "Maybe we should just post our schedule on the front door of the town hall."

"Doesn't look like we have to."

"How did he really know?"

"One of the cops might have told him. Everybody gossips. It's our national pastime. And on islands and in small villages…" Andreas rolled his left hand out into the air. "Or, he might have figured it out exactly as he said."

"Maybe he knew the monk?"

"I'm sure he did," nodded Andreas.

"Bet it wouldn't take much to get him talking."

Andreas smiled. "Probably no more than, 'Would you like to join us?'"

"So, what do you think the monk was doing running around outside the monastery at that hour?"

"No idea, but I'm pretty sure he was coming from, not returning to, the monastery. His body was found in the square by the entrance to the lane we took coming here. If he'd been walking through the square he'd have seen whoever was waiting for him. And even an old monk would have put up a struggle for his life. That would have left marks on his body. Besides, if he were returning to the monastery, whoever killed him would have waited up the lane where there were places to hide, and the body would have been found there."

"My bet is he was meeting someone."

Andreas nodded. "And I'd bet the answer to all this somehow ties into that meeting." He drummed his fingers on the table. "Was he giving or receiving? Telling or listening?" He shook his head. "No idea."

"Here's your coffee." Dimitri put two cups, a coffee pot, sugar, and milk on the table. A boy behind him set down plates of cakes and cookies. "Compliments of the house."

Andreas looked at Kouros. Kouros winked.

"So, Dimitri," said Andreas. "Would you like to join us?"

Dimitri launched into a running monologue on "all things monastery," supposedly to show "what to expect from the abbot." Andreas doubted Dimitri's views were shared by everyone; certainly not by the monks, but he was entertaining and obviously knew far more than any outsider about what went on inside the monastery. Dimitri had grown up within the literal shadow of its walls, had family who rose to prominence in the monastery's hierarchy, operated his business for years within steps of its main—and he claimed only—entrance, and fought almost daily with monks and the abbot over what he considered their unfair interference with his business.

Dimitri was quick to say that the murdered monk was one of the few not "written on my balls," a place far worse than any shit list. He agreed with the sergeant: everyone liked Vassilis, including himself, and he had no idea who might have killed him.

He talked about the history of the monastery only when he felt it necessary to put in context his views on what was currently going on "inside." "If you want history, buy a guide book," were Dimitri's exact words. He said he confined his history lessons to tourists who didn't realize that the Greek Orthodox Church was only a very small part, population-wise, of the three hundred million-member Eastern Orthodox Church dominating Russia, Eastern Europe, and the Christian populations of much of the Middle East. To them, he'd say that what gave the Greek Church its exceptional influence over the Orthodox churches of other countries were the many unique and revered sites within Greece, of which Revelation made Patmos perhaps the best known to the non-Orthodox world.

He described Abbot Christodoulos as "one right out of the history books." He'd taken his name from Hosios Christodoulos, who founded the monastery in 1088. That first Christodoulos obtained absolute sovereignty over the island and permission to erect the monastery in a direct grant from the Byzantine emperor in Constantinople. Since its early days, the monastery faced a seemingly endless flow of marauding pirates, meddling local bishops, and demanding foreign occupiers. Indeed, not until the end of World War II, when the Italians were ousted, did Patmos return to Greek rule. It took great leadership skills and delicate foreign alliances, including several with the papacy in Rome, to enable the monastery to safeguard its independence and treasures for nearly a thousand years.

"The monastery has always known how to reach far beyond this tiny island's borders to survive. Even today, it's not subject to the Church in Greece, its archbishop, or any other Eastern Orthodox leader. It owes allegiance only to the Ecumenical Patriarch in Constantinople, the worldwide spiritual leader of the Eastern Orthodox Church. At least that's what we Greeks like to consider him to be, a first among equals in the patriarchs responsible for leading their countries' Orthodox churches within Eastern Orthodoxy." Dimitri paused only long enough to take a sip of coffee.

"That makes this place no different from those monasteries on Mount Athos. They're all essentially their own little governments, subject directly to the Ecumenical Patriarch. They do as they like, as long as they have the money. And this one does for sure; it's one of the richest in Christendom."

Andreas wondered if Dimitri was about to launch into the major scandal that had helped hound Greece's ruling party out of power. Mount Athos was located on the easternmost of three peninsulas, an eight-hour drive northeast of Athens to one of two port towns where you caught a boat to go the rest of the way. It was the world's oldest surviving monastic community, revered as "The Garden of the Mother of God," and perhaps the last remaining place on earth still using the two thousand-year-old Julian calendar. An independent monastic state jutting out into the Aegean on a peninsula of roughly 130 square miles, the area shared its name with the marble-peaked, 6,700-foot-high mountain punctuating the far southeast end of the peninsula. Mount Athos was a rugged mountain wildness of unspoiled verdant beauty, myths and miracles, history and reality; a place where for far more than a thousand years hermits utterly withdrawn from secular life living in isolated huts and monks living within massive, fortified monastery walls shared a common commitment to God, prayer, contemplation, and protecting the cherished seclusion of their life on the Holy Mountain.

In the eleventh century, as many as 180 monasteries existed on the Holy Mountain. But times had changed, and today only twenty survived: seventeen Greek, one Russian, one Serbian, and one Bulgarian. A dozen smaller communities and innumerable other structures—ranging from large farmhouses to isolated caves within desolate cliff faces—sheltered monks and hermits, too, but generally as dependencies of one of the twenty principal monasteries sovereign over their twenty respective self-governing territories.

From the amount of press coverage the scandal received, you'd think Mount Athos were a place of two hundred thousand schemers, not just two thousand monks and those few civilians doing secular work willing to live confined to the Holy Mountain's capital of three hundred souls. What held center stage in a once never-ending media circus was the alleged involvement of high-ranking government ministers and the abbot of perhaps the most prominent of Mount Athos' primary monasteries in a purportedly fraudulent land swap and money laundering scheme arising out of the 2004 Olympics staged in Athens.

If that was where Dimitri was headed, Andreas wasn't interested. He'd heard it all before. Everyone in Greece had heard it all before. That scandal was the most talked about subject in Greece—until the country's massive, unrevealed debt crisis exploded across the EU, blowing everything else off the front pages. He was tired of it. All of Greece was tired of it. In fact, that's what some said was the idea: get everyone so tired of the subject that no one cared whether anyone was ever prosecuted.

"Christodoulos is as sharp as any of his predecessors. He's kept this monastery out of trouble and away from scandal, despite the efforts of everyone with a microphone and news camera to bring Mount Athos' problems here.

"Look, I'm not a fan of the abbot, I know he's the reason those bastards in the town hall won't give me the permit I need to expand my business, but I've got to give him credit. Patmos and Mount Athos are linked together by the Book of Revelation—it's the spiritual force behind much of what drives Mount Athos life. Some call Patmos the church's 'spiritual eye,' and monks through the ages have come here from Mount Athos to be closer to it.

"But, despite all that Patmos shares with Mount Athos, Abbot Christodoulos did not allow his monastery to share in its mistakes. Perhaps that's because he's a more astute politician or because his monastery exists in the midst of a cosmopolitan site filled with tourists, while Mount Athos remains virtually as it always has, accessible only by boat, and only to Eastern Orthodox men over eighteen given express permission to visit and the few non-Orthodox men approved for reasons of pilgrimage or study. Women are never allowed. And there's no TV. I'm not even sure they have Internet yet."

He shook his head. "Do I have to tell you what that sort of life can lead to? Especially the no women part. Why, even here—"

"Time to go." Andreas pushed back his chair and stood up. No reason to let him get into that subject. "You've been great, and I really like your place. Thanks." Andreas reached into his pocket to pay.

Dimitri put up his hand and gestured stop. "Please, all you had was coffee. It's on me."

Andreas knew it was a waste of time to argue. "I owe you."

"Great, you can tell that abbot when you see him to stop holding up my building permit."

Andreas smiled. "If he raises the subject I've got you covered."

As soon as they were out of Dimitri's sight Kouros started to laugh. "I think he was serious about us raising his building permit with the abbot."

"I'm sure he was. But I get the impression that's not a subject likely to endear us to the abbot."

They were on the far side of the *piazza* on steps leading up to a set of brown metal doors. "Yeah, like telling him we think one of his monks was assassinated will make us best buddies."

Andreas laughed and smacked Kouros lightly on the back of his head as they passed through the brown doors. A few paces later they stopped between two rectangular guard towers framing the entrance to the monastery, looked up, and stared.

Brown-gray and medieval, the monastery's soaring stone walls embraced a multi-level complex of courtyards, chapels, formal rooms, warrens of smaller rooms, and corridors, all arranged around the main church and built upon a once nearly inaccessible height. Its irregular exterior flowed with the land. At its greatest, the complex stood at 230 feet east-to-west, and 175 feet north-to-south.

In an arch above the doorway an icon of the ever vigilant Saint John stood as spiritual protector of the monastery. Toward the top of the wall sat an opening once used to rain hot oil and molten metal down upon invaders threatening harm of the secular sort. Andreas wondered what kind of reception the abbot had in mind for them.

He gave another quick glance toward the top of the wall, nodded to Kouros, and stepped inside.

Chapter Three

A gray-bearded monk met Andreas and Kouros just beyond the entrance and gestured for them to follow him, never bothering to ask who they were. He led them into the courtyard and with a quick turn to the left, into the main church. An elaborately carved, wooden *iconostasis* covered in icons separated the main part of the nine-hundred-year-old church from the altar area, and a large mural of the Second Coming seemed to grow up and out of the east wall. They passed through the main sanctuary into a small chapel lined with Byzantine paintings, then outside and down some steps to arrive at what seemed just around the corner from where they'd first entered the main church.

Andreas wasn't sure if the monk was taking them the quickest way, or one intended to impress them with the majesty of the place. As they followed the man up a flight of stone steps to a second floor, Kouros whispered, "Do you think we should drop some bread crumbs?"

Andreas stifled a laugh.

The monk turned right, stopped by a heavy wooden door, opened it, and gestured for them to enter. It was a large room with two windows. At the far end there looked to be more than enough chairs to seat every monk in the monastery. The monk pointed to two unadorned wooden chairs in front of a massive wooden desk, then left, leaving Andreas and Kouros alone. They sat and waited.

Andreas was a cop, his father was a cop. He was not into art and never had been, but Lila was. They'd met when he called upon her knowledge of ancient Greek art for help in an investigation. It almost cost Lila her life, and Andreas swore never to involve her in another case. So they talked about other things, and she laughingly gave him lessons on her passion for all things ancient. He was far from expert, but thanks to Lila's lessons, he realized this austere-looking abbot's chamber was anything but. The discreetly displayed icons, objects, and ancient texts were priceless, intended to deliver an unmistakable message to any visitor in the know: here was a very old, very holy, and very rich bastion of church influence.

The door swung open and a tall, lean man in traditional monk's garb strode in. "Welcome, my sons." He extended his hand.

For most, the ancient silver and wood cross about the abbot's neck would be the first thing noticed, but Andreas was drawn to his long, jet-black beard. The man was young, looked to be forty at most. Not that much older than Andreas.

Andreas and Kouros immediately rose and kissed his hand. "Good afternoon, Your Holiness," said Andreas.

"Please, sit." The abbot gestured with his right hand, then stepped behind his desk and sat in a tall-back Byzantine-era chair. "So, Chief Kaldis, how may I help you?" He was looking directly into Andreas' eyes and smiling.

"Thank you for seeing us. I know how busy you must be during Easter Week, and now, with all that's happened…" Andreas shrugged.

The abbot's smile faded and he nodded. "Yes, Vassilis was one of my favorites, all of us loved him. He will be missed." He drew in and let out a breath. "I cannot imagine who would have done such a thing."

"You anticipated my first question."

"It makes no sense. None at all." He shook his head.

"There must be something. Has to be."

The abbot gestured no. "I cannot think of a single person with whom he ever had even a cross word."

"What did he do at the monastery?"

"Do?"

"Yes, what were his duties?"

The abbot smiled. "He was a scholar. Loved the library. When we started modernizing—digitizing texts for computers—Vassilis insisted on taking part, 'so nothing went wrong,' he used to say. He made himself computer literate and kept the younger monks on their toes."

"Was it unusual for him to be out of the monastery so early in the morning?"

"Yes. I wish I knew why."

"So do I. Was something bothering him, was he complaining about anything?"

"We live in a monastery, there's always complaining. But Vassilis was one of the few who tried to discourage that sort of thing. He'd say, 'Stay focused on the positive, let God deal with the negative.'"

The abbot had an easygoing smile and way about him. He seemed of the unflappable sort that never quite allowed you to know what he was thinking. The perfect diplomat, the perfect churchman, thought Andreas.

"Sounds like someone who liked to avoid controversy," said Kouros.

"Yes, I think that's a fair way to describe him."

Andreas said, "Well, some things must have bothered him."

The abbot shrugged. "Not really. He even avoided discussions of politics. His sole focus was on the church and doing good."

Andreas decided he'd better ratchet up the rhetoric or they'd get nothing from the abbot but blessings. "With all due respect, Your Holiness, how could he be focused on the church for forty years and *not* discuss politics."

The abbot smiled again. "He was an unusual man."

"I see." Andreas nodded. "Is the monastery filled with unusual men like Vassilis?"

"I wish I could say that were so."

"Then I assume others talked politics."

The smile came, but not as quickly. "Some."

"So what sorts of things did they say that got Vassilis worked up enough to say, 'Don't focus on it, let God deal with it?'"

"Nothing of consequence."

Andreas shook his head. "I don't understand. You're saying that this 'unusual man' who 'liked to avoid controversy' would get worked up over 'nothing of consequence?'"

The smile was gone. The abbot stood. "I have other appointments."

Andreas did not stand. "Your Holiness, I didn't want to come to Patmos and, frankly, I'd prefer getting back to Athens. But somebody with enough clout to pressure my boss, the minister of public order, wants me here asking questions. So when I tell my boss it's a waste of time because you won't answer my questions, the worst that can happen to me is that I'm sent back to Athens to do what I want to do. I leave to your imagination what's the worst that can happen to you." Andreas left unsaid, *from whatever son of a bitch is behind this.*

The abbot stared for a moment and sat back down. "Good point." He smiled. "Our police captain warned me you could be persuasive." He paused. "Mount Athos."

"Excuse me?" said Andreas.

"Mount Athos. That's what was bothering Vassilis. The scandal in that Mount Athos monastery was consuming him. He was convinced it would be the ruin of the church."

"I don't understand. Claims of corruption in the church aren't new. Vassilis had to know that. Besides, this is isolated to one monastery. How could he think it was going to bring down the church?"

The abbot pointed to a framed map of Greece and Asia Minor on the wall to Andreas' left. "In 1054, at the Great Schism, the church of the West was fixed in Rome, and the church of the East in Constantinople. Our church has had a presence in Constantinople since the city's founding in the fourth century, and it has always been home to the Ecumenical Patriarch, the spiritual head of our church and my direct superior as abbot of this monastery."

The abbot leaned forward. "The occupiers of Constantinople have permitted our Ecumenical Patriarch to remain there, in what they call Istanbul. But there are requirements imposed by Turkey's constitution. Most significantly, the Ecumenical Patriarch must be a Turkish citizen and have a degree from an authorized Turkish university. For many years there was no problem, because Greeks on lands conquered by the Turks could attend the Ecumenical Patriarch's seminary, the Holy Theological School on the island of Halki in the Sea of Marmara."

Andreas started to fidget. Where the hell is he going with all this?

"But in 1971, Turkey passed a law forbidding private universities and closed the Halki School. There is no longer an Eastern Orthodox theological seminary in Turkey. Our blessed Ecumenical Patriarch sits in Constantinople because he meets Turkey's legal requirements, but after his time has passed…" The abbot shook his head, and looked up as if searching for a miracle. "Unless Turkey changes its constitution to accommodate Greece, I fear our next Ecumenical Patriarch must find a new home. Just think how the western world would react if Italy tried evicting the pope from Vatican City."

Everyone shrugged.

"Okay, we know that's never going to happen in Italy, but the situation in Constantinople is real, and a lot more than just the eleven million of us in Greece are worried about it."

"I don't follow you," said Kouros, sparing Andreas the same observation.

The abbot nodded, as if fielding a question from a visiting student. "The Russians have long claimed that the head of the Eastern Orthodox Church belonged in Russia. Russia and its former satellites have the most members of the faith, hundreds of millions. But for over nine hundred years our church has been linked to Constantinople, while for most of that time the Russian Church existed merely to appease the Russian masses. Under the tsars, the church was their servant. After the revolution, the only god allowed in Russia was the central government. That made

Russia a highly unattractive alternative to Constantinople, yet the Russian Orthodox Church long has sought to undermine, and indeed directly challenge, our Ecumenical Patriarch.

"The West also liked keeping the Ecumenical Patriarch isolated in Constantinople, removed from his resources and access to his followers. It minimized the risk of some powerful Eastern Orthodox leader emerging who might affect the western powers' view of 'world order.'" The abbot flashed his fingers for emphasis.

"But things are different now. Or at least that's what Moscow wants the world to think. Russia claims to have embraced the church anew, and that the sheer number of Orthodox followers within its borders entitles it to have the church headquartered there—*when* the Ecumenical Patriarch is forced out of Constantinople."

The abbot crossed himself. "Can you imagine our Ecumenical Patriarch driven out of Constantinople by the Turks and into the arms of Russian control and methods? Just think of the influence it would give the Russians over its former satellites. Forget about controlling their borders, Russia will control their peoples' souls."

Andreas wondered if that was part of the Greek Orthodox Church's pitch to the Eastern Orthodox community against the Russians. He also wondered how he could find the son of a bitch who got him into this mess.

The abbot continued. "No one but Russia wants that. But what's the alternative? Some have suggested Geneva, but the most obvious and natural choice is Mount Athos, a place holy and revered by all Eastern Orthodoxy. It is where the secrets of Byzantium remain safely hidden amid reclusive lives led much the same now as in the fourth century. Some say the entire Mount Athos scandal grew out of an effort by one monastery to establish itself as a world financial center in anticipation of an objection from Russia that Mount Athos was too unsophisticated and out of touch with modern times to be the physical center of our faith."

The abbot shrugged. "All I know for certain is that Moscow and Mount Athos are in competition to serve as our next Ecumenical Patriarch's home. Vassilis knew that too, and he worried that the scandal, with all its allegations of fraudulent property transactions, made Mount Athos seem far too tainted with corruption to serve as our Ecumenical Patriarch's home. Especially in light of all the real estate the Ecumenical Patriarch controls."

"As if Russia were any better." Kouros snickered.

The abbot nodded. "Yes, but Vassilis argued that corruption in a holy place is perceived as far more serious and sinful than corruption in a place of government or business."

"He had a point," said Andreas.

"What sort of property are we talking about?" asked Kouros.

"A lot…and lots of rents. The Archbishop of Greece controls all Eastern Orthodox Church property on land Greece freed from the Turks in our 1821 War of Independence, while all Eastern Orthodox Church property on land obtained by Greece when our borders were redrawn after World War I—that's most of northern Greece—is under the control of the Ecumenical Patriarch."

Andreas nodded, thinking that was some serious money. There looked to be a lot more than souls at stake here.

For the next hour Andreas and Kouros pressed the abbot for every detail he could remember of the past week that touched upon Vassilis in any way, and for a list of anyone with even the remotest contact with the murdered monk. They asked to see whatever files there were on Vassilis, but they proved useless. The background information was forty years old, everything else was praise, and the most recent entry was over twenty years old: a glowing accolade from the archbishop of Greece. Andreas figured whoever was charged with making entries felt there was nothing more to be said, and so no one bothered. Andreas made a mental note to have his secretary dig up what else she could on Vassilis' past.

"Yianni, start interviewing the people on His Holiness' list." Andreas looked at the abbot. "And, if you have no objection, I'd like to see Vassilis' room."

"Certainly." The abbot stood up and nodded goodbye to Kouros. "Follow me, please."

Vassilis' cell was in a whitewashed building by a pebble and stone courtyard filled with flowers. The building stood on the south side of the monastery and, if his cell had a window on the outside wall, enjoyed a terrific view of the valley below. What Andreas first noticed was the silence. Only birds disturbed the mood.

"His room is at the far end." The abbot pointed. "It's the one with the table in front." A photograph of a young, smiling monk sat next to a single white lily on a tiny, square-top table. "As soon as I heard, I gave instructions for no one to enter Vassilis' room until the police said it was allowed. We needed nothing from his room to prepare him."

"What time did you learn about the murder?"

"A little before three-thirty this morning."

"Did the police find anything in his room?"

"They haven't asked to see it."

Figured. "Has anyone been inside?"

The abbot looked at the door and pointed to a bit of wax running from above the lock onto the frame. "No, my seal is still on the door."

"Open it, please."

Inside was not what Andreas expected, and from the abbot's gasp, nor had he. The place was a mess. Books tossed everywhere in a way suggesting they'd been skimmed before discarded, a mattress sliced to pieces, every drawer emptied, contents scattered across the floor.

"Jesus—sorry," said Andreas.

"I was thinking the same thing." The abbot shook his head. "How could someone get in without disturbing my seal?"

Andreas didn't answer right away. He stood studying the mess. "What's missing?"

"I have no way of knowing."

"Think hard. Think about the man, think about his life, think about what he valued, what he used. It might help you to remember something."

The abbot stared at the floor, then at the bed, and finally at the desk. "No, I'm sorry, he treasured his cross, it belonged to his grandfather, but other than that I can't—wait a minute. Why, of course! His computer! It's gone." The abbot looked around again at the mess. "All his disks are gone, too. He loved his laptop. It was his pride and joy. We presented it to him last year as a gift in honor of his fortieth year with us."

"Are you sure no one else but you had access to your seal?"

"Positive. It is from this ring." He thrust out his right hand. "And it never leaves my finger."

Andreas nodded. "I was afraid you'd say that. Otherwise it would be all too simple."

"I don't understand."

"Since no one could have entered after you sealed the room, someone had to get in before you arrived. No way they got in through that window." Andreas pointed. "It's still locked shut and must be forty feet from the ground. Unless this is one of the great coincidences of all time, where a man's room is ransacked and his life taken in the same night in unrelated incidents, I'd say if we find who did this we find who murdered him." Andreas paused. "Unless, of course, you or one of his fellow monks did this after learning he was dead and before you sealed it."

"I was the first to learn of his death. And the room was sealed within minutes after that. As for my being the likely computer thief, Vassilis used a PC. I'm a Mac man." The abbot smiled.

Andreas nodded with a grin. "Fair enough. That leaves us with whoever killed him doing this either before the murder or in the thirty to sixty minutes between the time of death and when you sealed the room."

"What sort of person would murder and rob a man of God, then come into his room and steal yet more from him? Heaven help us."

Andreas didn't give the answer he was thinking: someone willing to take one hell of a risk—like a professional killer not finding what was wanted on the victim, or making damn sure no one else found anything. "Any chance of computer backup for what was taken?"

"We have a very elaborate backup system here, what with all the information we must protect in our library, but the work Vassilis did on his laptop he considered personal and much of it never made it onto our system."

"What do you mean by 'personal?'"

The abbot smiled, as if reminiscing. "Vassilis didn't like the idea of his every thought becoming part of what he called the 'information universe' before giving serious reflection to whether what he offered would help or hurt the purpose for which he lived. He worked offline from our network on those sorts of things until he had something he thought worthy to share."

Nothing's easy, thought Andreas. "Can you get me what you have of his on your backup?"

"Certainly."

Andreas bent down and picked up a plastic wrapper with three ten-by-twelve manila envelopes inside. They were unused. He looked around and picked up six more, all unused. "Where's the tenth?"

"Pardon?"

"The packaging says 'ten envelopes,' but I only see nine, and they're unused."

The two men scoured the room but found nothing.

"Come to think of it, I remember passing Vassilis on his way back to the monastery yesterday afternoon. He was carrying a plastic shopping bag. The envelopes may have been in it."

"Do you remember a name on the bag?"

"No, but he would have purchased them at Biblio, a shop just off the town square…" The abbot's words faded off at the mention of the square.

"Thanks. I think I'll give my partner a hand with the interviews." Andreas paused. "I'm sincere about the thanks. I know this must be very tough for you."

The abbot nodded. "You have no idea how much Vassilis meant to this monastery. Not only was he a true man of God, he was a mentor to us all. He wanted nothing of higher rank, yet there was no one above him in the Church of Greece who did not treasure his judgment as if he were a peer. He was their genuine friend and a trusted, respected confidant."

Andreas caught a glint of something in the abbot's eyes, as if his words had triggered a thought. But the abbot said nothing. He didn't have to. Andreas said it for him, "Perhaps he was *too much* of a 'confidant.'"

The abbot stared off into the middle distance. "God help us if that's the answer."

Andreas nodded. "Amen."

Chapter Four

It was nearly sundown by the time they finished interviewing those they could find on the abbot's list. A few visiting monks were out wandering about the island. The abbot said he would arrange for them to be available in the morning. Dozens of interviews had yielded two things: a mound of praise for a revered man, and zero leads. No one saw the monk leave, knew why he left, or had any idea of who might be involved in his death.

They were standing in the *piazza* by the monastery's gift shop. It was closed and the *piazza* virtually deserted. "No way some local did this," said Andreas.

"Way too professional," said Kouros. "But why?"

Andreas shrugged. "My guess is vengeance or fear. But it had to be a hell of a motive to lead to this."

"You think it might be tied to Vassilis' past, from before he became a monk?"

Andreas shook his head. "I doubt it. Can't imagine whatever drove this taking forty years to come to a head."

"Maybe one of the visiting monks noticed something?"

"Maybe," said Andreas, looking at his watch. "Jesus, I never called Lila to tell her I wouldn't be home tonight."

"Don't worry, I spoke to Maggie and told her to call."

Thank God for his secretary. Maggie ran Andreas' office. Most thought she ran all of Athens General Police Headquarters, better known as GADA. She'd been there longer than the building. Maggie's long-time boss had retired a few weeks before Andreas was promoted back to GADA from Mykonos, and when the human resources director suggested she retire with him, the political buttons she pushed had the director staring at his own retirement. That's how the legendary Maggie Sikestis came to report to Andreas—or, as it so often seemed to Andreas, vice versa.

Andreas let out a breath. "Thanks, Yianni." They started toward the stone path leading back to the town square.

"No problem." Kouros smiled. "But to be honest, Maggie said she'd already called her."

Both laughed.

"*My friends, please, come join me.*" It was Dimitri shouting to them from his open front door.

That guy doesn't miss a thing, thought Andreas. "Thanks Dimitri, but—"

"You haven't eaten yet, have you? And if they fed you inside," he pointed toward the monastery as he spoke, "you must be even hungrier."

Andreas looked at Kouros, shook his head, and smiled. "Okay, we give up."

They followed Dimitri into the restaurant and out onto the balcony. It was packed with tourists staring off into a pink, blue, and silver sunset.

"Here, please sit, I've been saving your table." He waited until they sat, then hurried back inside.

Kouros whispered, "Can't be too careful around that guy. I wonder if he's a spook."

"Wouldn't bet against it. Greece is full of spies. It's part of our history. The question is, a spy for whom?"

"The church?"

"If he is a spy, that would be my guess. That's who's most likely to want to know what's going on inside." Andreas gestured toward the monastery with his head. "And this guy has the best location on the island. He sees everyone going in and out, and between the restaurant and his personality, has the perfect cover for starting conversations with all of them."

"Who in the church do you think he's working for?"

"I don't even have an idea of *which* church. Is it the church in Greece, the church in Constantinople, the church somewhere else?"

"Like Rome?"

"Anything's possible, especially with all the power, money, and influence involved with this place. Then again, it could be just some political rival from another island or monastery. Who knows?"

"Here you are, something to start." Dimitri plunked down a bottle of *ouzo*, a small pitcher of water, a bowl of ice, and a plate overflowing with olives, sardines, cheese, sausage, cucumber, and tomato. "A bit of *meze*." Then he put down three glasses.

Andreas looked at Kouros, smiled, and thought, looks like this time we won't have to invite him to join us.

Dimitri pulled up a chair and sat down facing Andreas. "So, how did your visit go with His Holiness?"

"Your permit is on its way."

"Really?" He sounded legitimately excited.

Andreas shook his head. "No, sorry, the subject never came up. But if it does, I promise to push it."

Dimitri let out a breath. "The bastards." He poured himself some *ouzo*, added ice and water, and took a gulp. "I'll never get it."

Andreas thought, if Dimitri really is a spy he's terrific at maintaining his cover. "So, Dimitri, tell me what you know about any strangers hanging around the monastery recently."

Dimitri put down his glass. "You want to know about strangers on Patmos around Easter Week? You must be kidding me. It's one of our busiest times of the year. We are surrounded by strangers."

"Come on, you know what I mean. You watch everybody."

"If you're asking me if I've seen a great pair of tits I can answer the question, but other than a celebrity or two, there's no one I would call out of the ordinary. Besides, if you're looking for someone who came here for the purpose of eliminating Vassilis, don't you think he—or they—would be careful to blend in? They'd be pros, wouldn't they?"

Andreas stared at him. "Whom do you work for?"

Dimitri laughed. "*Touché.* As I think you asked me when we first met, 'Am I that obvious?'"

Andreas did not smile. "Yes."

Dimitri laughed again. "Well, I don't anymore, but I did a long time ago."

"For whom?"

"If it really matters I'm sure you can find out. I wasn't any sort of James Bond type, with deeply classified records. I just did the low level sort of analyst work, even got a pension. And a lot of people here know my background. I don't try to hide it. But I don't talk about it either." Dimitri's last words were said in a serious tone and without a smile.

Andreas nodded. "Okay. But just so we both understand each other, if I find out you had anything to do with what happened to the monk, or are holding anything back," he leaned forward, "the abbot will seem like your best friend compared to the grief I'll rain down on you."

Dimitri stared back. "Fair enough. But I'm not, so I'm not worried. Here, have an *ouzo*." He poured them each a drink. "*Yamas.*"

"*Yamas.*" The three touched glasses.

"So, who did you work for?" asked Andreas. No reason not to try again, especially with Dimitri drinking.

"Like I said, not telling."

"If everyone knows and I can find out, why keep it a secret?"

"It's one thing for you to know, another for me to tell you."

"You're one confusing son of a bitch."

"Thank you. My wife says the same thing." Dimitri laughed.

Andreas shook his head. "Okay, then give me your best guess on what happened?"

"My best is a wild-ass one."

"Go for it, you're local, it's probably better than ours."

"The Russians."

Andreas didn't respond. He sensed Dimitri was waiting for a reaction to see where to go next. He'd wait him out.

Dimitri picked up his glass and took another drink. "Some say the whole Mount Athos scandal was cooked up by the Russians to embarrass the Greek Church. Yeah, I know all about the Ecumenical Patriarch needing a new home thing. How could I not, living in the midst of all this?" He took another drink. "I also know how upset Vassilis was over that mess. We'd talk sometimes."

Andreas bet they did.

"He never said precisely what was bothering him but I could tell he thought things weren't as they seemed. And, from what I know of the Russians, when 'things aren't as they seem,' they're my best guess for why." Dimitri accentuated the point with his fingers.

"I think your logic has some Siberia-size gaps," said Andreas.

"Well, let me fill them in. In the 1990s, Cyprus emerged as the number-one destination for Russians and other Eastern Europeans looking for a place to launder suitcases full of cash. Banks thrived on that business, and unimaginable fortunes were made. A lot of ruthless Russian and Eastern European mobsters also set up shop there, driving local hoods back into legitimate businesses or into early graves." Dimitri reached for a piece of cucumber.

"During that same period the monastery involved in the big scandal rose to prominence, playing host to England's Prince Charles, the first U.S. President Bush, Russia's Putin, and many other big time movers and shakers in a style equal to any world-class, five-star luxury hotel. Mount Athos has always been a place where the world's powerful met in private without having to worry about 'special permission to visit' red tape. And like any other visitor to Mount Athos, they were free to visit any monastery they chose, but that's the one they picked—perhaps because its accommodations were better than the others."

Dimitri took another drink. "Some say it's just a coincidence that during its rise, the abbot of that monastery was from Cyprus. I'm not suggesting he did anything wrong. He was quite gifted at convincing the very rich from around the world—not just those who'd found their way to Cyprus—that charity toward his monastery smoothed the path toward salvation.

"Some also say it was a tragic coincidence when the patriarch of Africa, purportedly sent by the Ecumenical Patriarch to check that monastery's books, perished in a helicopter crash on the way to Mount Athos. Others say some of the monastery's Eastern European contributors were anxious to remain anonymous."

Andreas shook his head. "You sound like an old Greek sitting around a taverna spinning bits of old news, idle gossip, and off-the-wall speculation into international conspiracy theories. There's no proof whatsoever for what you're implying."

Dimitri picked up his glass and winked. "That you know of."

Andreas looked at Kouros, then back at Dimitri.

"How's all that tie into Vassilis' murder?"

"Don't know. But the Russians could have used their big money to burrow so deeply and secretly into that monastery's infrastructure that even its abbot wouldn't know what was going on. That would have made it relatively simple to embarrass the whole of Mount Athos by involving one of its oldest and most respected monasteries in a financial scandal and greatly increase the chances of relocating the head of the Eastern Orthodox Church to Russia. With all that's at stake, I wouldn't bet against the Russians doing whatever it took to pull it off, including murdering someone who might have figured it out."

"Vassilis?" said Kouros.

"Enjoy the *meze*, I'm going to get the fish." Dimitri stood up and walked away, taking his glass with him.

"The man sure as hell knows how to make his exit," said Kouros.

"And his point." Andreas drummed his fingers on the top of the table and looked west. "You know, if any of what he told us is true, or if he's working for somebody who's trying to make us think it's true, we could be in the middle of some very deep shit."

"Located in the middle of a very big minefield."

"Blindfolded. I think the time has come to find who put us here." Andreas reached for his cell phone.

"How are we going to do that? The minister sure as hell isn't going to tell us."

"He probably doesn't even know. My guess is this didn't pass through normal channels."

"So, like I said, how do we find out?"

Andreas dialed and waited. "Hi, it's me. We need to meet and talk about how you can help with a big surprise party." He hung up. "Answering machine."

Kouros said, "I hate the way we have to use cell phones these days. Can't say a damn thing on them directly. You'd think after that scandal over tapping the prime minister's phone they'd have figured out some way to make them secure."

Andreas shook his head. "If someone has the right sort of equipment there's virtually no way of preventing him from listening in on cell phones." He picked up a piece of cucumber with his fork. "And if something at all close to what Dimitri suggested is true…" he rolled his fork in the air, "I don't even want to think about it."

Kouros picked up an olive and popped it into his mouth. "Why, worried about mind readers?"

Andreas shrugged. "That's all we'd need, but thanks for reminding me. I better call Lila as soon as we get to the hotel." He put the fork in his mouth.

"At least GADA keeps all our landlines secure," said Kouros.

"Let's hope so. I'd hate to think of someone listening in on your late-night desperate bachelor calls from home."

Kouros grinned as he picked up another olive. "Jealous. So, what's next?"

"Looks like *barbouni*." Andreas pointed to Dimitri coming through the door carrying a platter of fried red mullet and a bottle of white wine.

"Here's something to get your minds off of business for a while. All that will wait."

Not really, thought Andreas.

Dinner with Dimitri was an experience. Between the great food, a bit too much wine, and endless bitching about every politician in Greece, Dimitri managed to sneak in a few subtle inquiries on the investigation. Andreas deflected them all, or so he hoped.

After dinner they stopped by the Biblio. Shop owners on tourist islands think like fishermen: if you want to catch anything, you better be there when they're running. So when tourists were massing on the island, everything stayed open late. This shop was barely wider than its door, but there was no telling how deep it ran, because every bit of space was jammed with open boxes stacked to the ceiling. No one seemed to be inside, although the door was open.

"Hello, anyone here?" said Andreas.

A shuffling sound came from somewhere deep within the mess of boxes, and a tiny person popped through what until then seemed just a crack between the cartons. It was a very old woman dressed all in black, with raging, uncombed gray hair, dark bright eyes, and a pencil behind her ear. She nodded.

"Hello, I am a policeman investigating the death of Kalogeros Vassilis." Andreas took care to address her formally and use the respectful title for a monk. "Abbot Christodoulos thought he might have purchased some envelopes here yesterday."

The old woman nodded yes, and pointed to a carton off to her right, about three feet above her head. He wondered how she reached them.

"Did he buy anything else?"

She nodded yes.

"What?"

She nodded toward a display of crosses hanging by lanyards on a pegboard next to the door.

"One of these?" He pointed at one of the crosses in the display.

She waved her hand to the left of where Andreas was pointing, and kept waving him to move his finger until it pointed at a silver-colored one on a black lanyard. "This one?" he asked.

She nodded yes. Andreas picked it up. It was square-edged, made of sheet metal, and its longer leg was at most three inches long and one inch wide. A thin, black lanyard passed through a hole at the top of the cross. More of the lanyard material was

wrapped tightly around the longer leg just below where it inter-
sected with the shorter one, presumably as a fashion accent for
a cheaply made tourist item. It was marked ten euros.

"Do you know why he bought this one?"

She gestured no.

"Did he ever buy a cross from you before?"

She gestured no, again.

"Was he alone?"

She nodded yes.

"What did he say to you?"

She pointed to the carton of envelopes and crosses, as if that
were the extent of the conversation.

"Can you think of anyone who might have wanted to harm
him?"

Another no.

Andreas looked at Kouros.

"*Yaya*," Kouros called her by the Greek word for grandmother
and smiled at her as if she actually were his *yaya*. "Can you think
of anything that might help us find who did this to Kalogeros
Vassilis?"

The old woman spread her arms wide, turned her palms up,
closed her eyes, and shrugged toward the heavens.

They thanked her and walked back to the car. Kouros drove.
He said, "That was helpful. Wonder if she can speak?"

"She probably speaks only Greek and is so used to commu-
nicating by gestures with tourists who don't speak her language
that she does it with everyone."

"Why do you think he bought that cross?"

Andreas shrugged. "Add that to our what-the-hell-is-going-on
list." He stared out the side window at the lights down below
in Skala and on the riggings of ships in the harbor. They all fit
together quite nicely against a sky alive with stars. "I have to
call Lila."

"Mavros said the hotel's about five minutes from here."

At the final right-hand bend on the mountain road back to
Skala they headed down a narrow road marked HOTEL THIS

WAY. A few blocks later they stopped in front of a white, three-story stucco building adorned with concrete slab balconies and the brightly lit sign, HOTEL. It was a style reminiscent of forgettable holidays.

"Too bad he couldn't find us anything in Chora," said Kouros. "He said everything's booked solid for Easter. This place belongs to his cousin."

Andreas shrugged. "It's only for one night." At least he hoped so.

The lobby was about as interesting as the architecture, but clean and tidy. The receptionist handed them keys to their rooms and an envelope. "Sergeant Mavros left this for you."

Andreas opened the envelope and peeked inside. It was photos and the videotape of Vassilis' body at the scene. "You look at these Yianni, I'll check them out later." Photos of a body lying dead in a street would change his mood; remind him of how close Lila came to ending up like that. She was in a coma for a week after being clubbed in the head. That was almost nine months ago. Thank God she was all right.

Andreas' room was small and had a view of parked cars. No matter, as long as it was quiet. He called Lila from his cell phone.

"Hello, my Prince Charming."

"Damn caller ID takes away all the mystery." Andreas was smiling.

"But not the romance, lover boy. So, how goes your island holiday off alone with Yianni?"

"Terrific, nothing but beautiful beaches, fine food—"

"And the bodies?"

Andreas paused. "I thought we agreed not to talk about that sort of thing."

Lila laughed. "I meant live ones. Find any to rival mine?"

"Sorry, I'm a bit edgy. No, none like yours. That person doesn't exist."

"Perfect answer. It's just what an almost nine months pregnant woman wants to hear. You're learning, Kaldis."

"I have a great teacher."

Lila laughed again. "So, when do you think you'll be back?"

"I'm hoping tomorrow."

"I hope so, too. I saw the doctor today and he said, 'Any day.'"

"Should I come home now?"

"No, it's not that close, but if you're planning to be away for more than a few days I can't guarantee the little one will wait."

"Don't worry, I'll be back."

"I know."

Neither spoke. It was one of those "should we marry" silences, or at least that's what Andreas thought. He was the son of a working class cop; she was from one of Greece's oldest, wealthiest families, and the young, socially prominent widow of a shipowner. Things had just happened between them. And the attack made him her protector. His move from his walkup apartment into her penthouse on the chicest street in Athens he saw as temporary, until the baby was born. Sooner or later Andreas knew she'd come to her senses and he didn't want her feeling bound to him by marriage. Until then, though, he'd continue to love her more than anyone on earth. He'd just not propose.

"So, is there anything else you want to say?" She always seemed to know what he was thinking.

Andreas paused. "It's terrible what's happened here." He decided it was safer to talk about the case than what was going through his mind. Besides, he'd only give details available to the media. "Everyone says the murdered monk was one of this world's few, truly good souls. Tragic."

"Then, thank God there are people like you who care what happens to the good ones."

"Lila, come on."

"Hey, big guy, I'm nine months pregnant, relegated to doing crossword puzzles and anagrams for thrills. Let me fantasize about the father of my child."

He wasn't sure if Lila was teasing or not, but decided to let it go. They spent the next fifteen minutes talking about all the things her parents and Andreas' mother were doing to make their baby the most appreciated in modern history. Then they said goodnight, with Andreas promising to tell her goodnight in person the next time.

He hung up and lay back on the bed. His cell phone rang. "I know, you forgot to tell me how much you love me."

"More than you'll ever imagine." It wasn't Lila.

Andreas didn't move. "I see you got my message."

"If I'd known how much you cared, I'd have called sooner. But I sensed you wanted to whisper sweet nothings in my ear personally."

"When can we meet?"

"I'll let you know when and where. What's your room number?"

"Two-two-eight."

"Night night, my love."

Andreas hung up and stared at the ceiling. It was time to get things running on a different track. He just hoped what he had in mind wouldn't end up with him tied to one right in the path of a freight train.

It was a pale sky. Filled with arrows. Back and forth they flew. Sharp-pointed black ones, with crimson feathers. The sky was never without them; they came and went in flocks. So often and so many that he no longer noticed. He'd grown used to them, accepted them as having a part in this place. They were not something to fear, but to understand so as not to be afraid. They flew all around him but could not harm him or those he embraced.

He thought back to before he'd come here. He'd heard talk of such serenity and knew of many who longed to find it, but he gave up on the value of the search when the only soul he thought could guide him there was lost. But to be fair, even had he tried on his own and by chance stumbled upon this station, the arrows flew everywhere; how was he to trust that not one could strike him if he remained?

Then, unexpectedly, he'd felt the stroke of some formless being, as light as a nursing baby at its mother's breast; a touch that gave him faith that a place of peace indeed existed, and the vision to see that he must overcome whatever of his past or present dared block the path to this rare sanctuary. It was his duty. It was the duty of a father.

Andreas jerked awake shaking his head. "Oh boy, definitely too much garlic in the *tzatziki*." He turned on the light, got out of bed, walked into the bathroom, closed his eyes and slapped cold water on his face. When he opened them he stood staring into the mirror.

He'd seen pictures of his father at his age. The father who killed himself when Andreas was eight, after a government minister had set him up, the trusting cop, to take the fall for bribes that went into that minister's own pocket.

"Yeah, Dad, we look alike. No doubt I'm your son. No doubt whatsoever." He shook his head and threw more water on his face.

"So, old man, was that your way of telling me to get on with my life and forget about how badly you fucked up your own family by checking out way before your time was up?" He watched his anger build up in the mirror but didn't look away.

"Smart move, Dad, come to me in a vision on Patmos. Makes it seem like the real thing, huh?"

Andreas paused, as if waiting for an answer.

"I need a sign, or else I'm going to chalk it up to the *tzatziki*. Make me believe in family, make me believe I won't mess things up as badly as you did. Go ahead, I dare you!"

Andreas stared into his own eyes. "See, I knew you'd let me down. Again."

He turned off the light and crawled into bed. He was back to staring at the ceiling when he heard a faint beep.

There was a text message on his phone:

I'M AWAKE, AND THOUGHT YOU MIGHT BE, TOO. JUST WANTED YOU TO KNOW JUNIOR AND I LOVE YOU VERY MUCH. L.

Andreas tried not to cry. He tried very hard not to cry.

Chapter Five

There was a knock on Andreas' door at seven in the morning. "Sir, a taxi driver just delivered an envelope for you. He said he'd wait for you."

Andreas had been up for an hour. But he wasn't expecting a taxi. "Slide it under the door."

It was a plain white envelope marked "Room 228." Inside was scribbled, *Tell the driver Lampi. See you soon.* He recognized the handwriting.

Ten minutes later Kouros and Andreas were in the taxi on their way to a beach called Lampi. It was a beautiful morning, almost no one else on the road. The taxi headed north through the old port, past harborside tavernas peppered with locals sharing coffee and gossip, and on through the new port edged by shops and places catering to the daily needs of island residents: car repair, hardware, furniture, clothing, electronics, cell phones, and pizza. As the road climbed out of Skala, eucalyptus replaced shops and the view turned to open land, marked by ancient walls, tiny villages, green and brown fields, and random homes and churches scattered across the hills among pines, cypresses, tamarisks, and pomegranates.

At a sign marked KAMBOS the driver slowed down to pass through a crossroads paved in rough-cut stone. "We're almost there. This is Kambos town. Kambos beach is up ahead."

Andreas had heard of Kambos beach. It was Patmos' most popular, the one where rich kids from around the world summering in their parents' homes and local kids in search of friends from a larger world grew up together. How well those friendships wore into adulthood largely depended on how well each appreciated the other's likely future: the rich would go on to assume their parents' lives and the locals would just go on.

"How much farther?" asked Kouros.

"About five minutes. We take a left just past the beach and it's on the other side of those hills." He nodded straight ahead. "Ever been to Lampi?"

"No," said Kouros.

"It's different than it used to be."

Why does every local, everywhere in Greece, say the same thing? thought Andreas.

"What do you mean?" said Kouros.

"The shiny colored pebbles that cover the beach. Many of them are gone. Too many tourists—and locals—take them, thinking they look better on a table somewhere or stuck in some mosaic. Damn shame how people destroy a place just to show they were there. Crazy how people think."

Yeah, crazy, thought Andreas, like the British and the Marbles from the Parthenon.

A bit later the driver nodded his head to the right. "There it is, over there." The road coiled down toward a long beach surrounded by unspoiled hills. Andreas could make out a taverna in the middle, under some trees. Or maybe there were two tavernas. A rented, blue Fiat Punto and a beat-up maroon Toyota pickup were parked at the edge of the beach. The driver turned the taxi around before stopping next to the Fiat. "Should I wait?" he asked.

"No, thank you," said Andreas, paying him.

The driver nodded. "Damn shame about the pebbles. Do me a favor, don't take any," and drove off before Andreas could reply.

Andreas smiled. The guy was right to say it.

"Over here." The voice came from the near taverna. It was about fifty yards down the beach.

"Wouldn't it have been easier to come by the hotel?" said Andreas, walking with Kouros toward the voice.

"You know me, never miss a chance for the dramatic."

Andreas hugged the man, and they kissed each other on both cheeks. Kouros and the man did the same.

"How's Lila?"

Andreas smiled as he thought about his dream last night and her message. "Due any day now."

"Can't wait."

"She'd probably tell you before me if it were up to her."

"If you're not back home when the baby's born she might never tell you." He smacked Andreas on the shoulder. "So, why has the chief of special crimes, based in Athens, dragged the chief homicide investigator for the Cycladic Islands onto a Dodecanese island outside my jurisdiction?"

Tassos Stamatos was well past retirement age, but no one in the ministry dared tell him. He knew where every body was buried, who buried them, and how to exhume any he might need to inflict the greatest possible harm on anyone who crossed him. It was called lifetime job security. "I'm guessing it has to do with the murdered monk."

Andreas nodded yes. "The only thing I'm sure of is this wasn't a mugging gone wrong. Whoever did it meant to kill him. And if even a little of what we've heard is true…" He rolled his right hand off into the air.

"Sounds like your kind of case." Tassos smiled. "I figured as much when you didn't want to talk on a cell phone. That's why I decided not to chance a landline either."

"How did you find me?" Andreas put up his hand to stop him from answering. "Maggie."

Tassos grinned. "You're the one who brought us back together."

That was pure coincidence. Andreas had known nothing about their romantic past when he played inadvertent matchmaker. He just was happy for them both: Tassos, the longtime widower, and Maggie, GADA's mother superior. Andreas shook his head and waved for him to continue.

"If anyone followed you we'd see them on the road." He looked up the hill. "So far, no unexpected visitors. And anyone here at this hour, besides Niko," he gestured toward an old man in a Greek fisherman's cap at the far end of the taverna, "is unexpected. This place doesn't open until noon. So, tell me what's going on."

It took about twenty minutes to fill him in on the facts as they knew them, and another five to spell out Dimitri's theory on Russians as probable bad guys.

Tassos just listened, and when Andreas finished he sat quietly for another minute or so. "I hate to say it, but Dimitri could be right. And if he is…" Tassos paused and shook his head. "Greeks and Russians are getting along pretty well these days, but killing our monks as part of some national plan to bring the Ecumenical Patriarch to Russia…" he didn't bother to finish. Just shook his head again. "Greece will go nuts. Make that the whole world will go nuts!"

"Welcome to my life," said Andreas. "Any idea on where to go from here?"

"Seems like something for the big boys."

"CIA?"

"Them, or MI6, or a few Middle East shops. They're the ones most likely, outside of Russia, to know if there's some basis for Russians possibly being involved. The Cold War never ended as far as they're concerned. They all keep an eye on each other, like jungle cats stalking the same prey. As for knowing for certain," Tassos shrugged. "Without a major leak or screw-up by someone directly involved, I doubt anyone will ever know. Killing monks isn't the sort of operation someone's likely to brag about, even to clandestine ops buddies."

Andreas drummed his fingers on the table. "If we bring this to one of the big agencies, no telling how they'll run with it."

"Or spin it," said Kouros.

Tassos nodded. "That's for sure. Once this gets out it won't be under your control. The big boys will play it to fit their agendas, which I guarantee you are a lot different from finding who killed an old monk on some tiny Greek island."

"I know, that's why I don't want to go that way. At least not yet. So far, all we know for certain is first, there's a monster of a damn mess out there, and second, someone went out of his way to put me in the middle of it. The only chance I see at getting an angle on what's going on is if I can find that 'someone.'" Andreas looked at Tassos. "That's why I need your help, old friend. Find out who got me into this."

Tassos smiled. "Would you like me to arrange for world peace while I'm at it?"

Andreas laughed. It had taken time, but Andreas had come around to accepting the value of Tassos' unorthodox police methods and backchannel contacts, as different as they were from his own. "You're the only one I know who actually might be able to do that, too. So, what do you say?"

"Can't think of a better thing to do at this point in my life than blindly jump into the middle of a potential religious war with Russia."

Andreas smiled and touched Tassos arm. "Thanks. Once again, I owe you. Big time."

Tassos grinned. "Have you picked out a name for the baby yet?"

Andreas smiled. "If a boy, after my father. If a girl, Lila's mother."

Tassos nodded. "Damn well better. Your dad was the best cop I ever knew." Tassos stood up and patted Andreas on the back. "Come on, I'll give you a ride back."

Andreas stood. "Are you sure you want to be seen with us?"

Tassos put his arm around Andreas' waist and steered him toward the car. "My friend, if the Russians are behind this operation they've been watching us by satellite all morning, and if it's somebody else…" he shook his free hand in the air. "Let's let them know that now they've got three of us to deal with."

Andreas smiled. "I feel so much safer now."

Tassos took his arm from around Andreas' waist and smacked him on the back of the head.

On the drive back, Andreas called the abbot to set up interviews with the monks they'd missed the day before.

The abbot was apologetic. "I'm sorry Chief Kaldis, but I never had the chance to tell them you wanted to speak with them. I only learned this morning that they'd taken a late boat Sunday night in order to be back in their monasteries in time for Easter observances."

Andreas let out a deep breath.

"I'll e-mail you their names and how to get in touch with them as soon I get that information. I'll also send you copies of whatever computer backup we find for Vassilis' work, but so far our network administrator has found nothing for him newer than two months ago. Sorry."

"Thanks, just get everything to me right away. Okay?"

"Certainly. Goodbye."

Andreas looked at the bright side: there was nothing left for him to do on Patmos, at least for the moment. He turned to Yianni in the back seat. "Looks like we get to go home." Then he looked over at Tassos. "Would you like us to give you a lift to Syros? The extra weight is no problem for the helicopter, it's a big one." He smiled.

Tassos gave him the middle finger gesture. "Thanks but no thanks. I'll drop you at the heliport. It wouldn't be fair to my friend who sailed though the night to get me here by dawn if I left him to make the four-hour return trip home alone."

For most men, twenty minutes or so in the air versus four-plus hours on a choppy sea back to the island capital of the Cyclades was a no-brainer choice. That, Andreas thought, was another reason Tassos had so many well-connected friends willing to do so much for him: he never took them for granted. Andreas hoped somewhere out there one of those friends had an answer. Any answer.

Tassos dropped them off at the heliport and drove down toward the harbor. He knew this wasn't a simple murder and that

Andreas knew it, too. There was something almost spooky about this one. And a lot of toes to step on: Greek, Russian, and God knows what else. He didn't mind that so much; he just wished there were a head he could bust or an arm he could twist to get a lead, some place to start. He let out a breath. It would come to him, it always did. God willing.

◇◇◇

"Surprise, I'm back. See, I kept my promise."

Lila chuckled into the phone. "I know. Tassos called. He said he'd made sure to ship you home."

"He's such a bastard." Andreas laughed.

"So, when do I get to see you?"

Andreas looked at his watch. "We're on the way to the office—"

"So, sometime before midnight?"

"No, honest, I should be home this afternoon." He looked at his watch. It wasn't even noon.

Lila laughed. "Yes, I'm sure. Don't worry, do what you have to do. Just knowing you're nearby is all the comfort I need. Kisses."

Andreas hung up and stared out the window, wondering what he'd done to deserve her. And how much longer could she stand a life with him. He didn't want to think about that.

Fifteen minutes later he was back at GADA. Athens was a place more than five million called home, and where few ever seemed to be asleep at the same time. Some never seemed to sleep at all. GADA was in the heart of the action, across the street from the stadium of one of Greece's two most popular soccer teams, down the block from Greece's Supreme Court, and next to a major hospital.

No sooner did Andreas sit behind his desk than Maggie came bouncing through his office door. She dropped an envelope on the desk. "So, what did he have to say?"

"What did who have to say?"

"Tassos."

"Of course, how could I have thought this was about police business?"

"It is about police business, I don't need to ask you what he has to say about other things." Maggie smiled. "I want to know if he can help you find the guy you're looking for."

Andreas stared at her. "Is there anything you don't know?"

"When he called to find out where you were, I knew it had to be serious if he wouldn't talk to you over the phone, and since we both know what he's good at," she seemed to swoon at a different thought, "I figured you were looking for someone."

Andreas shook his head. "You'd have made a terrific cop."

"Too limiting." She turned and left.

He watched her bounce out the door; five-feet, three-inches of red-topped, endless energy.

Andreas opened the envelope. It contained the photographs he'd given Kouros of the crime scene. He took them out and spread them on his desk. There were dozens. What a tragedy. Time to focus: on each photograph, on each section of each photograph, on everything in context with all else. Looking, studying, hoping to find a clue, anything that might help. But all he kept seeing was the same thing: a sad-looking, silver-haired monk, lying dead on a street, clutching a cross. What a terrible end for such a wonderful life, for any life.

He stood up and walked over to the window. What was going through that monk's mind when faced with the end of his life? To accept his death…to fight…to pass along a message? There were no signs of a fight or a message, and he was clutching his cross. His choice seemed clear. Acceptance.

Andreas had reached a dead end. Now it was up to Tassos.

Chapter Six

Andreas was in the middle of a dozen things on a half dozen different cases when Maggie buzzed him. "It's *him*."

He didn't have to ask whom she meant; he just picked up the phone. "Are you about to make me as happy as you're making my secretary?"

"I hope so—but differently."

"Where are you?" Andreas looked at his watch. It wasn't even two. "You can't be back on Syros."

"No, we stopped for lunch on Ikaria."

"Ikaria?" It was a northern Aegean island, a little less than halfway between Patmos and Syros. "Why Ikaria?"

"I have a lot of friends here from the old days."

Andreas knew that for Tassos the "old days" meant Greece's military dictatorship years, between 1967 and 1974, and his time spent as a rookie cop in an island prison guarding the junta's political enemies. He'd taken great pains to befriend all the politicians under his care as a hedge against Greece's return to democracy. That made him great friends among both outright fascists and hardcore communists. No doubt the ones on Ikaria fell into the latter category. It was a bastion for communists long ago forced to relocate there from other parts of Greece.

"I have what you want. I'm on a landline, do you want to chance it?"

"What the hell, if every phone line in this country's tapped, we're wasting our time trying to save it anyway. Shoot."

"It was a lot easier than I thought. The person who called the
minister of public order to get you assigned to the case didn't try
to hide who he was. Everyone in the office knew."

"Why don't I think I'm going to like what's coming."

"Oh, it's not as bad as you think." Then Tassos told him the
name.

"Great, a former prime minister. How's that *not* bad news?
Who's possibly going to make him talk? He's untouchable,
another dead end."

"Are you finished?"

Andreas slammed his hand on the desk.

"As I was saying, it was easier than I thought. You see, the
person who got him to make the call also must have figured that
a former prime minister was untouchable, that no one possibly
could force him into revealing a confidence, and so he didn't
bother to use an intermediary when asking for the favor. What
he didn't know was that the prime minister owed a few favors
of his own."

"I could kiss you."

"Don't pucker up quite yet. The prime minister has, as he
admits, 'a weakness for contraband antiquities,' and that's had
me bailing him out of more than one politically sensitive night-
mare. But he's of the kind that doesn't like being reminded of
favors owed. When I told him what I wanted, he raged on about
'How dare I ask him to betray his word,' 'Who did I think I was
asking him to violate a confidence,' etcetera, and he threatened
to hang up." Tassos paused. "But he didn't."

Andreas could almost see a grin through the phone.

"We reached a compromise. He said he couldn't give me the
name because there'd be no way for him to deny he was the source.
Instead, he gave me a phone number. Said it's for the man who
wanted you assigned to the case. Our distinguished former prime
minister's exact words were, 'Take this number and lose mine.'"

"The next sound you hear will be a kiss—"

"Hate to wreck your style, but I've a boat to catch. I checked
out the number, it's in Thessaloniki." Thessaloniki was Greece's

second largest city, located in northeast Greece. Tassos quickly read off the number, then repeated it. "Bye-bye."

"Thanks, kiss, kiss." Andreas stared at the number, then pressed the intercom. "Maggie, come in here, please."

She was in before he hung up.

"I need you to find out what you can about this number." Andreas held out a piece of paper.

She didn't take it. "It's a Thessaloniki number, no further information."

He stared at her. "You ran it for him, didn't you?"

Maggie shrugged. "He was on a boat in the middle of the Aegean, and we knew you'd want to know. What's the problem?"

Andreas put the paper down. "No problem. Just wondering why I'm always the last to know what's going on in my own office."

"You're too busy handling the big things." She smiled. "Besides, we want to try to get you home in time for dinner, don't we?" She turned and left.

Andreas stared at the door. Now the women in his life were teaming up on him. He stood no chance.

He shut his eyes and sat quietly for several minutes, then picked up the phone and dialed. It rang six times and he was about to—

"Hello." It was a formal, resonant, male voice.

Andreas swallowed. "It is I."

"And whom would that be?"

"The chosen one."

"I'm afraid I don't know what you're talking about, or how you got this number."

"You should."

"Why?"

"You chose me."

There was a pause. "I heard you were good. Chief Inspector Kaldis, I presume."

Andreas thought to reach out for the man's name, but decided it better to act as if he already knew his identity. "So, where do you want to meet?"

"Why should I meet you?"

"Oh, you're definitely going to meet me. I'm just giving you the choice of having me show up on your doorstep with a brass band, or doing it less conspicuously at a location of your choosing." Andreas held his breath. If the man hung up, he was nowhere.

"Give me a minute."

It seemed like an hour.

"How's seven tonight at the Sofitel?"

"At Venizelos Airport?"

"Yes, call this number when you get there."

"See you then."

"Looking forward to it. Goodbye." The line went dead.

Andreas didn't hang up. He dialed Lila's number. So much for making it home this afternoon. He still might make it for dinner, if it wasn't an early one.

Andreas and Kouros were at the hotel by four. A team sat in a van directly across from the hotel entrance with instructions to photograph everyone going in and out, as well as anyone in its outdoor café adjacent to the entrance. The hotel's front door was fifty yards from the main terminal and the place had a virtual monopoly on anyone needing a room at Athens' international airport. It also was convenient for travelers looking for a place to meet with locals. Many simply sat at the café, did their business, and left without ever going inside the hotel. Andreas guessed this guy would want privacy and get a room for their meeting. A male-female team was instructed to hang out in the lobby, photographing everyone getting off the elevators, just in case he'd already checked in.

At precisely seven Andreas strode into the lobby and dialed the number.

"Hello."

"I'm here."

"You need a room key to get the elevator to stop at my floor. I'll send someone down to meet you."

"What does the 'someone' look like?"

The man laughed. "I'm sure you'll figure it out."

Andreas wondered if he should reconsider his decision to meet without backup. He thought to say something to his team in the lobby but decided against it; someone might be watching him now that he'd made that call. He walked to the elevators. The only thing waiting for him was a massive reproduction of a classic, white marble Cycladic statue of a female form, arms crossed below the chest. It stood against the far wall at the end of the elevator bank. He was staring at it when an elevator door next to him opened.

A couple in jeans, tee-shirts, sneakers, and matching baseball caps stepped out, speaking English and clutching a map. Nope, not them. Another elevator door opened. This one was at the far end, next to the statue.

A man stepped out and turned to face Andreas. The statue vanished. The sun would have disappeared behind this guy. He was a giant, but not just any giant, a graying blond one in full Eastern Orthodox cleric dress: hat, cross, and all. Backup no longer seemed relevant. They'd need a howitzer to stop this guy. Andreas stepped inside the open door and the cleric followed. He put a room key into the slot by the floor buttons and pressed six.

If this guy's taking me to room 666 I'm not going in. His private Book of Revelation joke had Andreas smiling to himself, but then the man opened the door to room 616. The man waved him inside without saying a word or entering the room, then closed the door behind Andreas. Another man was inside, alone in the room, sitting on a chair by the window. The sunlight passing through the window made it difficult to make him out.

"Welcome, my son." The man did not stand, just extended his right hand.

He was wearing a finely tailored, dark blue suit, like the Italian one Lila had bought Andreas for his birthday. He wasn't sure if he should shake or kiss the man's hand. Perhaps this was a test to see if Andreas actually knew who he was. Andreas moved slightly to the left as he approached him, just enough to shield the sun a bit and get a better look. The man was old but looked fit. His silver hair was pulled into a tight bun behind his head, in the fashion of Italian movie stars. And Greek clerics. Andreas bent over and kissed the man's hand.

"Thank you for seeing me, Your Holiness."

"So you do know who I am."

Andreas nodded, even though he didn't. "Hard to miss, considering your entourage." He pointed back over his shoulder toward the door.

"Ah yes, Sergey. A very loyal follower of the faith."

Andreas had heard rumors of such loyal followers of the faith making it into receptive monasteries directly out of Balkan military forces. Whether they entered seeking true salvation or sanctuary from a past they and the world would rather forget, he did not know.

"Frankly, I don't like traveling, as you say, with an 'entourage,' but after what happened to poor Vassilis," he crossed himself, "do I have a choice? Or to dress as I am to journey to meetings such as this?" He pointed at his suit.

Andreas took that as an opening for avoiding preliminary chit-chat. "What are you afraid of?"

"I wish I knew."

"Please, just tell me what you do know."

"How much history do you want?"

"All of it." Andreas sat down on the edge of the bed across from him and listened. An hour later, he wondered if he'd said the right thing to an old man who'd just lost a very dear friend. Nothing he'd told Andreas seemed relevant to the case. The ancient intrigues of the church were of interest only to scholars, reminiscences of his days shared with Vassilis in the seminary were almost fifty years old, and their shared views on modern theological problems of the church raised not even a hint of a motive for murder.

Thank God I'm wearing a wire, Andreas thought. If I'd been taking notes I'd have lost patience long ago. He sneaked a peek at his watch. At this pace, a late dinner with Lila was out of the question; breakfast might even be iffy. He had to find some way to move this along onto something relevant.

"Excuse me, Your Holiness, would you like some water?"

The man seemed surprised at hearing another's voice. "Uh, why yes, thank you, my son." He paused. "I hope what I'm telling you is helpful."

Andreas went to the minibar and took out two bottles of water. "Yes, very." He walked back to the man and held out the bottles. "Gas or no gas?"

The man took the flat water. "Thank you."

"Why did you ask that I be assigned to this case?"

The man took a sip of water. "I was just about to tell you."

Andreas hoped that meant within the next hour. He sat back down on the edge of the bed and opened the other bottle of water.

"Vassilis was a scholar and patient observer. He saw things others missed. A debate with him was an exploration of thought." He shook his head. "He never should have left his theoretical world. I told him to stay out of it."

Andreas leaned forward. "Out of what?"

"This Russian thing."

A chill ran down Andreas' back. "Go on, please."

"I'm certain that by now you are well aware of Russian interest in relocating the Ecumenical Patriarch."

Andreas nodded.

"And of Vassilis' obsession with how the scandal at Mount Athos might affect that issue."

Andreas nodded again.

"If the Russians could be shown to have played any part in creating that scandal, it would destroy the credibility of their attacks on Mount Athos' fitness to serve as the new home for the next leader of the church. In fact, if Russians were involved, the moral value of our claim is strengthened. It would make us the innocent victim of vicious intrigues by a former superpower."

From his use of "our" and "us" in describing Mount Athos, Andreas presumed that was where he called home. It also fit

with Andreas' guess about sanctuary for Sergey, because anyone accepted into monastic life on Mount Athos acquired Greek citizenship without further formalities.

"I told him to let it be, that there was nothing he could do, but he would not relent in his quest for proof." The man paused. "I assume you know all that, too."

Andreas nodded as if he did.

"There's one thing I'm certain you do not know." He paused and took a sip of water. "Vassilis was coming to meet me when he was murdered."

The man took another sip, then crossed his legs and sat quietly watching Andreas, as if waiting to measure his reaction.

"I didn't know that."

The man nodded. "He called me on the morning of the day before he was killed. He said he had proof things were not as they seemed."

The same state of mind Dimitri had used to describe Vassilis, Andreas thought.

"He was excited, but also frightened."

Probably something like the feeling Andreas now had.

"He said I 'must' see what he'd found 'immediately.' I tried calming him down, but he wouldn't listen. He invoked Revelation, saying I must see it now, 'for the time is at hand.' He was quoting from the opening lines of Revelation, the part some say first warns of the coming Apocalypse." The man drew in and let out a breath. "I told him to e-mail me whatever it was. He said he knew my assistant screened my e-mails and he couldn't risk anyone other than us knowing what he'd found. 'Too dangerous,' he said. I never dreamed it might cost him his life." He shook his head.

"Did you tell your assistant about your conversation with Vassilis?"

"No, I told no one. You're the first person to whom I've mentioned any of this."

"Who else knew what Vassilis was looking for?"

"A better question is, 'Who didn't?' As I said, Vassilis was obsessed, as if he'd been called upon to be a savior of the church. He contacted anyone he thought could possibly help get him an answer. Frankly, I was worried some might stop taking him seriously, begin indulging him as if he were an old man who'd lost it."

"Had he?"

"No, not a bit."

"So, what happened?"

"He insisted he must see me in person, but could not possibly come to me without being observed and that 'would be dangerous for us both.' He told me I must come to him and made a joke about his friends being only 'poor fishermen with brightly colored, slow moving boats,' while mine were more from the 'stealthy, fast, silver helicopter' crowd."

The man rubbed at his eyes with his right hand. "So we agreed to meet at three the next morning in the house of a friend of his, off behind the Patmos town hall. The friend was away and we'd be alone. The only people who knew I was on the island were the American pilot who flew the helicopter, the taxi driver who brought me to Chora, and of course, Vassilis. The pilot had no idea who I was, and the taxi driver thought I was some old monk with 'a relative in the military' important enough to get me 'a lift to Patmos for Easter Week.' Even my secretary didn't know where I was going.

"I was in the house by two thirty, waiting for Vassilis to show up. He was late and that wasn't like him. Then I heard someone shouting, and when I realized what he was saying…'Kalogeros Vassilis was murdered in the square'…I didn't know what to do." He looked down at his hands. "I'm ashamed to say it, but I was afraid."

Andreas leaned over and touched the man's knee. "No need to explain, you were right to be afraid."

The man nodded. "I called my secretary and told him what happened. He said to stay where I was and he would arrange for 'someone' to accompany me back home."

"Sergey?"

"Yes, and through the help of another friend with another helicopter, Sergey met me at the house, disguised me, and got me out of Patmos before the sun came up."

Damn sight more efficient than the Patmos police, thought Andreas.

"He is very concerned that anyone even remotely suspected of knowing whatever led to Vassilis' murder is in grave danger."

Thank you for inviting me to the party, thought Andreas.

"May I have some more water?"

Andreas got up, went to the minibar, and brought the man another bottle.

"Thank you. I still have no idea what Vassilis planned on showing me." He twisted off the cap and took a sip. "I can assure you that sitting afraid and alone in that house, not knowing what might happen before help arrived, I tried thinking of anything he conceivably might have found explosive enough to get him murdered." He shook his head. "I came up with nothing. But I reached a decision. No matter what it took, I swore I'd see those who killed him brought to justice." He crossed himself, perhaps as an apology for the show of anger.

"That's how you got involved. I called my friend—I assume you know the former prime minister?"

Andreas shrugged. "Not really."

The man shrugged back. "No matter. I told him there was no more heinous and pressing a crime to solve in all of Greece than that morning's murder of a revered holy man in the middle of the town square of the Holy Island of Patmos during Easter Week. He agreed and promised to use 'all of his influence' to get the country's 'best investigator' assigned immediately. I told him whoever was chosen must be incorruptible and not afraid of treading on political toes."

Andreas laughed. "Should I be flattered that he picked me?"

The man smiled. "I'm not sure. If police are like churchmen, you're probably in the minority."

Andreas laughed again. "Of all the people in the world, you're the one Vassilis chose to confide in. Why do you think he did that?"

"We were *simpatico*. We thought the same way about a lot of things."

"So, what's your gut instinct on why he was murdered?"

"I wish I had one. All I have are thoughts. Just random, unsupportable thoughts." He stood for the first time since Andreas had entered the room. He was as tall as Andreas, but very slim. He turned and stared out the window.

"So much of life is illusion, driven by masters of manipulation who incite passions, instill mortal fears, justify actions. They've always existed, always will. But those to fear, to guard against—and yes, to pray against—are illusionists who act without conscience, without values, without any moral compass."

Time to bring him back to the here and now, thought Andreas. "What are you trying to say, Your Holiness?"

"I don't know, I sincerely don't know." He turned from the window and looked into Andreas' eyes. "Whoever killed my dear friend does not fear God…or, worse, might see his murder as serving God in some way."

This is getting freakier by the minute. "Any names come to mind?"

He gestured no. "The Russians certainly qualify—in both categories—but it could be a lunatic, a zealot, the antichrist."

Andreas believed in flesh and blood bad guys, but thought if the Russians were behind this he might stand a better chance against the spirit world. "It had to be someone who felt threatened enough by Vassilis to kill him." Andreas paused. "And no doubt would kill again if threatened."

"I know, that's why I keep Sergey closeby."

"A wise decision." Andreas looked at his watch. Time to make another wise decision. He stood and handed the man his card. "If you get any more thoughts or ideas you think might help, please give me a call. And do you have a card so I may reach you with what I'm sure will be more questions?"

"You have my phone number, don't you?"

"Yes."

"That's the best one to use, calls to that number come directly to me."

"Fine, and thank you for your time."

"Thank you, Chief Inspector." He walked Andreas to the door. "I will call my friend to thank him for getting you assigned to the case. You're definitely the right man for the job." He patted Andreas on the back and opened the door.

Andreas stepped out, and turned to acknowledge the compliment.

"And, of course, to thank him for setting up this meeting." His Holiness shut the door.

Oops.

◇◇◇

"Do you really think he'll ream out a former prime minister?" Kouros was driving them back from the airport, and Andreas had just finished filling him in on the meeting.

"Don't know what their relationship is like. Don't even know who the guy is, but for Tassos' sake, I sure as hell hope not. I think he just was letting me know I wasn't fooling him."

"What's your take on him?"

"He's definitely smart and didn't get where he is in the church making bad political decisions. He doesn't come across as a potential bad guy, but he's certainly no country bumpkin priest either. He's a politician, a church politician at that. I want you to find everything you can about him, but I also want you to dig up what you can on that giant Sergey. I'm betting he's here on asylum and we'll get a better measure of the boss when we see what sort of 'loyal follower of the faith' he's protecting."

"Why do you think the boss didn't want to identify himself? He must know we'll find out."

"I think it was just a case of nerves. He has real reason to be afraid, and if not telling me his name gave him comfort, so be it. The real question is, how did the bad guys know Vassilis was on his way to meet him?"

"Perhaps they didn't know?"

"Then how did they know Vassilis was carrying something worth killing him for?"

"Like I said, maybe they didn't know, just decided to take him out as a precaution."

Andreas shook his head. "I don't think so. Even an idiot would realize murdering a monk on Patmos during Easter Week would unleash the kind of political pressure we're getting to find the killers. A 'precautionary' murder," he flashed his fingers at Kouros, "is a drug-induced heart attack or a tragic automobile accident. This is what you do in desperation, when there's absolutely no other alternative."

"So we're back to 'How did the bad guys find out?'"

"If we figure that out, it might give us who they are. I wish we knew what they're so damn afraid of." He stared out the window. "Have Maggie start in on transcribing the tape first thing in the morning. No one but Maggie."

"She'll just love you for that."

Andreas smiled. "I'm sure, but we can't afford gossip in the typing pool about Russians or the antichrist running around killing monks."

Kouros cleared his throat. "Yeah, it's beginning to sound like one of those books by that American guy, Dan Brown."

Andreas turned and stared at him. "How long have you been sitting there, waiting for an opportunity to say that?"

"It was spontaneous, came to me in a 'Revelation.'"

Andreas shook his head and looked out the window. "And Lila thinks my sense of humor is twisted."

"I've always admired her instincts."

Andreas shot a quick left jab at Kouros' right shoulder, not hard enough for him to lose control, but enough to make him smile; and realize how much his boss appreciated him.

Andreas then decided to express his appreciation in words. "Drop me off at home, asshole."

◇◇◇

The original plan was to return home tonight, but he was tired. All the talk about Vassilis had left him sad. They'd known each other since they were children. Now he was the only one left. He decided to go straight to bed and leave early tomorrow morning. No one but the policeman knew he was in the hotel, and Sergey was in the adjoining room, just in case. As he lay in bed, he wondered if perhaps he'd come down too hard on the policeman. Obviously, Kaldis had done something to get the former prime minister to betray a confidence. But what good would it do confronting the minister, except fire him up for retribution against whomever he could blame but himself for the embarrassment?

Besides, he thought, I'm the one who insisted the minister find someone capable of getting to the bottom of things, no matter what it took. Can't have it both ways; at least not all the time.

And there was another reason for keeping the minister's indiscretion to himself. A confrontation was likely to make the minister indignant and less likely to help the next time; but, if properly stroked, the minister's guilty conscience over this incident might yield even greater favors in the future. He decided to leave things be, turned off the light, and shut his eyes.

Not all manipulation is bad, he thought, as he prayed for sleep to come quickly.

Chapter Seven

Lila Vardi's home was next to the Presidential Palace, the entire, sixth-floor penthouse in one of downtown Athens' rare old residential buildings. It was perhaps Athens' most exclusive and breathtaking address, offering unobstructed views of both the Acropolis and its majestic sister hill, Lykavittos.

When Andreas first moved in with Lila he imagined every doorman, elevator operator, and porter thinking, "So you're the superstud cop who knocked up one of Greece's most sought-after women and now lives the high life." The thought kept gnawing at him, and one night he shared it with her.

Five minutes later, after Lila stopped laughing, she said, "If that's what they're thinking, it's only because they're jealous as hell. So don't worry about it, my 'superstud cop.' Just keep earning your title." Then she laughed some more.

That's when he stopped worrying about what others thought. The truth was, as far as Andreas could tell, he was always treated with the same respect as every other resident in the building, and indeed, the staff referred to Lila as his "wife" and him as her "husband." The press took to doing the same. Lila still was among the most photographed women in Greece, but in deference to his position in the police and potential threats to his safety, rarely did a photo of him appear; when one did, he was identified only as "her husband, Andreas."

It was as if they were married in everyone's eyes but their own.

"Hi, honey, I'm home," Andreas said in the sing-song comic way everyone seems to use at one time or another.

A voice answered from another room. "She's in the bedroom, Mr. Kaldis." It was the maid, rather, one of the maids. He still wasn't used to that part of his new life: someone always there ready to do whatever he needed done. He wasn't sure he'd ever get used to that.

"Thank you, Marietta."

He walked through rooms filled with antiques and paintings, none of which he noticed anymore. They'd become part of his surroundings, like people you see every day and stop noticing because you expect them to be there. Andreas wondered if that's why no one noticed anything unusual at the monastery: everyone expected to see monks in a monastery, and that made anyone dressed as a monk virtually invisible. What did Vassilis see that the others did not? What spooked him into believing 'the time is at hand?' First thing tomorrow Kouros had better chase down those unaccounted-for monks.

He peeked into the bedroom. The drapes were open to a view of a brightly lit Acropolis, and Lila was sitting up in bed. "Guess who?"

"Daddy's home." She patted her belly.

Andreas walked to the bed, leaned over, and kissed her; then kissed her belly.

"Daddy's going to take you out to play soon," she said.

He rubbed her belly, and winked. "Too bad I can't stop up for a visit."

Lila smacked his arm. "Don't even joke about sex. Rent movies." She smiled.

He kissed her belly again, and then her forehead. "See, I made it home before midnight."

She looked at the clock on her bedside table. "Wow, ten-thirty, you're a man of your word! Do you want something to eat? I couldn't wait for you."

"No problem, I didn't expect you to. I'll make something later in the kitchen."

Lila shook her head and picked up the intercom handset. "Marietta, would you please prepare a plate for Mr. Kaldis and bring it into our bedroom. Thank you." She put it down and said, "When are you going to get used to having help around the house?"

Andreas shrugged, kicked off his shoes, and flopped onto the bed beside her. "I feel more at home among the monks. Doing things for myself."

"Let's not go there. I said no more talk about sex."

He laughed. "But I really admire someone who finds a life so rewarding and purposeful that he willingly gives up what so much of the rest of the world considers so damn important."

"Moderation, I'm afraid, is a thing of the past, even among churchmen. There are very few I know who have given up much of the material world in the pursuit of their faith."

"But there still are some who believe 'nothing in excess' is the right way to live."

Lila turned and stared at him. He'd just quoted from one of her lectures. "That was carved in Delphi by Athenians 2,500 years ago. It's Apollo's Creed."

"And a favorite of a scholar I much admire." He kissed her on the cheek. "But I'm talking about monks, not all churchmen, and one monk in particular."

"The murdered one?"

"Yes. He must have been a rare soul. Amazing how no one had a cross word to say about him." Andreas pushed up on his elbows and stared out the window at the Parthenon. "Imagine feeling so much a part of something, a part of something so much bigger than yourself that when your time has come you're totally at peace." He smiled and took her hand. "I guess it's sort of how I feel at this moment."

Andreas stared at her hand and wrapped his fingers around hers. "He died at peace…embracing his past…clutching his cross." He let the thought drift off.

Lila spread her arms. "Come here with…" she looked down at her belly "…us."

Andreas smiled and lay down next to her. Lila rested her head against his chest. Neither said a word.

Andreas drifted off into that state just before sleep when the senses recede and thoughts become meditative. He pictured the cross in the monk's hand. The cross of his grandfather, the cross with which he might well have shared virtually every day of his life. Andreas' eyes popped open. He felt as if a silent bomb had gone off in the room.

"*His cross,*" Andreas cried out and jumped out of the bed, almost sending Lila tumbling off onto the floor. "It wasn't his cross he was holding when he died. His cross, the one he treasured from his grandfather, was left dangling openly around his neck, free for anyone to take. The one he chose to grip, to guard when he knew he was dying, was a cheap, ten euro piece of junk he'd bought only hours before! How could it possibly have meant so much to him that his last act on earth was to protect it?"

Andreas paced back and forth in front of the window. Lila said nothing, just watched him.

"He didn't die accepting the end of his life. He died sending a message. But what message?" He turned to Lila, "I've got to get back to Patmos, right away."

"'Right away'?"

He didn't miss the disappointment in her voice. Andreas drew in and let out a breath. "'Right away,' as in 'first thing tomorrow morning.'" He sat next to her on the bed, took her hand, and kissed it. "Tonight I'm spending with my baby." He patted her belly. "Both my babies."

Tears started forming in Lila's eyes. She dabbed at them with her fingertips. "Sorry, pregnant women get this way at times."

"No need to say more." A knock at the door signaled it was time for dinner with his family. "I belong here." He doubted any soul would disagree, certainly none like Vassilis.

Patmos was a place of rich beauty, deep conviction, and pious tradition. It also was an island, and island people were different from mainland folk. Separated from the rest of the world, they grew up facing dangers without expecting help from the outside.

Instead, they relied upon each other and learned to honor their neighbors' families by attending their baptisms, weddings, and funerals. During Easter Week there would be no baptisms or weddings, but funerals were different. They were prohibited only on Good Friday.

Vassilis was not from Patmos and had no surviving family to honor him, but from the crowd overflowing his funeral that morning you'd think Kalogeros Vassilis was the father of each soul on the island. Virtually every Patmian-owned business closed for the funeral. It was an unimaginable honor, paid by a business-savvy people during one of their busiest weeks of the year.

Andreas arrived in Skala while the funeral was underway in Chora. That made it hard for him to shop for what he wanted. But, finally, he found it in a store run by an Athenian. From there he went directly to the police station. No one was expecting him and that was how he wanted it. Two young cops seemed to be the only people in the place. Everyone else must be at the funeral, he thought.

Andreas identified himself and told the cop sitting at the front desk that he was there "to review the physical evidence in the Kalogeros Vassilis case."

The cop turned his head toward the other cop standing by the hallway to the captain's office. From their exchange of looks it was obvious neither knew what to do.

"I'm sorry sir, I'm not authorized to allow you access," said the cop behind the desk.

"Who is?" Andreas was crisp and formal.

"The captain, sir."

"Then call him."

"I can't, sir, he's at the funeral."

"Then open the door to his office."

"I said I'm not allowed, sir." There was a slightly testy edge to his voice.

Andreas leaned over and stared. "That's Chief Inspector Kaldis, Special Crimes GADA, to you, rookie." He paused. "Now, open the goddamned door before I kick it in."

The two Patmos cops looked at each other as if each hoped the other would do something. Andreas waited five seconds, then walked around the desk and headed toward the captain's office. The cop by the hallway stepped in front of him and held up his hand.

"Stop!" He paused. "I'll get the key."

"Wise decision, officer."

Three minutes later Andreas and the cop with the key were in the captain's office standing around the evidence table. Neither said a word to the other. Andreas wanted the cop there; that way there'd be no charge of tampering with evidence.

Carefully, Andreas laid out every piece of evidence in front of him: the robe, the hat, the undergarments, the sandals, a cross.

"Where's the other cross?"

The cop shrugged. "I guess they took it for the funeral service."

"Who authorized its removal?"

He shrugged again. "The captain?"

Hope the idiot doesn't bury it with him, thought Andreas. Thank God he took the silver one.

Slowly, Andreas began examining every stitch of every garment, as if a Rosetta stone-type secret were woven into the fabric. After twenty-five minutes of this, Andreas noticed the cop was getting antsy. He'd stopped watching every move Andreas made and began glancing around the room. Five minutes later Andreas said, "Officer, would you do me a favor and open the shutters, I need a bit more light in here if I'm ever going to finish."

The cop seemed excited at the chance of finally getting to do something besides watching Andreas' hands. He stepped behind the captain's desk, popped open the shutters and returned to the table. By then Andreas had moved on to the cross. He was holding it up to the new light. "Thanks, that helped a lot."

The rookie nodded.

Ten minutes later Andreas said he was finished. He told the two how much he appreciated their cooperation and said, if they preferred, he'd not mention his visit to their captain. They looked at each other and, in Greek chorus fashion, nodded and said, "Thank you."

Andreas walked back to his car imagining what he'd do to anyone under his command that let himself be bullied into opening up his office. No telling what could happen. He touched the item in his pant pocket that he'd purchased less than an hour before in the shop. Well, not really the same item, but one just like it. Someone might even switch crosses on you, he thought.

The first thing Maggie saw on her desk that morning was a sealed envelope wrapped in red ribbon with a scribbled note:

> *Please transcribe <u>ASAP</u>. Only you are to do it, and only you are to know. There are two voices on the tape, one is still unidentified and the other belongs to the person who made me do this to you. xox, Yianni.*

She smiled. They were good kids. Dedicated cops, too. Not many like them. She put aside the things on her desk, opened the envelope, and took out the tape. There wasn't a decent software program for converting Greek speech into the written word, so she did it the old fashioned way: she put the tape into her transcription machine, adjusted her headphones to minimize damage to her permanent, and hit the foot pedal to start things off.

Maggie could type as fast as they spoke, and once she caught the rhythm of their voices it was easy. She was breezing along listening to the other man's scholarly description of ancient church intrigues and enjoying every minute of it. She was deeply religious and more aware than most of church history. She quickly realized that the other man was someone who truly knew what he was talking about. She also noticed something familiar about his voice. Probably, she thought, because she'd heard the subject discussed many times before.

The man was five minutes or so into his thinking on modern theological problems confronting the church when she screamed, "*Kalogeros Giorgos! I can't believe it's you.*"

Maggie transcribed the rest of the tape in rigid, concentrated silence. Nothing in life surprised her anymore, but she prayed he wasn't involved. Not all sacred cows should fall to slaughter. Certainly not this one, she prayed.

Kouros looked at what the abbot had e-mailed as being all his information on the three unaccounted-for monks. It was about as helpful as saying, "Huey, Dewey, and Louie live in Disney World." Maybe less so. All were from a monastery on Mount Athos that was among the poorest, least developed, and strictest there. Its monks prided themselves on rigorous discipline and endless prayer. They slept on wooden plank benches without mattresses, and regarded as far too liberal a neighbor monastery well known for its strict interpretation of all things and the inscription "Orthodoxy or Death" over its entranceway.

They had no television, no Internet, no telephone, and barely communicated with the outside world. The only way to make contact was by mail or to show up on their doorstep and literally pray for them to let you in. Kouros sighed. He saw a pilgrimage in his future.

Kouros decided to take a crack at something more within his control and ran a check on the Patmos police captain. It came back clean except for a number of citizen complaints that his personality bordered on asshole—coming from the dark side. No surprise there. But an otherwise clean record didn't necessarily mean anything more than he was careful. Some of the dirtiest cops he knew looked terrific on paper. They'd pull more quality arrests than any other cops in their jurisdiction. Of course they did, because they were paid by their bad-guy partners not just to protect them, but to shut down their competitors through tip-offs. It was a double hit for crooked cops: glory for the collar, cash for the protection. Still, there was nothing to suggest this Patmos cop was dirty. It would require an undercover operation in the middle of nowhere. He'd leave that call to his chief.

Chapter Eight

Stealing evidence wasn't his proudest moment, but Andreas saw no choice. He had to study it in detail, and if he did so in front of Patmos cops there was no doubt his interest in the cross would get back to anyone on the island with an interest in his investigation. Vassilis died protecting whatever secret it held and Andreas wasn't about to help give it away.

Switching crosses wasn't all that difficult, even though he'd relied more on improvisation and luck than practiced skill. He'd casually slid his left hand into his left front pant pocket and gripped the duplicate cross as the cop went behind the captain's desk. The instant the cop turned to open the shutters, Andreas grabbed the evidence from the table with his right hand, and with his left, yanked the replacement out of his pocket and thrust it up in front of him. By the time the cop looked back, Andreas was slowly twisting the duplicate in the light, drawing the cop's eyes to it while slipping the original into his right front pant pocket.

The only real downside he saw to what he'd done was that unless something truly nasty turned up in the Patmos captain's file that Andreas could not overlook, a potentially crooked cop was home free. Andreas knew if he pushed for an investigation that ultimately led to prosecution the rookies would tell their captain everything, and his visit would become a key element in any defense. That one incontrovertible fact would be partnered with a lot of made-up ones to yield stories and headlines along the lines of "Chief Cop Plants Evidence on Local Cop." It was just that sort of take-no-prisoners media approach that broke his father. He wouldn't risk subjecting Lila and the baby to the craziness. No reason to revive the bad memories for his mother either. No smoke, no investigation. Make that no roaring fire, no investigation.

Andreas sat in his rented car outside the police station and pressed his hand against his pocket. Still there, he thought. He didn't dare take it out here; one of the cops inside might get suspicious. After all, why would he leave their captain's office to sit in the parking lot staring at something unless he'd taken evidence? No, he'd find some other place to study it.

This must be what it felt like to be a thief, he thought. No, make that a novice thief who thinks everyone is watching him. Truth was, no one probably cared, but he couldn't take the chance. He had to find the right place to study the cross and think. But where? He drove up the mountain toward Chora.

The Patmian School was halfway between Skala and Chora. Begun in 1713, it was among the world's most renowned schools of Greek language and Orthodox theology, and now served as a seminary. Surely, a man sitting outside contemplating a cross would not be out of place.

He was almost at the school when he noticed a long line of buses idling along the roadside. They were just sitting there; doors closed, passengers inside, waiting for something. Then Andreas realized where he was, made a quick U-turn, and pulled up next to a pair of black wrought-iron gates hung on broad stone walls. This was the place to do his thinking. He got out and walked toward the entrance. A handwritten sign in five languages casually hung by a string tied to one of the gates, and two boys in the uniform of the Patmian School sat next to it. They were courteously telling the more aggressive visitors that the sign meant what it said: CLOSED FOR FUNERAL UNTIL 11 a.m. It seemed every place and person that mattered to Vassilis in life was honoring his funeral.

Andreas stopped in front of the boys, and one of them said, "Sorry, sir, we're closed for another half hour."

Andreas showed them his badge. "Official business."

The boys jumped up and opened the gate. "Yes, sir," said one.

"God bless you, and welcome to the Holy Cave of the Apocalypse," said the other.

It was the abbot's duty to say the words that must be said when a monk goes to sleep with the Lord. But it was not his duty to prepare him. That was a job for others: to sponge—not bathe—him with warm water in the sign of the cross upon his forehead, chest, hands, knees, and feet; dress him without gazing upon his nakedness in socks, pants, and necessary vestments; cross and tie his hands, and place a prayer rope within them as his spiritual sword for defeating the devil; cover his head with his cap and his face with his hood formed in the shape of a cross; put on his shoes and belt; place him on a bed of straw; cover him with his cassock and sew it closed about his body with black thread, and with white thread sew three crosses, one at his head, one at his breast, and one at his feet; and as he was a priest, not just a monk, place the stole showing his rank upon him.

Kalogeros Vassilis' body had rested on a wooden bier in the entrance to the main church, beside a burning candle, in the continuing presence of those with whom he'd shared his life who were now taking turns reciting from the Book of Psalms. The monk lay in the middle of the church, his icon on his chest, his fellows holding candles. This service would be a long one, in keeping with a departed monk's long service to God. When it was over, his body and a procession led by acolytes bearing lanterns would follow on a journey, filled with prayers and stops along the way, to his final resting place within the monastery's walls. Only his body, no casket or bier, would go into his grave, and once his body was blessed by a priest with the sign of the cross made by thrown earth and holy oil, the gathered monks would complete their thousand prayers for his soul and the Thrice Holy Hymn recited.

Only then it would be the abbot's time to speak: to praise the virtues and spiritual struggles of the monk who had died.

The abbot was wrestling throughout the service with how to describe Vassilis' struggles without addressing those tempests of the church that haunted every moment of his final days. They might even hold the answer to the reason for his death. How could he not speak out? But would it truly honor one who had built such a magnificent and meaningful life on earth to point out imperfections in the material he'd chosen for its construction? No, that would honor neither the man nor his life's work. He would speak only of how Kalogeros Vassilis honored his church, how he labored to make life better for so many in keeping with its teachings, and how his reward was now to be with God in heaven. After all, why should my words praising the man do less for his church?

Besides, the abbot knew one did not advance in the church by being impolitic.

Bringing a stolen cross, even a just "sort of" stolen one, to this holy, sanctified site might seem wrong to some, but to Andreas, it was the only place to come. He took his time walking along the wide stone path, lined on its sea view edge by stone benches, pines, and a low wall. A hundred yards dead ahead of the gate stood the gray, natural boulder steps and simple entrance to the centuries-old Monastery of the Apocalypse, and the beginning of Andreas' descent to the Holy Cave enclosed within its whitewashed walls. A few steps down to a gift shop and a quick left back outside had Andreas in an inner courtyard. From there, steps twisting down brought him to the shared entrance of the Church of Saint Anna and the Holy Cave of the Apocalypse.

The cross still was in Andreas' pocket, though he'd been gripping it from the moment he entered the monastery. He stood at the entrance and read the inscription: AS DREADFUL AS THIS PLACE IS IT IS NEVERTHELESS THE HOUSE OF GOD AND THIS THE GATE OF HEAVEN. He drew a deep breath, pulled the cross out of his pocket, and stepped inside. A stone arch divided the church into a modest front section and even smaller rear area. Each section of the church had a small window along its left wall, revealing olive groves meeting an azure sea. The distant landscape was one of rolling brown hills, tiny islands, and a bright blue sky.

The simple elegance of the place caught him off guard. Yes, priceless icons adorned a richly carved iconostasis inlaid with gold against the far wall, ornate silver chandeliers and oil lamps hung from the vaulted ceiling, and silver candle stands stood next to finely carved cabinetry beneath precious paintings; but he'd seen all that before, and much more, in so many other churches.

What commanded attention and drew so many pilgrims was what was *not* here: there was no right wall to the church. Running parallel to each other, the church and holy cave were essentially one, joined side by side. This was not a place for show. Plain wooden benches sat haphazardly on the cave floor. This was a place where one came for prayer and meditation.

It was four steps from the entrance to the front section of the church and another dozen to reach its far end. Andreas stared into the far right corner of the cave, his eyes drawn to a familiar icon, the Vision of Saint John. Strange, he thought, how it was beneath a copy of this icon that he'd snatched the cross from the cave-like office of the police captain, and now he stood looking at the original, in the cave of its inspiration, seeking answers from what he had taken.

Beneath the icon, at floor level and tucked behind a bit of discreet, brass tube fencing, was the soccer ball-sized niche where history records Saint John rested his head while receiving the Revelation. The niche was surrounded in hammered silver, and to its right a few feet above the floor and outside the fencing was another silver-wrapped, smaller niche. Here he placed his hand when rising from the floor.

Andreas stared at the simple cross; it seemed so out of place. He drew a breath and walked toward six tall-arm wooden prayer chairs against the left wall. He sat in the one closest to the window and stared at the cross.

He went over it as he had so many times before in the photographs: each leg was about one inch wide by one-quarter inch thick, and the longer no more than three inches in length, with a thin, black leather lanyard tightly wound and glued in place about it just below its intersection with the shorter leg. Andreas kept turning it over and over in his hands. Staring, looking for some clue, some hint of meaning.

"Why this? You had to know they'd find the envelope and take it, so why were you clutching this so fiercely?" Andreas realized he'd said the words aloud. He looked around, but no one was there.

He stood up and began to pace. Is this a symbol? Something tied to the monk's past? Maybe it's some obscure link to an esoteric scholarly reference? How am I ever going to figure it out? "*How!*" He knew he was frustrated. He took a deep breath and decided it was time to leave.

Andreas looked toward the holy cave. I ought to go inside, he thought. I might never have the chance again. Six or so steps from the left wall he had to duck to enter the cave's space. It was much smaller than he'd imagined and the rock ceiling angled down more steeply that it seemed. So much so that he easily could touch the fabled cleft in the ceiling rock through which God spoke to Saint John.

Andreas wondered how many countless tourists and pilgrims over the centuries had wondered what Saint John saw from his place in this cave. Andreas crouched down between the two silver-collared niches and leaned over so his head was close to the ground in front of the fencing. Still clutching the cross in his right hand, he looked back toward the window. He saw sky. He stayed in that position for about a minute, thinking about nothing but what it must have been like. "Better get up," he said aloud, and pushed off from the floor with his free hand. He got up so quickly that for an instant he felt dizzy and stumbled back toward the cave wall. Instinctively, he reached out with his right hand to catch himself, driving the cross into the stone and dropping it to the floor in the process.

Andreas resisted an immediate urge to curse. That's all I need to do, commit the sacrilege of destroying a cross—in this place of all places and with a baby on the way. Lila would be a nervous wreck if she knew. He bowed his head. "God forgive me," he said and crossed himself three times. He picked up the cross from the cave floor and kissed it. He noticed that the bottom part of the longer leg gave way under the pressure of his lips. It had separated from the rest of the cross somewhere beneath the lanyard wrap.

"I can't believe I broke a cross in the Holy Cave of the Apocalypse. And not just any cross, the stolen cross of a holy man during the time of his funeral." This was something he never could tell Lila. Instinctively, he tried to fix it, get the longer leg back in place under the lanyard.

Andreas knew he was standing in the place of Revelation, and perhaps that's why he wasn't so surprised when the thought hit him. He stopped trying to fix the cross. Instead, he slowly wiggled the longer leg, carefully separating it from the lanyard and glue, then with a firm tug, pulled it away from the rest of the cross. He looked at the broken piece, poked at it a couple times, and broke into a smile almost as wide as when Lila told him she was pregnant.

"You wily old bas…" Andreas didn't finish his curse, but still crossed himself as he shouted, "It wasn't just the envelope, you were trying to get him this!" and held up to the light a tiny USB flash drive—a computer storage device small enough to conceal a million envelopes of information within the body of a hollow cross.

Chapter Nine

The funeral had ended over an hour before, but it took until now for the abbot to retreat from all those wanting his ear and escape to his office. He needed time to be alone with his thoughts. No such luck. Waiting for him in a chair across from his desk was Patmos' police captain. He rose as the abbot entered but did not kiss his hand.

"Your words touched everyone, Your Holiness."

"Thank you." He didn't know whether to believe him but hoped he meant it. "Vassilis was a special soul. I tried to do him justice."

"I knew him practically all my life. He will be missed by everyone."

The abbot nodded. "So, what is on your mind?" He knew there was something.

"It's that cop, Kaldis, from Athens. Someone saw him on the island during the funeral."

"I didn't see him."

"No, that's just it. He was on the island but not for the funeral, and left before it was over."

"Any idea why?"

"No. I was hoping you might have one. You see, he and I didn't get off on exactly the right foot, and I don't want to give him any reason to be more…perturbed with me than he already is."

The abbot took the captain's effort to avoid a harsher word as a sign of respect. "Why would you think I possibly could be cause for him being 'perturbed' with you?"

"I'm just asking if you can think of any possible reason that might be lurking out there." He waved his right hand in the air. "As farfetched as that may seem."

Now the abbot sensed the captain was patronizing him. His temper flared. "I think you forget who you're talking to."

The captain shrugged. "Sorry, no offense intended, Your Holiness. But let's be frank, your truly wonderful eulogy left out a few things. Like the fact Kalogeros Vassilis was murdered in the middle of our town square after ranting like a wild man for weeks about Russians trying to destroy the church."

The abbot's face tightened. "How I chose to memorialize one of my monks is absolutely none of your concern."

The captain nodded. "True, but it makes me wonder if there might not be a few things you do know that could help with the investigation of his murder. And if you do, and Kaldis finds out you've been withholding them, I don't want to be pushed up any higher on his shit list because of you." This time he made no effort to choose a gentler word.

The abbot stared at him. "I am more concerned with how I am recorded in God's book. If I have erred, my mistake will be judged by the Lord, not you."

The captain leaned over the desk. "I mean no disrespect, but if something goes wrong, don't come to me this time looking for backup. If God is your judge, get his army to bail you out, not mine. If you're hiding something, you're not getting any further help from me. I stonewalled that cop once because you asked me to help keep the monastery from being drawn into a mess unnecessarily. Well, whatever mess is percolating out there is certainly not of my making, and if it's yours or you're making it yours for God knows what reason, good luck. Last chance, are you going to tell me what you're hiding or not?"

The abbot stood up. "*Kalo Paska*, my son."

The captain stood up. "Then so be it. And Good Easter to you too, Your Holiness."

◇◇◇

When Andreas walked into his office Kouros was sitting on the couch next to the window, reading.

"Maggie finished the transcript. Interesting stuff. There's a note—"

"Can't wait to see what's on this." He held up the flash drive. "I found it inside that cheap cross Vassilis bought the day before his murder."

"Amazing. What's on it?"

"Don't know. Didn't dare do anything with it until one of our computer guys tells me if it's booby-trapped to delete something if the wrong person tries accessing it. *Maggie!*" He didn't bother with the intercom.

The door swung open before he'd reached the other side of his desk.

"You rang?"

"Get one of our computer geniuses up here. I need to know what's on this flash drive, and tell him it might be tricky. Could be booby-trapped. And make sure it's somebody with a top-level security clearance who can keep his mouth shut."

She nodded. "Right away. I assume that means your morning helicopter jaunt to Patmos was successful?"

He nodded yes.

"I'm glad to hear that. Anything else you need from me?"

"Maggie, please, I'm in no mood to chit-chat. Just get that computer guru up here now. Please."

She didn't seem the least bit offended at his brusqueness, just smiled and winked at Kouros as she closed the door behind her.

Kouros burst out laughing.

"What so funny? Doesn't she get how important this is?"

Kouros laughed again. "Oh, I'm sure she gets it, Chief, and—may I speak freely?"

Andreas waved him to continue.

"She's got your number, too."

"What the hell are you talking about?"

Kouros leaned forward and slid a piece of paper across the desk toward Andreas. "This was clipped to the transcript." It was in Maggie's handwriting:

In case you're interested, I know who the mystery man is on the tape. Just ask. I don't dare put it in writing.

Andreas stared at Kouros. "Why didn't you tell me about this before?"

He smiled. "I tried, but you cut me off, then launched into Maggie before either of us could tell you."

"Bastard, both of you are bastards. *Maggie,* get in here."

Five seconds later, "You rang again, master?"

"Okay, okay, so shoot me. I apologize. I'm just wound up about that flash drive."

Maggie nodded. "I spoke to our resident computer whiz. He's like a modern doctor, won't make house calls. Said you'll know if there's a potential problem when access requires a password. Otherwise, just use it. If it's password protected, you'll have to bring the drive down to him because that's where the equipment is that he needs to get around it."

Andreas let out a deep breath. "Thank you, Maggie, that was very efficient of you, as always."

"Keep going, I love it when you kiss my butt."

Kouros laughed again. Andreas shot him a glare, and Kouros laughed some more.

Andreas put up his hands. "Enough already. I give up. Now, please, tell me who's the other guy on the tape?"

"Fine, just be patient, okay?"

Andreas nodded. "Okay, promise."

She looked out the window. "I just pray he's not a bad guy." She turned back to Andreas. "You know how interested I am in our church's history."

Andreas nodded.

"I don't think I've missed a lecture in Athens on the subject in years, unless I've heard it before or know the speaker will bore me to death." She let out a deep breath.

"One speaker in particular fascinated me. I never missed one of his lectures, even went to Thessaloniki twice to hear him. He didn't speak very often, possibly once a year, at most. But he was mesmerizing." She nodded. "Yes, he's your man."

"What's his name?"

"The name isn't important, you won't recognize it. It's who he is that's…mind-blowing." She paused. "The twenty principal monasteries on Mount Athos are ranked in a hierarchical order that cannot be changed. He's from one of the five most senior monasteries. He must have been well liked and respected by his monastery because I remember at one lecture he was introduced as his monastery's representative to the Holy Community."

"What's that?" asked Kouros.

"Mount Athos is a self-governing monastic state within Greece, made up of twenty self-governing territories, each with a ruling monastery and each with a representative to the Holy Community, the governing body of Mount Athos. They're monks who must be at least thirty years old, but usually much older, and well versed in church law and doctrine. They move from their monasteries to Karyas, Mount Athos' capital, where they meet in the tenth-century Church of the Protaton, the oldest church on the Holy Mountain, and from what I hear, enjoy modern communications with the outside world and a pretty fancy lifestyle. At least for monks."

That explained the Italian suit, thought Andreas.

"Anyway, he didn't seem to be lecturing anywhere, and I was worried he might be ill or, God forbid, passed away." She crossed herself. "So, I went to a lecture by another representative and asked him if he knew what had happened to the other monk. You'd have thought I'd asked him to commit blasphemy. I thought it was because I was a woman, and that *really* pissed me off."

Pity the poor monk who did that, thought Andreas.

"I called the head of police in Karyas and asked him to find out what happened to the monk. I couldn't believe it. He knew, but wouldn't tell me, either. I reminded him who I worked for and that unless he wanted to be reassigned to duty on a bread-and-water prison barge off the coast of Turkey in August, he'd better start talking."

"I didn't know we had that sort of place," said Kouros.

She smiled. "We don't, but he got my point and told me what I wanted to know. The monk was alive and well, but in a position many on Mount Athos preferred playing down. A group of four monks, called the Holy Administration, serves as the executive committee of the Holy Community. One member of the group must come from one of the five senior monasteries, the other three from the remaining fifteen. He was one of the four overseers."

She paused and shut her eyes. "But he was more than just a member of the Holy Administration. He was from a senior monastery." Maggie opened her eyes. "And that made him *protos*, the head of it all. He's their president, the most powerful churchman on Mount Athos."

Andreas picked up the flash drive and stared at it. He'd guessed right about the man being from the Holy Mountain, but never imagined that it was *his* mountain. "You know, Maggie, somehow I'm not as excited as I once was to learn what's on this thing." He fluttered his lips. "But what the hell, what's the worst that can happen?"

He slid the drive into his computer's USB port, hoping the answer to his question was not eternal damnation.

The Protos wasn't used to arriving home in secret. But Sergey was adamant. No one should see them arriving so early in the morning from the mainland. Karyas was a small village and gossip its primary pastime—especially among civilians working for the civil governor appointed by Greece's ministry of foreign affairs and charged with supervising the area's secular matters. It was their way of impressing coworkers back on the mainland that what they did really was important, even if they seemed to be living in the middle of nowhere.

A simple, "It's Easter Week and the Protos was away last night," would spawn endless speculation on his whereabouts, and perhaps a "My cousin Nick drives a taxi and thought he saw the Protos at the Athens airport," followed by more speculation over the reason for the trip at such a busy time. That was not the sort of gossip Sergey wanted to risk reaching the ears of nervous killers.

By mid-morning they were back at the Protaton, in the Protos' Church, a place of serenity and prayer. Yet the Protos' thoughts were on its martyrs, for here a *protos* and monks loyal to him were slaughtered on orders of a ruler who had replaced Orthodoxy with another faith and sought retribution against that *protos* for denouncing his new faith as heresy. But that was in 1282, in a time of savage zealots murdering monks in the name of God.

The words repeated through the Protos' mind: "a time of savage zealots, murdering monks in the name of God." He shook his head and thought of Vassilis. *Old friend, why did you get us into this?*

◇◇◇

Three faces stared at the computer screen. Twenty-one faces stared back. Make that forty-two: twenty-one on each of two photographs. That was all Andreas, Kouros, and Maggie found on the flash drive. That and a few cryptic lines typed on a one-page document. The reluctant computer whiz that Andreas had Kouros "drag up here by his geek whatever" had no better luck. He swore nothing else was on the drive and left.

They'd been staring at the photographs for what seemed eternity, and must have read the words a hundred times. The document bore no sender or recipient, only two lines: THE END WILL COME AS A THIEF IN THE NIGHT. PREPARE, FOR THE TIME IS IN THEIR HANDS.

"Okay, I get the 'thief in the night' reference to Revelation," said Maggie. "No one knows when the end may come, so be prepared spiritually and morally for that moment, but the part about time being 'in their hands' makes no sense. Eastern Orthodoxy doesn't believe mortals can bring about or even anticipate the end."

Kouros smiled. "Sort of sounds like the answer I get every time I ask a Greek bureaucrat about the status of anything. 'It will happen when it happens, it's in God's hands.'"

Andreas laughed, Maggie stuck out her tongue.

"So whose 'hands' are we talking about?" said Kouros. "It has to tie into the photographs; otherwise, why did he put it on the drive?"

"Well, we know one of them is the Protos, so unless he's a bad guy, it can't be all of them." Andreas kept switching between the two photographs; each showed twenty-one clerics, identically posed in full regalia in three rows of seven, as if attending the same ceremony. The photographs looked to be taken at the same time, although in one a tiny oriental rug was centered at the feet of the clerics in the front row and an empty chair sat at the right end of each row. He shook his head. "There's something not right about this." He brought the photos up onto the screen together, one above the other.

"Look here." Andreas pointed his left index finger to the top photo, at the cleric on the left end of the bottom row, and his right index finger at the one in the same position in the bottom photo. Slowly, he moved his fingers across each row, cleric by cleric.

"My God," said Maggie.

"It's the same bodies in each photograph," said Kouros.

Andreas nodded and leaned back in his chair. "Someone spent a lot of time and care putting new heads on old bodies."

"But why?" said Kouros.

"The answer to that probably answers everything." Andreas leaned forward and stared at the photographs. "And why the three empty chairs and that carpet in one, but not the other? Were they added to the one or deleted from the other?"

Silence.

"Maggie, do you recognize any of them?"

"A few. These are abbots from monasteries at Mount Athos." She pointed to five faces on the photograph without the empty chairs. "But I have no idea who the others are. Some men from my church might know; they're regulars at Mount Athos."

Andreas gestured no. "Nobody but us can know about this. If there's a message hidden in all this, and there must be, we can't risk letting it out to the wrong people. And I have no goddamn idea who the wrong people are." He picked up a pencil.

Maggie smiled. "Is this snap-and-throw time? You're averaging two dozen a week."

Andreas put down the pencil. "Cute. Now would you please ask our computer guru which photo is the original?" He pressed a button on the keyboard, pulled out the drive, and handed it to her. "And this time, you can take the drive to him. Just copy everything first."

"Will do. Bye-bye."

"Bye. So, what do we do now?" asked Kouros.

"Only thing I can think of is to ask the Protos if he sees anything in all this. After all, he's in one of the photos and Vassilis was taking everything to him."

"Or so he says," said Kouros.

Andreas nodded. "Good point. But I don't see any other play, do you?"

"No."

Andreas paused. "But first." He picked up the phone and dialed.

"Tassos, can you talk?"

He pointed to the extension and gestured for Kouros to pick up.

"Sure. My office line is secure," said Tassos.

"Good, Yianni and I have something to run by you. It's about that guy who belongs to the phone number you got for us." Andreas briefly told him of his meeting with the Protos and that they'd found what he believed Vassilis was passing on to the Protos.

"How do you know he's the Protos?"

"You mean Maggie didn't tell you?"

Tassos' tone turned serious. "Maggie and I have a wonderful relationship. She refuses to tell me anything about the other men in her life, and I don't ask." He laughed.

Andreas chuckled. "Fair enough. She recognized his voice when transcribing the tape. He's the Protos, for sure. Do you know him?"

"Yes, but he's in his seventies, and I knew him when he was a lot younger. I'd just started out on the force and he wasn't *protos* then, just a priest visiting my guests."

Andreas knew Tassos was referring to his time guarding political prisoners. He wondered if the Protos had followed Tassos' strategy of making friends with the inmates, so that if they returned to power he'd still have friends in government.

"He was pretty respected, though, even back then," said Tassos.

"By whom?"

"Everyone, as far as I could tell. After all, the junta let him visit prisoners. And they were paranoid about visitors serving as messengers, especially clerics."

"So they trusted him?"

"As far as I could tell. Why, is that what you're worried about, trusting him?"

"You're as bad as Lila, always reading my mind."

"Hopefully you're thinking different thoughts around her."

Kouros laughed.

"Glad one of you likes my humor. And to answer your question, I never heard anyone suggest, 'Don't trust him.' But that could mean one of two things: either he can be trusted, or is so devious no one could tell that he can't be."

"So which is it?"

"Damned if I know. And the fact he's as important as he is in the church doesn't prove anything one way or the other."

"Tell me about it," said Kouros.

Andreas rolled his eyes at Kouros. "Spare me, please." He cleared his throat and said to Tassos, "What's your instinct?"

Tassos let out a deep breath. "Can't say, haven't spoken with him in years, and rarely does he appear in public anymore. Don't even know whom to ask without it getting back to him for sure. I think you'll have to go with your gut. If you're so worried about trusting him, I assume it's critical."

"It's the whole game. If he's on the wrong side…I don't want to think about it."

"Good luck."

"Yeah, thanks."

"Love to Lila."

Andreas hung up and stared out the window. He spoke as if thinking aloud. "Why would the Protos have pushed so hard for an investigation if he was involved as a bad guy? Then again, if he was worried someone might make the connection—like by finding what's on that flash drive—that kind of move gave him a former prime minister to vouch for him as the champion of the impartial investigation. What a super-smart move. And ballsy."

Andreas let out a breath, turned to Kouros, and shrugged. "*Maggie*, get in here. Please."

The door swung open. "If you want to know about the photos—"

"Is everyone reading my mind today? How the hell did you know I wanted to ask you about the Protos?"

Maggie walked over to his desk, leaned over, and exaggeratingly enunciated, "I said 'photos,' not *protos*. The guru said he didn't have to look at the photos again. The photo with the Protos was the original. Everything else was added on."

"Why didn't he tell us that in the first place?" said Andreas.

"My guess is, he didn't like being 'dragged' by his 'whatever,' so if you guys didn't ask, you didn't get." Maggie handed him a pencil. "Here, snap and throw one, it will relax you."

Andreas just stared at her. "I need your knee-jerk instinctive yes-or-no reaction to something."

She nodded.

"Do you think the Protos could be one of the bad guys?"

"No."

He nodded. "Okay, that's good enough for me."

"Please God," Maggie added, and crossed herself.

Chapter Ten

Easter was the main event in Eastern Orthodoxy. No day was as hallowed or meaningful, and it was preceded by more than a week of significant religious observations and cultural traditions. As much as Greeks complained about the workings of their church—along with every other hierarchical institution touching their lives—there was no question whatsoever of their deep loyalty to their faith. No more so, perhaps, than on Patmos, except of course for Mount Athos. In fact, you couldn't pick a worse time than Easter Week for trying to get the attention of churchmen in either place. That made Andreas' complicated investigation even trickier.

He wondered if that was coincidence, or part of some, he hoped, not divine plan.

Still, using the Protos' private number Andreas was able to get him on the phone and pressed him to meet immediately. At first the Protos resisted, saying he couldn't possibly leave Mount Athos again this week. His absence would attract too much attention. Andreas said that for the same reason it was not wise for him to come to Mount Athos. "Attention is something neither of us wants, considering what I have to show you."

At that the Protos suggested they meet in Ouranoupolis, a seaside village at the threshold to the Holy Mountain, ninety miles slightly southeast of the city of Thessaloniki. It was about as close as you could get to Mount Athos by road, as one of its ancient laws forbade "a road upon which a wheel can run" to connect it to the rest of the world. The village—whose name meant "city of the heavens"—was where pilgrims presented their required visiting permits to the Athos Bureau and waited at the edge of the sea for boat passage, inevitably staring up at the mysterious fourteenth-century Byzantine Tower of Prosforiou dominating the harbor. The Protos said he could explain it as a quick, necessary trip to the bureau office.

Three hours later it was Andreas' turn to sit in a room in a stranger's house waiting for a monk to arrive. It was one of many whitewashed, red tile roof houses multiplying along the green hillsides edging the port village.

I'm a sitting duck, Andreas thought. All alone in the middle of nowhere, waiting to show something to someone that got the last guy who tried the same thing sliced ear-to-ear. Terrific. Maggie, if your instincts were wrong—

The front door burst opened and sunlight filled the doorway. Andreas instinctively stood up. Someone stepped inside. He couldn't make out a face against the light, but from the eclipse the figure caused Andreas knew who it was. "Afternoon, Sergey."

No answer, but Andreas made out a nod. The Protos stepped out from behind him. Andreas waited until Sergey had left and closed the door, then he stepped forward and kissed the Protos' hand. "Thank you for seeing me, Your Holiness."

"I understood it was important." He seemed focused on wanting to hear what Andreas thought so serious.

Andreas nodded. "I know you're very busy, so let me get right to the point." He reached under his shirt and pulled out a large manila envelope tucked flat into his pants. "No reason to attract attention." Andreas had decided to keep any parallels to Vassilis' fate to a minimum—and a 9mm strategically concealed in a holster over his family jewels. He pulled out two eight-by-sixteen photographs and handed them to the Protos. "Here."

The Protos looked quickly at one, then the other. He held one up, looked at it more closely, and handed it to Andreas. "That one was taken the day I became *protos*." He studied the other for about a minute. He shrugged. "It's a little hard to make out details, my eyes aren't what they used to be."

Andreas reached into the envelope and pulled out a magnifying glass. "This should help." Thank God for Maggie. She thought that might happen, even with the greatly enlarged photos.

The Protos nodded thank you, and sat down on a chair by a table beneath a window draped in white lace. Andreas didn't move. He preferred standing, watching the Protos carefully study each face.

After five minutes or so, the Protos put down the magnifying glass and pointed to a chair next to him. "Please, my son, sit."

Andreas did, but on a chair on the other side of the Protos, facing the door.

The Protos didn't seem to care. "Where did you get these?"

"They were on a computer flash drive Kalogeros Vassilis had hidden in a cross he was carrying when he was murdered."

The Protos smiled. "Ah, Vassilis, resourceful until the end. Always hiding things in the most obvious, yet overlooked, places." He pressed his finger against the photo four times. "Just like here, I'm certain of it."

"What did you find?"

"May I see the other photograph again?"

Andreas handed it to him.

The Protos bobbed his head through a face-by-face comparison of the photographs. "Yes, just as I thought. The faces superimposed on the abbots of the twenty monasteries attending my ceremony are of monks from those same abbots' monasteries. But, with the exception of three who have succeeded to a position of abbot, none of the others holds any significant hierarchical position in his monastery."

"What about the three new abbots? Were they important before in their monasteries?"

The Protos paused. "No."

"Then how did they become abbots?"

"The monks in their monasteries elected them."

"Weren't you surprised?"

He nodded. "As a matter of fact, yes. Our abbots are elected to serve for life, and there seemed so many more qualified, seasoned candidates available." He shrugged. "But such is the way of democracy."

"How did the three they replaced die?"

"Die? Oh no, only one died." He spoke as if Andreas were implying they'd been murdered. "And he was very old. Another moved on to a different monastery away from Mount Athos, and the third…uhh…resigned."

Andreas knew from the newspapers about the third one's resignation. He was the abbot caught up in the scandal that haunted Vassilis. "Can you think of any reason why these twenty-one men are in this photograph?" He pointed to the doctored photo.

"I only recognize twenty faces. And I have no idea why they appear."

Andreas asked for the names and monasteries linked to the superimposed faces, and took great care to write them down—so as not to make completely obvious that he was recording their conversation.

"Which face don't you recognize?"

He looked grim. "The face replacing mine." He pointed to a blurred image. "It looks familiar but I can't quite make it out. Do you have a better copy?"

"No, it's exactly as it appeared on the drive."

"Knowing Vassilis, I'm surprised he'd have made such a significant mistake."

"Maybe it was meant to be that way?"

The Protos shrugged. "Perhaps."

"What do you make of the empty chairs and the carpet?"

The Protos picked up the glass and looked again at the photograph. "Not much, they seem the typical gold tone and red velvet chairs so favored by our monks. It's a style you see in almost every abbot's office."

"And the carpet?"

He shrugged. "Again, a patterned oriental of a type I see everywhere."

Andreas reached into the envelope. "There was something else on the drive." He handed him the note. "What do you think this means?"

The Protos read it quickly, then read it again much more slowly. He picked up the doctored photograph and magnifying glass. Andreas noticed the glass start to shake, then the photo. At first ever so slightly—

"My God." The Protos crossed himself three times, apparently not realizing he was holding the glass in his hand as he did. He held up the photograph to Andreas. "The chairs, the twenty-four chairs. Saint John saw twenty-four elders in twenty-four chairs immediately after the beginning of his vision. Their meaning is a source of rich debate, but in this photograph I have no doubt what Vassilis is trying to tell me." He waved the photograph at Andreas.

"This symbolizes the twenty-four survivors of Armageddon who will represent the church's resurrected faithful when the Kingdom of Heaven has come. I'm not saying that is Vassilis' view, but it's the message he's passing me through symbols from Revelation he knew I'd recognize." He paused. "And he sees them in the presence of great evil."

"Okay, now you've completely lost me." Andreas felt a bit like a kid caught unprepared for Sunday school.

The Protos' expression did not change. "Every symbol, every word, and certainly every number in Revelation has spawned endless interpretations, many with significant distinctions having little in common with each other. 'The pearly gates,' 'streets of gold,' 'harps in heaven,' 'seven seals,' and, of course, '666' are just some of them. But that is the way of apocalyptic writing. It is highly symbolic and can be made to serve many purposes, some good, others not."

There was a subtle change to the Protos' voice; he was sounding more and more like a teacher. "Perhaps it would be helpful, my son, to give you what many call 'the bottom line.' Without the additional chairs, there are three rows of seven men in seven chairs. There are a lot of sevens in Revelation. Indeed, the very

Book of Revelation is written as a message to seven churches. My guess is that Vassilis added three abbot-style chairs to a picture of twenty one to take attention off the distracting number seven, and put it on the number twenty four which, to someone familiar with Revelation," he smiled at Andreas, "could only mean the twenty-four elders."

"Okay, but—"

The Protos held up his hand. "I know, I'm still going too fast. For some, the twenty-four represent the leadership of the church that will emerge after the coming of our Lord."

After all hell's broken loose as I recall, thought Andreas.

"That was not his thinking, but I'm sure Vassilis replaced the faces and added the chairs to make clear to me when I read 'the time is in their hands' that the men in the photo are seeking to change the church."

Andreas let out a breath. "Okay, let's assume you're right about what Vassilis was trying to tell you, and that he's right about the monks in the photo wanting to be the new leaders of the church, I still don't see how any of that makes any of them 'evil.' At most it sounds like they may be out of step with prevailing church politics."

The Protos shook his head. "This is not a question of politics. And I'm not saying the men in that photograph are 'evil,' nor did Vassilis. What I said is, 'He sees them in the *presence* of great evil.'"

"I'm sorry, Your Holiness, I need another 'bottom line' moment here."

The Protos pointed to the carpet in front of the image that replaced his own. "If you look closely at the carpet you can make out a pattern. It took me a moment to recognize it, but once I did I immediately realized that the face replacing mine wasn't from a photograph, it's from a famous painting." He let out a breath and put down the glass. "The carpet pattern is of a dragon, and both the dragon and the blurred image represent the same thing." He crossed himself. "Satan." He crossed himself again.

Andreas just stared at the photograph. This was turning into one of those days he wished he'd become anything but a cop.

How do you tell this man, respectfully, to come back to the real world so we can solve a real world crime?

"Okay, I hear you, Your Holiness, but what flesh and blood proof is there for any of this?"

The Protos looked up and stared into Andreas' eyes. "My son, Vassilis is dead."

◇◇◇

"I haven't felt that stupid in a long time." And on that note, Andreas finished describing his meeting to Kouros.

"Yeah, I guess, 'Vassilis is dead,' was sort of the obvious answer to your question."

"Sort of? I felt as if I were back in elementary school getting taken apart by a teacher."

Kouros kept his eyes on the road. "Just trying to make you feel better."

Andreas smiled. "Thanks, but it's not working."

"So, where do we go from here?"

"The Protos has gone back to Mount Athos, promising if anything else comes to mind he'll let me know. As for where we go, it's back to the office and the sexy side of police work."

"Sitting in a car for hours eating *spanikopita*?"

"Better. Reading everything we can find on every monastery and every monk in Mount Athos. Which reminds me, what did you dig up on the Protos' buddy, Sergey?"

"Nothing bad. Yeah, he was one mean motherfucker in his army years, but no war crimes stuff. Seems to fit the profile for many who lose themselves in monasteries. They've seen it all, done it all, and now want to forget it all."

Andreas nodded. "And what about that computer backup the abbot promised to send us?"

"Maggie said it arrived this morning, but nothing on it as far as she can tell except for esoteric comments by Vassilis on church doctrine and liturgy. She actually likes that stuff."

"Well, I'm about to make her even happier by getting her started on pulling things off the Internet." He picked up his phone and dialed Maggie's number.

"Should I get them here or wait until after the helicopter lands in Athens?" asked Kouros.

Andreas was holding the phone to his ear, waiting for Maggie to pick up. "Get what?"

"The spinach pies. I think five dozen should be enough. After all, twenty major monasteries, no telling how many related places, and a couple of thousand monks. How long can that possibly take?"

"Like I said, thanks for trying to make me feel better, and the next time you—Hello, Maggie…"

They'd gone through almost two dozen *spanikopita* and three pots of coffee. Andreas was glassy-eyed and Kouros claimed to be numb "for a lifetime" to anything clerical. Maggie, on the other hand, seemed in virtual heaven. She said she couldn't believe she'd been asked to immerse herself in the study of her church as part of her job, and get paid overtime for doing it. A lot of overtime.

"I can't read another word. I just can't." Kouros pushed himself up from Andreas' couch, stretched, and jumped up and down.

Andreas lifted his eyes from the pile of documents on his desk. "Stop that, you're wrecking my concentration. I'll forget where I am."

"That's what I want to do," said Kouros, jumping three more times before stopping. "So much of this is all the same sh—" he glanced at Maggie, "stuff, just written differently enough that I have to read it again and again and again. I see nothing."

Andreas stretched. "I thought the first thousand or so articles were pretty interesting, myself."

Maggie looked up from the chair she'd been glued to for hours. "Stop that, you two. This is very interesting. It's the history of our church and of those special souls who dedicate their lives to honoring our past and our traditions in order to keep our church alive in the present."

Andreas looked at Kouros, then at Maggie. "Cut us some slack, will you? We're trying to find a clue to a murder, not impugn the church, and it's…" he looked at his watch, "…four o'clock in the morning."

"Like I said, Chief, I've had it," yawned Kouros.

Andreas threw his pencil on his desk. "Okay." He ran his hands through his hair. "Before we call it a night, do either of you have anything to tell me that might be helpful? Anything?"

Kouros shrugged.

Maggie scowled. "Okay, wiseasses."

Andreas smiled. At four in the morning Maggie finally was letting them know who really ran their office.

She handed Andreas a single sheet of paper. "Read this."

He looked at it. "I've read this or something like it a hundred times already. It goes monastery by monastery according to hierarchical rank, describing each one's history, location, size—"

"Well, read it again, and this time more carefully."

Just what he needed, another teaching moment; but he did as she told him. It described a monastery ranking near the bottom of the twenty, but it had more monks than virtually any of the others. It also was one of the strictest and most severe. He read it twice, then looked up. "Okay, what am I missing?"

Maggie took the paper from his hand and began reading out loud. "'The monastery withdrew its representative from the Holy Community decades ago and does not take part in its assemblies.'"

Andreas gave her a blank stare. She turned to Kouros. He shrugged and then yawned.

"If one of the twenty monasteries refuses to participate in assemblies of the Holy Community of Mount Athos, why then are there twenty abbots in the photograph with the Protos at his installation—instead of nineteen?" She said the last three words very slowly.

Kouros shrugged. "No idea. And I'm too tired to make a joke."

Andreas stared at Maggie. "Twice in one day."

"What 'twice in one day'?" said Maggie.

"That I've missed the obvious."

Kouros reached for another *spanikopita*. "Don't forget about the cross."

Andreas nodded. "Fine, okay, three times." He looked at his watch. "Too late or early to call the Protos?"

"Both," said Maggie. "He's probably in the middle of morning prayers."

"I'll take that as a sign to get some sleep." Andreas stood up. "At least now we have a question to ask."

"Do you think he'll talk to you over the phone?" asked Kouros.

Andreas shrugged. "Won't know until I try. He gave me his landline numbers when we were in Ouranoupolis. They're probably more secure than the prime minister's, but if it's something he doesn't want to talk about I'm sure he'll let me know."

Andreas looked at Maggie. "Any idea of what his potential answer might be?"

"Probably something obvious, like everyone came out of respect for the office of *protos*."

"Sort of like warring families getting together at a church social?" Kouros was smiling.

Maggie shook her head. "You can't help yourself."

"Would you prefer something more earthshaking? How about, 'The devil made me do it'?"

Guessing at answers was a big part of every cop's life. In Andreas' experience some were better guessers than others, but even the best of them rarely were right on the mark, just close enough to point the way. Great, he thought, the devil made somebody show respect for the Protos.

Ever so quietly he crept into the room. Like a thief in the night. But a naked one, on tip-toe. Andreas had dropped his clothes on the floor outside the bedroom. Muscle memory brought him around the bed, extreme care lightly onto it. No covers tonight, he thought, the movement might wake her. Ahh, made it.

PLOP. An arm dropped across his bare chest. "Anything interesting happen today, my love?"

"I can never sneak in on you, can I?"

"Nope, and don't you ever forget it." She patted his chest.

He rolled over and kissed her. "Missed you."

"I bet. After all that time alone with monks even Mother Theresa would look good."

He laughed and touched her belly. "How are you guys doing?"

"Great." She snuggled up to him. "Now that daddy's home."

He kissed her forehead. "Me, too."

"Tassos sent us the strangest gift today."

"What was it?"

"It came from a florist, but I guess he was trying to tell me to learn to cook."

"Huh?"

"It was wrapped with pink and blue ribbon—to cover all possibilities I assume—with a lovely note, but I can't figure out why he sent what he did."

"What did the note say? I might have a better fix on his sense of humor."

"Something like, 'May your home always be filled with joy and love, and may this protect your family from all that is not.'"

"What did he send, a gun?"

"No, wise guy," and she gently squeezed his nuts.

"Careful, they're not used to much action these days."

Lila didn't listen; instead held them in her right hand, lightly squeezing and gently rubbing. Andreas adjusted his position on the bed. She started feathering him with the tips of her fingers and, after a while, strayed on to something much firmer and erect to the touch. Back and forth she ran her fingers, from top to bottom and back again. She stopped when she felt him start to pulsate, then gripped him tightly, and slowly and deliberately began pulling up and down.

"I'd love to take you in my mouth, but I just—"

"Don't worry, this is just fine. Oh, yes, just fine." Andreas put his arm under her body and pulled her against him. He was flat on his back and thrusting in synch with her hand.

She squeezed extra hard and pulled twice, very slowly.

Andreas moved his hand to where he could touch Lila's bare ass and squeeze it in rhythm with her stroke. He began to moan, she kissed him and stroked faster. He moaned more, twisting beneath her hand, then paused for an instant before thrusting his hips forward and holding them there. "Don't stop, please don't stop."

She didn't.

"Ohhhh, ohhhhh…"

Lila kept pulling, even after he'd finished. Andreas had to hold her hand to get her to stop. "Easy there, my love, we'll need to use it again some day."

She kissed his cheek. "You like?"

"Yes…I like." He kissed her neck. They lay silently holding each other for a few moments, then Andreas left for the bathroom.

"So don't you want to know what he sent us?"

"Who, my mind is completely blank at the moment. Just the way I like it."

"Glad I could clear your head."

Andreas was laughing as he walked back into the bedroom. "Okay, what was it?"

"The strangest thing. Garlic. A dozen heads, wrapped tightly together in a line, and in a gold mesh bag no less. Such a silly thing. But a lovely thought."

His first thought was thank God the room was pitch black, so Lila couldn't see his face.

Andreas swallowed. "Yes, a lovely thought." His mother used to do the same thing, hang garlic in their house. But it wasn't for cooking: it was to keep the devil away.

Andreas remembered the day she gave up that superstition. They'd just returned from his father's funeral. She was a young mother of two children whose husband had chosen to commit suicide rather than subject his family to any more of the shame brought on by the bastard minister who'd set him up to look corrupt.

It was a moment burned into his memory. His mother was tearing down the garlic and ripping it to shreds. "It doesn't work. Nothing works if the devil wants to take you. Nothing."

Andreas crossed himself in the dark and prayed his mother was wrong.

Chapter Eleven

"Hello, Your Holiness, it's Andreas Kaldis. Sorry to bother you again."

"No need to keep apologizing, my son. We're way past that. So, what fresh hell have you brought me today?" There was a lightness to the Protos' voice. It wasn't what Andreas expected.

"I'm glad to hear you're sounding better."

"It is Easter Week, our holiest time, and all our trials must be measured against the ultimate sacrifice. Besides, I may never have the chance to use that Dorothy Parker 'fresh hell' line again."

"I hope you're not right about the 'hell' part," whoever Dorothy Parker was. "I understand one of the monasteries is not part of the Holy Community."

"Yes, sadly that is true. Although we are hopeful they will return."

"But there are twenty abbots in the photograph taken at your ceremony. Did its abbot attend?"

"Yes. In fact, that day was the first step toward a hoped-for reconciliation."

"What made your rogue monastery suddenly see the light?"

The Protos cleared his throat. "I would not call it a rogue monastery, just slightly overzealous in pursuing its alternative beliefs on church policy."

Spoken like a true politician. Andreas waited, there had to be more coming. Teachers were like that.

"We owe it all to Kalogeros Zacharias."

"Who's he?"

"A monk in that monastery, but a very special man. Although relatively young, he has great patience, humility, and skills. He gained the trust of his abbot and ultimately convinced him to attend the ceremony out of respect to the 1,100-year-old office of *protos.*"

Guess Maggie was right.

"That was not an easy feat to achieve. That abbot was the reason his monastery withdrew in the first place, and he is a man of, shall we say, strong opinions. He never got along with any *protos* before me. Some say our few steps forward are my doing, but they are all thanks to Zacharias."

"What do you know about Zacharias?"

"He's very well educated, speaks a half-dozen languages, and came to Mount Athos in the mid-nineties."

"From where?"

"I don't know his origins, but his passport is Swiss. I know because he once asked me if he should obtain a Greek passport now that he was a Greek citizen."

"What rank does he hold in his monastery?"

"None, he does not want rank. Which perhaps is why he's so well thought of by so many. He presents no threat."

Andreas thought, this guy Zacharias seems too good to be true. What's he doing in the outcast monastery if he's so talented? "Do you happen to have a file on him?"

The Protos paused. "What you're asking is highly irregular."

"So is the murder of a monk. And I'm trying to keep it that way."

The Protos let out a breath. "You have your own special way with words."

"Can you arrange for me to come up and meet with Zacharias?"

"When?"

"Today."

"Impossible, this is Holy Week."

"Your Holiness, I appreciate all that but like I said—"

"My son, I understand what you're about to say, but you don't understand. That monastery has the strictest rules of any on our Holy Mountain. No one, and I mean no one, is allowed access during Easter Week. From Sunday to the following Sunday at noon it has no contact with the outside world. There is no telephone and even electricity is forbidden during that holy period. There is no way you can visit or communicate with Zacharias until Sunday afternoon."

Andreas let out a deep breath. "When can you get me his file?"

"The one I have, right away, but it contains little more than what I've said. Any additional information would be in his monastery's file."

"And not available until Sunday."

"Assuming the abbot cooperates. Sorry."

Andreas thought *damn*, but said, "Thank you, Your Holiness."

"You're welcome, my son." He paused. "And I appreciate all that you're doing. Bless you and your family."

"Thank you."

Between the garlic and the blessing things were looking up. Now if only he had some idea of where the devil to look for an answer, or something like that.

This was the time of year he liked least. Most held the opposite belief. They lived for the pageantry and depth of Orthodox Easter. He couldn't stand being cooped up for almost eight days, and counted off every day, every hour, until Sunday noon, his own resurrection day. But he never let on. Never. He had their trust and wasn't about to lose it with a casual gesture or word. No, he wouldn't let down his guard for a second.

Gaining trust wasn't as hard as many thought, at least not for Zacharias. He'd been doing it for years, long before finding his way into monastic life. Through time and patience he'd take the measure of one he wished to befriend, then with an easy smile, become exactly what the other wanted him to be, allowing his target to take center stage and credit for whatever mattered to

the other. And when the potential friend questioned Zacharias' motives—and that time always came—Zacharias was at his best.

He'd confide a past that made him less than perfect, one that encouraged rescue and, in a monastery, a shared desire for salvation. His story forged a relationship in spiritual steel. The other now "knew" Zacharias' weaknesses and understood him completely: Zacharias was a soul seeking redemption and a place in heaven through a revived life of selfless good works and prayer.

And to keep all of them believing that, he'd keep on praying.

"These still are pretty good." Kouros was eating one of the *spanikopita* from the night before.

"Obviously, you're a bachelor," said Andreas.

"And proud of it." He finished off the last bite and reached for another one.

"Stop already, I'm getting sick watching you eat that crap."

Kouros didn't stop. "So, how did your early morning call go to the Protos?"

"Just terrific, everything's absolutely perfect in paradise. The answer to our question on the surprise appearance of the twentieth abbot at the Protos' ceremony turns out to be a dead end. We've got a savior monk reuniting the gone-astray monastery with the flock. And I can't even talk to that monk until Sunday morning."

"Sunday, why Sunday?"

"No person or communication is allowed to enter or exit that monastery from Palm Sunday through noon on Easter Sunday."

"Bummer. Which monastery is it?"

"The one Maggie and I were talking about last night."

"Chief, you never mentioned the name. The two of you were looking at some paper and I was falling asleep."

Andreas shook his head and said the name.

Kouros stopped in mid-bite. "You're kidding me?"

"Why?"

"That's the monastery of the three missing monks. The monks we never got to interview on Patmos."

Andreas sat up in his chair. "The same ones Abbot Christo-doulos said left to return—"

"Sunday night. But if what the Protos told you was true, no way they could have made it back to that monastery in time to take part in Easter Week."

Andreas nodded his head.

"Maybe you misunderstood what the abbot said?"

"No way." Andreas paused. "But maybe he didn't know that monastery's rule and just thought that's where they were going."

"Maybe, but before the abbot came to Patmos he was on Mount Athos for a half dozen years. If that monastery was as strict as the Protos said, he must have known they couldn't have made it back to their monastery in time."

"Kind of makes you wonder." Andreas picked up a pencil, stared it, and put it back down on his desk. "Let's see what the abbot has to say for himself."

Lila always liked time to herself and had no doubt that's what helped keep her from going mad when, after her husband's death, virtually every eligible man in Athens and beyond was after her. She detested all the phony posturing and hustle of the dating scene, and learned that "eligible" could be a relative term to many a currently married man who saw landing Lila as a unique opportunity for "trading up" the social ladder. She'd even tinkered with the idea of escaping her suitors by hiding away in a monastery for nuns. But the fates were Greek and they had their own plans for her. Or so Lila now liked to say.

At the moment, though, Lila was not alone. Her mother had stopped by and they were sitting in Lila's kitchen having coffee. As a child, Lila would sit in her mother's kitchen and watch her hover around the cooks, making sure everything was prepared "just like your father likes it." Even though her mother never had to cook or touch a dirty dish, she was as much an old-school Greek wife as any you'd find in the remotest mountain village:

husband ruled, wife did all else—albeit, in Lila's mother's case, with a houseful of servants to help.

Kitchens were where Lila and her mother liked to talk when alone. They preferred the cramped intimacy of a cluttered kitchen table to the formality of china- and silver-filled dining rooms.

Lila sighed. "I never expected this to happen."

Her mother glanced at Lila's belly.

Lila stroked her tummy. "No, mother, not the baby, I mean this." She waved her hands around and over her head. "I didn't even know Andreas ten months ago. Now we're about to have a baby together."

Her mother nodded. "Are you afraid?"

Lila's lip quivered. "Yes. And I feel so ashamed that I am." She started crying.

Her mother handed her a handkerchief. "If you weren't somewhat afraid it wouldn't be natural. You're close to the most intimate moment of a woman's life, giving birth to a being you will love more deeply than yourself for the rest of your life." She reached over and stroked Lila's hair. "It is a moment for great joy. And great fear. But you are blessed. Andreas is a wonderful man and will be a terrific father."

Lila threw the handkerchief on the table. "But he won't marry me. He won't even talk about it."

"Why do you think that is?"

From her mother's tone Lila could tell she had asked the question with a pretty good idea of the answer. It was her style of parenting: don't tell, lead and elicit. "He's afraid, too."

Her mother nodded.

"But why? He must know that I love him."

"Of course he does. He's just not sure that's enough for you."

"Why do you say that?"

"You come from different backgrounds. He fears you later may regret your decision, that your feelings for him now are tied into having a baby together."

"Are you trying to tell me you think the same way?" There was angry tone in Lila's voice.

Her mother smiled. "One of the things I like most about Andreas is how he's learned to deal with this confrontational streak of yours. No, I don't think that way. Besides, it's not my life that will be affected by second thoughts and 'what ifs.'"

"I have no such issues."

"Good, then don't push things."

"But it's difficult to act as if I don't care whether or not he marries me."

"I know, but trust me, he'll come around. After all, how could he resist the best person in the world?" She stood up and kissed Lila on the forehead. "And the mother of his baby." She patted Lila's belly. "Got to run."

Lila smiled and took her mother's hand. "Thanks, I love you."

She's right, Lila thought. I shouldn't push. Instead, maybe I should try hitting him over the head with a frying pan until he proposes? No chance, he'd never feel it. She chuckled despite herself.

◇◇◇

The abbot was not pleased at the surprise visit. Even less so when Andreas insisted that the procession of monks entering his office, dropping to their knees before him, crossing themselves, and kissing his hand must end, and those already seated in his office told to leave.

"We are reviewing the plans for tomorrow morning's Holy Thursday Ceremony of the Basin. We have very important things to discuss."

"So do we, but unless you want to risk washing dirty laundry in front of everyone here today, I suggest you excuse them for now."

Andreas could see the abbot was angry, but he told his monks to leave.

"This better be important."

Andreas was in no mood to be politic with anyone. "If I were you, I'd hope it isn't."

"What are you saying?"

"Do you remember telling me that the three monks we wanted to interview had left Patmos before you had the chance to speak to them?"

"Yes."

"And that they'd left by boat late Sunday night?"

The abbot hesitated slightly. "Yes."

"And that the reason they left was so that they could 'be back in their monasteries in time for Easter observances'?" Andreas emphasized the last words with quotation marks from his fingers.

The abbot glared in a way Andreas figured he reserved for withering a most out-of-favor monk. Andreas looked at his watch, crossed his legs, and smiled.

The abbot blinked and let out a breath. "Okay, so you learned they couldn't have returned home in time to celebrate Easter Week within their monasteries."

"That's *monastery*. They all came from the same one," said Andreas.

The abbot bristled. "They are men who have found salvation and repentance in God and whatever they may have done in the past has nothing to do with Vassilis."

Andreas shook his head. "Interesting, a monk who lived in your monastery for forty years gets his throat cut and you take it upon yourself to protect strangers who might be able to help us find his killer. I admire your sense of loyalty." Andreas watched the abbot struggle to retain control.

"The three, they are from the Balkan conflict. They came to Mount Athos and earned the right to a new life. That is nothing new. For centuries Byzantine and Serbian rulers have sought and received refuge there. But police may not agree, and I saw no reason to involve them in this."

"Or perhaps embarrass whoever gave them sanctuary?"

"That is none of your business."

The abbot's back was up and he seemed ready for a fight. Andreas stared straight into his eyes. "I think you're way out of line on this, and in way over your head. I don't know what you're thinking or who you're afraid of, but one thing is for sure, you're going to end up on the wrong side of things if you don't tell me what you know, and I mean tell me *now*." It was a wing and a prayer bluff, but one aimed at most politicians' knee-jerk propensity for protecting self-interest over all else.

The abbot's face looked as if he'd missed that possibility, and for the first time he sounded unsure. "I cannot tell you a name, but I'm not refusing out of fear. It would betray a deep confidence of a true friend. I never will reveal his name. He put those three men onto the true path of the Lord, and I trust his judgment completely. I'm sure Vassilis would have agreed."

"Did Vassilis know him, whoever 'he' may be?"

"Vassilis knew of him and of my regard for him, but we never talked about him." He paused. "Although I think he knew Vassilis."

"Why do you say that?"

"Because the three you seek sought out Vassilis. I assume to convey his regards."

Andreas struggled to hold back what he was dying to say.

"He is a spiritual gift to our life. I would never betray him," said the abbot.

Andreas bit his tongue. "I admire loyalty, but blind loyalty can lead you into the abyss. Now, where are the three men?"

The abbot stared out the window. "Honestly, I have no idea. All I know is they are gone from here."

"From Patmos?"

He paused. "From here."

Andreas took that to mean he was finished with protecting them, but also with cooperating. Time to let him get back to preparing for tomorrow's ceremony. Andreas wondered who got to play Judas.

What Zacharias missed most was his cell phone. The abbot forbade them in the monastery, and they didn't work inside anyway. He'd tried, many times. If only he could convince the abbot that modern communication was not a thing of the devil. He'd tried that, too, many times, but the abbot was firm. As long as any telephone number contained the combination 666, the abbot considered all phones linked to Revelation's Beast of Satan.

With so much in play on the outside at the moment, being incommunicado for more than a week was taking its toll on Zacharias' good nature. He had to work extra hard at showing he was easygoing and stress-free.

Just take it one day at a time, he was thinking as he chanted prayers with his brethren. Stay under the radar, do not draw attention to yourself. It was a mantra he'd picked up many years before during another period of confinement, surrounded by lines of razor wire and watched over closely by men with guns.

That worked for him then; it's what made him invisible and allowed him to escape. And it's what was working for him now; it enabled him to remain in the shadows, quietly amassing a group that shared his vision or, to be more precise, a message he knew would sell. In his other life Zacharias had learned another important truth: it wasn't the message that mattered, it was whether people were willing to buy it. All he needed was a malleable ally in each monastery, one he could promote to the other monks, and the message would carry itself. So far, so good—three tries, three new abbots.

And his vision was so very simple, only a slight variation on the message of Revelation to the seven churches: Let us find someone who will resolve our monasteries' problems, lead us back to our first love of God, address the heresy that has infiltrated us, set our priorities back on the right path, and help us to reach out to save our fellow man.

It was a message that gave Zacharias a lot of flexibility. Yes, he definitely knew how to go with what sold.

"'Into the abyss.' You actually said that?" Kouros was shaking his head. They were standing in the *piazza* outside the monastery.

"I don't know, the place is spiritual, the words just came to me." Andreas grinned. "At least I didn't ask if the name of his mysterious best friend was 'Zacharias.'"

"I admired your discipline."

"Yeah, the moment of satisfaction wasn't worth it. I can guarantee you that bringing up Zacharias' name to the abbot would get back to him. And with all the powerful friends he seems to have, the last thing we need is Zacharias thinking we're interested in him. We know he's covering up a past and probably has a lot of favors he can call in to help keep it that way."

"On Sunday."

"In these days of text messages and cell phones, who knows? Better to play dumb and see what we can learn elsewhere."

"Where do you suggest we start looking?"

"Hungry?"

Kouros smiled. "Thought you'd never ask."

They started walking. "So, what did you find out about our new favorite taverna owner?"

Kouros answered, "He's what he said. A former spook everyone knows about."

"For whom?"

"Not for us. He didn't work here, he worked in Eastern Europe, speaks four of their languages. The story is that he worked for the highest bidder."

"Figures."

"But like he said, not field stuff, just analysis."

"In other words, he was one of those guys who decided whether it was worth the risk of someone else getting his nuts shot off," said Andreas.

"You could put it that way."

A minute later they were in Dimitri's.

"My friend, how are you?" Andreas spoke with his arms spread wide.

Dimitri seemed surprised to see them. "Hmm, things must be heating up. You're here every day now."

"So you heard about my visit yesterday?"

He shrugged. "Force of habit. I like to keep informed."

"Great. Is there a place we can talk?"

"Sure, you're regulars now. Let me show you to your table."
He told a passing waiter to bring coffee and sweets, and dropped
into a chair next to the table. "So, what can I do for you?"

"We're looking for somebody," Andreas said.

Dimitri nodded.

"But this has to be hush-hush. We're not even sure the guy's
on the island, but if he is and learns we're looking for him, *poof,*
he'll disappear."

"Okay, I get it."

"If you can help us we'd appreciate it, really appreciate it.
But, if after we talk word gets out that we're looking for someone…" Andreas shook his head in a way that made voicing a
threat unnecessary. "So, if you offer to help, great. If not, no
hard feelings."

"You really know how to make a guy feel welcome." Dimitri
laughed. "No problem, I get the picture. As long as he's not a
relative…unless I don't like the bastard. But no matter who he
is, I promise not to tip him off."

Andreas looked at Kouros. Kouros nodded.

"Okay," said Andreas. "Your word's good enough for us. Well,
it's really three guys."

"Eastern European, big?"

"How the fuck…" Kouros caught himself.

"One guy would be tough, but three guys hanging out
together in a place they don't belong get noticed, and people
start to talk."

Andreas shook his head. "Go on, please."

"Yesterday, was it yesterday—yeah, yesterday—I went over
to this farm on the far north end of the island. It has the best
fruits and vegetables on Patmos, but this time of the year I go
for the eggs. Anyway, I get there and the farmer had three big
guys working on repairing a shed. They were strangers; and I
asked where they were from. He said he didn't ask for passports;
they just wanted to stay for a few days and were willing to work
for food and a place to sleep."

"Ever see them around the monastery?"

He shook his head. "Not that I recall, but like I told you before, there are a lot of people visiting the monastery now. Big ones, small ones, you name it."

"When did they get to the farm?"

"He said 'yesterday,' which would mean Monday. Monday morning."

Andreas nodded. "Can you tell us how to get there?"

"Sure. But are you sure you want to go?"

"Why?"

"I don't want to get your *macho* juices running, but these guys are three muscled motherfuckers. I saw them working with their shirts off."

Andreas shook his head and said, "No problem," then turned to Kouros. "I guess that means I get to wait in the car while you ask the questions, detective."

Zacharias was a student of human behavior. He prided himself on reading a mind from a glance. But there was nothing new to learn from this confinement. He'd grasped the essence of these men long ago. They were non-evolved examples of what writers had observed in antiquity: Greeks only buried their differences to unite against an external threat. Every man for himself until called upon to unite for the glory of Greece. They were like men in many parts of the world, and perfect for his purposes.

As for those who despaired because they believed corruption and self-interest made success in Greece a matter of random chance, he agreed with them—but only for those unwilling to manipulate the odds. He had no such reluctance and so for him that made success a matter of certainty, not chance.

If only he could be as certain of what was happening on Patmos.

Chapter Twelve

The road north took them back to Kambos, but instead of going straight at the crossroads they went left. Dimitri's directions were precise, in a Greek sort of way: keep going until you see really spectacular country, then take a right at the first big road heading downhill; it's the farm off in the distance, next to the sea, with no tractors, only donkeys. Dimitri was willing to wager his pension that the family running the farm had no idea who the three men were. He said the family rented the land from the church and raised everything by the labor of their own hands. Such hardworking people were rare these days. And they never overcharged, which made them even rarer.

The farm was right where Dimitri promised it would be and just as he'd described: a cluster of white buildings surrounded by tall cedars and pines, above fields of sprouting green running down to a long stone wall that set the farm off from a sandy beach and the cove beyond. On the far right side of the cove, a short jetty cut into the sea, running parallel and close to the beach; a dozen small, brightly-painted Greek fishing boats were tied bow-to-jetty, stern-to-shore, and tiny sheds for fishing nets and other needs of the trade filled the seaward side of the jetty.

There was no way to approach the house unnoticed. It no doubt was built with that in mind generations ago by wary folk wanting warning of the welcome and not-so-welcome entering their isolated paradise. Besides, the dogs would announce their presence long before they reached the house. To make it tougher, the only practical way to get there was by foot or aboard some four-footed creature.

"Yianni, stop here." They were on a dirt road running down toward the sea, above and as close to the house as you could get from the road. From here they had an unobstructed view of the house, and vice-versa. The shed Dimitri had described was on the other side of the house and not visible from the road. A small coffee hut serving locals and the occasional tourist was farther down the road, blocking vehicle access to the sea below.

"Looks like the church wants to keep this bit of paradise serene," said Kouros.

"Let's hope we don't change things."

Kouros nodded. "If they're the ones who murdered the monk, they have nothing to lose."

"I don't doubt for a second they'd kill everyone in that family if they had to."

"And us," added Kouros.

Andreas nodded. "Let's just sit here for a while, and make sure they know we're here."

"Sounds like a plan. Too bad I'm not in uniform, I could get out and parade around."

"I think they'll be able to tell from the car." Andreas knew Kouros was teasing; they were driving a marked, blue-and-white Patmos police car.

"That Patmos captain sure came around. He couldn't help us enough. Like he found religion or something."

Andreas nodded. "Or something." Andreas fluttered his lips. "Well, I guess it's time."

"Damn sure hope this works."

Andreas didn't respond; he was concentrating, preparing himself. "Remember, show no guns. Just make sure you've got them ready."

"Three of them."

Andreas looked at Kouros. "Okay?"

Kouros nodded. They bumped fists, and stepped out of the car.

They made their way through a break in the tightly packed brush and over a stone wall, then slid down a twelve-foot hillside to a wide path running parallel to the road above. Dogs started barking the moment they started sliding. A smaller rock-and-dirt path began there and ran straight up to the outbuildings next to the house. It was lined by three-foot-high stone walls and unevenly spaced cedars.

The two cops walked very slowly, as if strolling down a country lane. Chickens scurried along the path toward the buildings.

"Do you think they saw us?" Kouros' voice was tight.

"I sure as hell hope so." Andreas resisted the temptation to pat where he'd hidden two of his semiautomatics. It would be a literal dead giveaway to anyone watching. And he knew, if they were the killers, they were watching. They had to be. The path ended just beyond a small barn where a narrower path started off to the left. The new path ran between the house on the left and a group of small sheds and coops on the right before winding down out of sight toward the jetty side of the beach.

"Where the hell are they?" whispered Kouros.

"Where the hell is anyone?" whispered Andreas. He paused then yelled, "*Yiasas*. Hello. Anyone here?" They'd not seen a human since stopping the car. No way he wanted to surprise them.

No answer.

Andreas nodded toward the sheds on the right. Kouros jumped the fence and stepped inside the first one. He stuck his head out and gestured "nothing." He checked the other two, each with the same result.

Andreas whispered, "My turn, cover me." Andreas drew his gun and pointed at the door to the house. He peered in the window next to it, gave a glance and a nod back at Kouros, pressed himself against the wall between the window and the door, leaned over, and pounded five times on the door. "Police! Open up!" No answer. He banged away again. "Police! Open up!" Still no answer.

He looked at Kouros, nodded toward the door handle, and turned it. It was unlocked. He threw open the door, sending it slamming into a table next to it, and pots crashing onto the stone floor. No one inside could have missed that arrival. Andreas wanted it that way. He shouted, "Anyone here?" No answer.

Andreas went in with Kouros right behind him, and together they scanned the downstairs rooms. Either his plan was in play or it wasn't. If not, and the bad guys were inside, things were likely to get very hot very quickly.

Not a soul was in any room. Andreas pointed upstairs. He put his foot on the first step. There was the sound of something falling on the floor above them. His heart skipped a beat. Fear. Good, he thought, it made him focus. Only idiots and fools weren't afraid at times like this.

Kouros' face was grim. They crept up the stairs on opposite sides, at angles widening their fields of vision with every step, hoping to get a glimpse of anyone who might be at the top waiting for them. They took their time, prepared to fire instantly. The men they were hunting were professionals, not likely to spook. This was a time of cautious moves, and prayer.

They were almost at the top when a new sound came from the same place. It was like muted stomping. Andreas put a hand on Kouros' chest to warn him. It could be a trap—like whistling when the deer you're stalking starts to run, distracting the creature just long enough to take your shot. Andreas opened and closed his left fist three times, then went low and fast around one corner at the top of the stairs, gun barrel first, as Kouros did the same on the other side. Again, no one.

Andreas pointed to a closed door across and to the right of the stairs. The sound was coming from in there. Andreas stood on the right side of the door, his left hand on the doorknob, his right on his gun. Kouros stood on the other side, nodded, and Andreas flung open the door.

A bound and gagged young girl lay on the floor, next to a bed, kicking away at the floor with her bare feet. Four middle-aged women and one old man were lying face up on the bed, bound and stacked like strapped-together firewood at a city market. Andreas and Kouros did a quick search of the room and every closet. There was no one else in the room. Andreas whispered to Kouros to keep an eye on the door and went to the girl on the floor. She wouldn't stop kicking. She looked to be no more than eight and scared to death. Andreas put his finger to his lips, and pulled his ID out from beneath his shirt. "Shhh, it's okay, my child, we're police, you're safe now."

She kept shaking. Andreas said, "I'm going to take the gag off, but it will hurt a bit. I'm sorry." She was haphazardly wrapped in duct tape of the sort every farmer kept handy for quick repairs.

As soon as he freed her mouth the girl started talking. "They ran into the house, they made us come up here. They said they'd kill us if we screamed." She seemed too frightened to cry.

"Is there anyone else in the house?" Andreas asked.

"No, the rest of the family is out on the island. Easter is very busy for us."

Andreas smiled at how precise she was.

"It's just us."

The five tied to the bed were wide-eyed and nodding at every word the girl said.

"Where are the men who did this to you?"

"There were three of them. Big men. I heard them running out the door, toward the sea."

"How long ago did they leave?"

"I don't know." She shook her head. "But they brought us here and tied us up right after the police car stopped on the road. I was downstairs with my grandfather watching the car come down the road."

Andreas looked at Kouros. "I guess it worked," then gestured for him to untie the others. He asked the girl, "How did you free yourself?"

She gripped his hand and let out a deep breath. "I'm smaller than the others, and wiggled my way out when I heard you shouting."

Andreas patted her on the head. "Smart girl."

The first one untied was the grandfather. "They took my boat. They took my boat."

Andreas raised his hand. "Easy, don't worry about it."

"What do you mean don't worry about it? I heard them say they were taking my boat. You're the police. Go stop them. It's your job. Do something!"

The first thing that came to mind was to tell Kouros to retape his mouth, but Andreas knew the old man was covering up fear and frustration with indignation. A man doesn't like being helpless when his family is threatened, no matter how old and frail he may be. Besides, thanking cops for just having freed your family was not as Greek as complaining about what they hadn't done.

"Don't worry, *Papou*." Andreas helped the old man off the bed and over to one of the two windows overlooking the cove. It was a peaceful late afternoon sea, glorious for a voyage. You could see the old man's *caïque*, plodding out to sea. The perfect escape scenario for professionals wanting an exit strategy to another island or a faster boat elsewhere. Or so Andreas had hoped.

"They're getting away. Do something."

"Relax and enjoy." He patted the old man. The women crowded up to the other window. Kouros stood next to Andreas. Andreas picked up the girl so she could see.

The grandfather's boat was just about to where the cove opened into the sea when the Greek Coast Guard cutter came into view, accompanied by two swift moving Zodiacs equipped with mounted machine guns. The *caïque* made a desperate turn to the right, headed directly toward the shore, but within seconds one of the Zodiacs cut it off, while the other closed in from behind to the sound of a bullhorn echoing off the water.

"What are they saying?" said the girl.

Andreas patted the grandfather on the back and winked at Kouros. "Probably something like, 'It's not nice to steal *Papou's* boat.'"

Andreas and Kouros left the farmhouse carrying shopping bags full of cheese, eggs, sausages, preserves, vegetables, and homemade wine. The women insisted. The grandfather wouldn't stop shaking Andreas' hand and thanking him for saving his boat.

As they walked between the stone walls back to the car Kouros said, "Do you really expect them to believe your wild-ass story about this being the Greek police and coast guard working together to protect our citizens from known boat thieves? I don't think even the kid believed you."

Andreas grinned. "I didn't hear you coming up with a better one. Besides, the old man believed us, and he's who'll be telling the story in the coffee shops. And it only has to hold up until we get the bad guys to talk."

"Well, let's hope it works as well as your 'let's be obvious' plan did."

Andreas smiled and started up the slope to where the car was parked. Neither spoke as they angled up the steep, slippery hillside and over the wall onto the road. They made it without dropping a thing out of the bags. "Yeah, no way I wanted to go up against those guys hand-to-hand, even if the family wasn't at risk."

Kouros shook his head. "They must have thought we were the dumbest cops alive the way we came strolling up to the house."

"Thank God they did. Flushed them right into the waiting arms of the coast guard. No way for them to run off and hide in the middle of the sea. I was praying they'd go for the boat. Otherwise, it would have been one hell of a chase through the hills. And forget about trying to keep that sort of operation quiet."

"Yeah, Maggie said she keeps getting calls from the press trying to get an angle on where you are and what you're doing."

Andreas shook his head. "I don't understand why they keep looking for me. The minister made it clear all media on this goes through him."

Kouros smiled. "That's what she keeps telling them, and they keep saying, 'Yeah, but we want to talk to someone who actually knows what's going on.'"

Andreas smiled. "I prefer having the entire Greek military at our disposal and letting the minister have the press."

"What did you say to inspire him to get us that kind of help?"

"I told him we thought we'd cornered the killers, but unless we had immediate coast guard cooperation, there was a guaranteed hostage situation involving professional killers and the likely deaths of more innocents on Patmos during Easter Week."

"So he got the hint."

"And the chance to claim credit for the capture, but I told him not to put it out to the media until we're certain they are the ones we are looking for. Because if they aren't, they're monks from Mount Athos on a true pilgrimage and wrongfully accusing them of killing a fellow monk would get career-ending pressure from the church for everyone involved."

"I assume he got that point, too."

Andreas nodded. "So now it's time for us to join our coast guard friends and their new guests. We're meeting them on one of those virtually deserted islands between here and Turkey."

"Why there?"

"Can't risk word leaking out that we might have caught Vassilis' killers. The media would be all over us. No way the press will find us where the coast guard is taking them. The only ones living over there are isolated families subsidized by the Greek government to stay put, so that the Turks can't claim the islands are abandoned." Andreas opened the back door of the police car and put some of the bags inside.

"How do you plan on getting them to talk?"

Andreas lifted the rest of the bags. "Something will come to me, but if not, I'm sure you'll come up with suitable ideas."

Kouros burst into a broad smile and nodded in a way reminding him of Tassos.

"Yianni, remember, innocent until proven guilty." He said that as much to remind himself. But no cop really believed it. Not if they wanted to stay alive among scum like those three murdering bastards.

Evening prayers during Easter Week always exerted particular strain on Zacharias. The sound of the mallet striking the long wooden cymbal-like *symantron* signaled another long night alone in his cell wondering what was going on outside the monastery walls. Tonight he simply couldn't concentrate until, in a glance from the abbot, he sensed that his disinterest might be showing. Instantly, his demeanor changed, and once more Kalogeros Zacharias was among the holiest and most dedicated of the prayerful. A fact he actually believed was true.

The rapes, the murders, the genocide had not been committed by him but by some nonexistent being out of a past cleansed pure by his dedicated piety, rejection of the corruptions and temptations of the temporal world, and single-minded commitment to spreading those same values throughout his church. But that required an army of brave men, thirsting for change, inspired by a goal. Those were not of the sort to be found among the powerful, for their zeal ran only to protecting their privileges. No, he knew where to find his warriors; the same places as he had in the past: on the fringes of life, men who felt powerless, waiting for a message to unite them in common cause.

And with the "we must find a savior" message he'd fashioned from Revelation, he found his men among each monastery's neglected and overlooked and unified them around a passionate, shared priority: Mount Athos must become home to the Ecumenical Patriarch, and the vast riches of the church made to pass through the largesse of a lens of moral piety, not bartered away in marketplace corruptions.

He knew their goal faced serious obstacles, but he saw only two: rivals in the church, and the Russians. The first was proving not as insurmountable as he once thought. Jealousies among the monasteries and disillusionment of their monks primed many for change, and the endless scandals rocking all of Greece provided a roaring catalyst. The country no longer trusted its leaders, and many prayed for a strong, decisive deliverer. The growing influence of his flock in virtually every monastery amazed even Zacharias. A united front was building, one difficult for other rivals in Greece, and indeed, elsewhere in the Orthodox world, to oppose.

The Russians presented a more difficult problem. They did not play by the same rules of morality. So be it.

Chapter Thirteen

The place the coast guard picked was among a cluster of barely inhabited, rock-strewn, hilly islands about ten miles north of Patmos. Though small, it still was big enough so that whatever went on in a cove to the northwest wouldn't disturb the family of goat herders living at the southern end.

One of the Zodiacs from the operation, minus mounted machine gun, met Andreas and Kouros at the port in Skala and had them on the island twenty minutes later. Only a bit of daylight was left by the time they started up the beach toward a tiny, all-white structure. It had a round roof and sat nestled on a ledge about twenty yards above the shore.

"You'd think they could have found a better place to do this," said Kouros.

Andreas smiled. "I don't know, I think it might be fate."

Light was coming from inside the building through the only window they could see. There were no windows on the front side, only a blue door facing west—in the tradition of all Greek churches, even those in the most remote of places. A man in his early twenties, about Andreas' size, was standing next to the door watching them approach. Andreas waved as he walked up to him, then patted him on the shoulder. "Great job, sailor."

The man nodded. "Thank you, sir. The captain is inside with the prisoners." He pushed open the door.

The space inside the church was cramped, but neat and clean, as if tended to every day. A military issue, battery-powered lantern stood on a small table next to the door. The required icons were in their proper places, but there was no candle stand. As if reading Andreas' mind, the captain said, "We took it out. No reason to give our friends here anything to swing at us in case they decide to get frisky." He smiled. "Again."

The three prisoners sat in a row at the captain's feet, legs tied together straight out in front of them, and tied again to each other's. Their hands appeared tied behind their backs. On either side of the row stood a sailor, each armed with a twelve-gauge short-barrel semiautomatic shotgun. They were the best for close work and gave an unmistakable message to the three on the floor: the end is near and here if you want it. From the way the three looked, Andreas doubted they were anxious to test that possibility.

Andreas pointed to the man in the middle. "Looks like his face ran into a door a half dozen times." The others didn't look much better.

The captain laughed. "They're big boys, and I guess they thought my little guys couldn't handle them. They took a run at these two," he pointed to the sailors holding the shotguns, "when we brought them on board the cutter from the *caïque*. They were wrong." The captain smiled again, then kicked the one closest to him on the bottom of one foot. "Assholes."

"Captain, thank you very much. We'll take it from here," said Andreas.

"You want us to leave you alone with them?" He sounded worried.

"Don't worry, we can handle it. Just leave a shotgun with my buddy here. He once was one of you." Andreas nodded toward Kouros.

The captain smiled. "Another sea-sucking *lokazides*?"

Kouros grinned and gave the captain and the two other sailors some archaic hand-slap that must have meant something to the shared DYK special ops brotherhood of Greece's equivalent of U.S. Navy Seals.

Andreas had insisted to the minister that the operation use only coast guard vessels so as not to attract unusual attention, and that the men involved must be able to handle trained military types willing and capable of killing without hesitation. So the minister sent in the big boys.

"We'll be right outside. If you need anything, just holler." The captain glared at the three on the floor and followed his two men out the door.

Kouros took up a position looking straight down the line of prisoners, leaving no doubt what would happen if they tried anything with the new guy holding the shotgun.

Andreas smiled. "You guys have had quite a day. First a stroll in the country, then a boat ride, now a bit of prayer and meditation. But, oh yes, I forgot you're used to that. So, do you miss the monastery?"

No answer.

"Okay, I understand, these are not the best circumstances for us to get to know each other, but it's all the time we have."

Silence.

"Now, now, you're not going to tell me you've taken a vow of silence are you?"

Not a word.

This was going nowhere, thought Andreas. Time to take another risk. "I don't understand, Kalogeros Zacharias wouldn't have sent you if you had."

It was as if someone had touched the three with an electric cattle prod. The prisoner in the middle said something in Serbian to the others.

Andreas shook his head. "Fellas, the party is over. We know where you came from, and you know where you're going. The only question is whether it's prison for the rest of your lives— for war crimes." He guessed that at least one of them had that worry, possibly all of them.

Kouros shrugged and tightened his grip on the shotgun.

"No matter. Besides I'm sure you boys know more about that than I do."

"Fuck you." It was the prisoner in the middle.

Must have guessed right. "Nice to meet you, too. The name's Andreas."

"We have nothing to say."

Andreas nodded, and walked over to a bag he'd brought with him. Carefully he lifted it from the floor and stood holding it in front of the three men. He shook his head. "Would you like to see what I have in here for you?"

The middle one spoke again. "Fuck you, we're not afraid. We've been tortured before."

Andreas looked surprised. "Torture, who's talking torture?" He reached into the bag, pulled out and pointed a cylinder in the man's face. "Here, bite this."

The man jerked his head back and away from the thing, studied it, leaned forward, and sniffed at it. Then he took a bite.

"Good, huh?" Andreas gave the others the same choice, and each accepted. Then he went up and down the line until the sausage was finished. "I know it's a little awkward doing things this way, but I'm sure you understand why I can't untie your hands." He reached into the bag, pulled out some bread, and repeated the process.

"Cheese?"

The three nodded. One even said, "Thank you."

After another round of sausage, Andreas opened a bottle of wine. "Hope you don't mind sharing." Carefully, he held the bottle up to each prisoner's lips, allowing each man to comfortably drink as much as the man wanted. Andreas kept this up until the bottle was empty. Then gave them more sausages, another bottle of wine, more cheese, another bottle of wine, more cheese, and more wine. It took about a half-hour for the feast to finish.

"I hope you liked it. The farmer you worked for gave it to us."

"Yeah, it was good." It was the prisoner who'd said thanks.

"They were good people," said the one in the middle. "Sorry we had to do that to them. I hope they're okay."

Andreas was always amazed when professional killers of innocents showed such seeming genuine concern for their prey; as if murder were just a job to them, unrelated to their feelings for those whose lives they ended. "Sure, no problem," said Andreas. "How did you end up there anyway?"

The prisoner who'd been quiet looked at the others. "It's nothing he doesn't already know." The two others shrugged. "We found the place the first day we got there. Just in case we needed to leave the monastery."

"Smart," said Andreas.

The thankful one said, "And when we heard you wanted to talk to us, we decided it was time to move on."

"And, of course, you couldn't go home to your monastery until Sunday."

He nodded. "Yes. The farm seemed as safe as any place."

"We were going to leave by boat next Saturday morning," said the quiet one.

"That's how you got to Patmos in the first place, by boat."

The middle one nodded.

"So, who wants to tell me?" said Andreas.

"Tell you what?" said the middle one.

"Why did you have to kill him?"

No one answered; their faces like carved stone.

"Okay, guys, I know the rules, no confessions, ever. But here we have a special situation." Andreas looked at Kouros. "Tell them."

Kouros looked each of them in the eye before speaking. "If you stick with the good soldier's 'name, rank, and serial number' routine, you'll be prosecuted as international war criminals and spend the rest of your lives in prison. No tribunal would even consider a lighter sentence, not after what you did to a priest. You're all as good as dead."

Andreas raised a finger. "However, there is an option. If you cooperate I can promise that instead you'll be tried in a Greek court for murder."

"Some promise," said the middle one.

"It's a better deal than you think. First of all, Greece has no death penalty. Secondly, with the right lawyer and the right amount of money, in time you'll probably get out." Regrettably, thought Andreas, all that was true.

"I want a better deal," said the quiet one.

"I hoped you'd say that," said Kouros. "It will give me great joy to deliver you personally to a war crimes prosecutor."

"We didn't plan on killing him, honest." It was the middle one.

Thank God it worked, thought Andreas. "What happened?"

"We were just supposed to watch him. See what he was up to."

Andreas nodded. "All that stuff he was saying had attracted a lot of attention."

"It was all over Mount Athos," said the quiet one.

"We only were supposed to watch him," the middle one repeated.

Andreas grinned. "Must have been pretty boring watching an old man do his thing."

"Yeah, pretty routine," said the thankful one.

The middle one looked down. "Then he went out that night."

The quiet one said, "It all happened so quickly. He just up and left the monastery at two-thirty in the morning, carrying an envelope. We didn't know what to do. We couldn't reach—"

"Out to God for an answer," the middle one finished the sentence.

The quiet one seemed startled, then nodded. "Yes, to God."

"Fellows, God wouldn't tell you to cut his throat." Andreas said the line flatly.

"We know," said the quiet one, glaring at the middle one.

The middle one glared back.

Guess now we know who wielded the knife, thought Andreas.

The quiet one continued. "We ran out behind him, and when we saw him take the high road past the taverna toward the town square we took the path down to the bus stop and ran back up again into the square."

"We didn't intend to kill him. The was a man of God."

That was becoming the middle one's mantra, thought Andreas.

The quiet one said, "When he came into the square, we grabbed him and took the envelope. Then we saw what was inside. He didn't struggle, just stood there, clutching his cross as we held him."

"We had no instructions, and no way of receiving any," said the thankful one.

"Communication was forbidden by then," said Andreas.

The middle one nodded. "We'd been told, 'Use your judgment.'"

Andreas nodded and decided to take another chance. "The photographs must have surprised you."

"Yes," said the middle one. "If what he knew ever got out, it would mean the end of God's mission on earth. It was God's will for us to protect that mission with our lives if necessary. It would be a humble sacrifice."

The thankful one bowed his head. "After it was done, we decided to make it look like a mugging." He looked up at the middle one. "But I wouldn't let them take his crosses."

"His death was a necessary sacrifice to the Lord," said the middle one. "He knew it too, he immersed himself in prayer, accepting his fate."

Andreas heard the shotgun safety click twice. He took it as Kouros' suggestion that they consider ending this interrogation with an attempted escape.

Andreas went on. "That's when you tossed his room?"

The quiet one nodded. "Yes, I did that. The others watched to make sure no one saw me."

"Where's his stuff?" Andreas asked the quiet one.

The thankful one answered for him. "We threw it in the sea when we fled to the farm."

"Where?"

"I don't know, some place between here and there. It all looked alike to me."

"Anything on it surprise you?"

"Never had a chance to look at it."

Andreas didn't believe any of that, but the subject was going nowhere. "So, fellas, how about you telling me again just how you came to follow Kalogeros Vassilis."

Andreas drove them through their story six more times, twice in reverse. It all came out about the same. They were sent by one they would not name to keep an eye on a monk they'd been told posed a threat to God's mission on earth, one which they must be prepared to die to protect, and if anything unanticipated occurred, to "use your judgment." In other words, the power to decide life or death was delegated to men best trained in ways to kill. Whoever sent them was clever: give ambiguous advice to men who saw only black and white, and thus gain absolute deniability for yourself.

There was no way the person giving those instructions could be held accountable for this murder, even if the three named their dispatcher. But they didn't have to. Andreas was certain it was Zacharias.

As far as Andreas was concerned this investigation was over. The fate of the three killers was out of his hands. They'd been caught and their confessions were on tape. Time to get back home to Lila. The rest was a mess for the church to sort out, not him. His job was done.

At least that's what he kept telling himself on the helicopter back to Athens.

Chapter Fourteen

At four a.m., all would gather by candlelight for morning prayers. For Zacharias it meant an end to a restless night filled with thoughts of what was happening on the outside. The world might be in the midst of all-out war and this place wouldn't know about it until missiles started landing in the monastery's courtyard—assuming the abbot allowed them in before Sunday morning. Consciously, he knew there was nothing to worry about; all his bases were covered, no matter what. But in that falling-off-to-sleep time, when the subconscious started playing with the conscious, concerns leaked out.

What if that Patmos monk actually did know his plans? But how could he know? He'd only be guessing. Still, the others respected the old monk, and a good guess would present problems, raise suspicions, put him on everyone's radar. Anything that made him visible was unacceptable. He could not allow one monk to destroy it all. That's why he sent the three: to watch the monk, to learn what he knew, and, if necessary, to resolve an unacceptable situation.

Zacharias knew what "use your judgment" meant to such men, but a public airing of the monk's suspicions would be lethal to his plans. He just hoped there'd be another way; at least that's what his subconscious was trying to tell him, no doubt grasping about for justification for the likely outcome if events he'd set in motion developed as he feared. He drew in a deep breath and fed his subconscious what it was hunting: the old fool brought it on himself by snooping into matters that didn't concern him. So what if a holy man died? A lot have died in the past, and many more would in the future. Martyrs were everywhere. He let out the breath and his thoughts now were at peace. He drifted off to sleep, promising to pray for them all at morning services. Kalogeros Vassilis, too, alive or dead.

◇◇◇

"Breakfast in bed on a weekday with my super-stud cop, what a treat." Lila rolled over onto her side, kissed Andreas on the cheek, and picked a grape off the plate balanced on his chest. His eyes were fixed on the newspaper held out just beyond the grapes. "And a famous one, too."

"Yeah, if you get beyond the front page and bother to read the next-to-last paragraph."

"At least the minister knows who's responsible."

"Yeah, so he can blame me if anything goes wrong. Like word getting out that the three killers he told the press were 'posing' as monks actually were monks. The minister's job description might include covering up embarrassing truths for important friends, but it's sure as hell not part of mine." Andreas closed the paper and tossed it on the floor. "Why am I complaining? The minister takes the credit and lets me do what I want. It's our deal."

"If you didn't complain, you wouldn't be Greek."

Andreas kissed her on the cheek. "Okay, how's this: The minister must have told the paper to hold the presses for a major story, written it for them, and released it the moment I told him the three guys were the ones we wanted. No other way it could have made this morning's edition."

"I'm sure the other papers are crazed over being scooped. He must owe this one a big favor."

"Or want one."

"Shall we see what the TV is saying?"

"No, I don't need to hear how our minister's 'hands-on approach to confronting threats to our way of life' once again saved the planet."

"At least he gave you the day off."

"No, I gave myself the day off. And I gave Yianni the rest of the week off." Andreas lifted the fruit plate off his chest and put it on the bedside table, then rolled over so they were face-to-face. "So let's make the most of it."

"Oh you sweet talker, you. If only—" she jumped. "Whoa, baby's really kicking, guess the little one wants out."

"Is it time?" There was alarm in Andreas' voice.

"No, I've been getting soccer-style kicks for the last few days. The little bugger just wants to let us know there's someone in there."

He kissed her on the forehead. "You're going to make a great mother."

Lila smiled. "I'd also make a terrific wife."

Andreas froze. She'd never said it directly before, though she'd hinted at it many times. He didn't know what to say so he let the moment pass. He knew she wouldn't push it. Why should she? She could have any man in the world she wanted. Once the baby was born and Lila faced the reality of what her life would be like with him, she'd come to her senses and move on. It was just her maternal hormones talking now. Andreas was certain of that. How could it be otherwise?

Lila rolled over and pressed the intercom. "Marietta, could you please pick up the tray? Thank you." She rolled back over and faced Andreas. "So, my man, what would you like to do today?"

"This works just fine for me."

She patted his chest. "Not really." There was a knock on the door. "Come in."

The maid entered and started gathering up the plates and cups. "Mr. Kaldis, your office would like you to call as soon as you have the opportunity."

"I guess that answers what you'll be doing today."

"Not a chance. Today, I stay home." He picked up the phone, "I just have to call Maggie," and dialed. "Morning."

"Hello, next-to-last-paragraph star."

"Glad to see my glamorous life hasn't affected your view of me."

"But you're all over TV. Well, sort of. You're getting prominent mention under the code name 'key personnel,' as in, 'the minister was assisted in his operation by key personnel of the police and military.'"

"What else is new?"

"As a matter of fact, you have a call from that guy you met on Patmos."

"What guy?"

"The ex-spook, Dimitri."

"What did he want?"

"Wouldn't say, but said it was very important, something some farmer wants you to have. He left me his number."

Andreas was tempted to say don't bother. "What is it?"

She said the number and hung up.

He looked at Lila. "Just one more call."

"Sure." Her voice was flat.

He dialed and waited. Then heard the unmistakable voice of a salesman. "Hello, Dimitri here."

"Hi, I understand you're looking for me."

"Sorry to bother you, Chief, but I have something for you from that farmer you saved. Or rather your minister rescued." He laughed. "Bureaucrats are all the same."

Andreas was not about to discuss his boss on a public phone. "The farmer and his family have been more than kind. Thank them, please, but I really don't need any more of their food."

"It's not food. But something I'm pretty sure you'll want to chew on. Is this line safe?"

Jokes and drama, this guy knew how to sell, thought Andreas. "Yes, but is yours?"

"Yep, I'm talking from an old friend's office."

Then I'd better be real careful with what I say, Andreas thought.

"In all that excitement the farmer's hens got out and started laying eggs everywhere. After you left, the little girl was looking for the eggs and found something hidden under empty feed-bags in the shed where the three men had been working. Her grandfather called me. He thought it might be something you'd be interested in seeing."

"How did he know to call you?"

"Because I'd told him I was the one who sent you in the first place. You think I was going to let your minister take all the credit? Besides, it might get me a better price on eggs." He laughed.

Andreas shook his head. Always an angle with this guy. "Well, just send it on to my office."

"Better yet, I'll drop it off."

"Huh?"

"Just got into Athens this morning. Spending today and Good Friday with my sister."

"No need to rush. I won't be in today."

"Yes, you will."

"Don't bet on it."

Dimitri laughed. "Let's put it this way. I wouldn't wager anything you really care about."

Andreas wanted this to end. It was old news. "Okay, what did the little girl find?" He waved his hand in the air to Lila, as if to say, I want this guy to get off the phone already.

"A laptop computer and a pile of disks. I didn't look at them, but I have a hunch you'll want to."

Andreas didn't respond.

"Hello, did you hear what I said?"

This is old news. I don't want to know what's on Vassilis' computer. "What time can you have them in my office?"

Lila rolled over and got out of bed.

Holy Thursday's morning Ceremony of the Basin was a powerful moment in Zacharias' monastery. The abbot played the part of Christ washing his disciples' feet after the Last Supper, but the monks cast in those roles knew better than to view this as anything but a brief, ceremonial exercise by the autocrat who ruled within these walls.

Zacharias had been through more than a decade of these ceremonies. He watched the abbot move along the row of bare feet. Amazing how much he'd aged. *He was very lucky I came along when I did. He needed me.* Someone had to organize this place and speak enough different languages to communicate with the world beyond these walls. Still, the abbot never would have taken me in if I'd not sworn to reject all my worldly possessions—and turn them over to his monastery. To Zacharias that just proved anyone could find a place in the world, assuming of course you had the price of admission, which in his case was a very expensive ticket.

The abbot was about to wash Zacharias' feet. *How fitting he's doing this*, Zacharias thought. *After all I've done for him without taking a bit of credit…or a euro or a dollar or a ruble. But then again, that's our arrangement, the same as I have with all I've helped rise to power in our monasteries. I get them what they want without seeking anything for myself, except of course, their friendship and access to them whenever I want. What more do I need of money? I have all I'll ever require in life safely away in Swiss bank accounts. The vast wealth of the Ecumenical Patriarch shall serve another purpose, for with it will come the earthly power to bring much needed order to the world, once he is on our Holy Mountain…and under my guidance.*

Zacharias smiled.

The abbot noticed the smile and smiled back, as if reflecting on their past together.

Oh, yes, Your Holiness, I remember our first ceremony together, thought Zacharias. *I was the youngest, and that meant I played a special role. I was your Judas.*

Lila didn't act upset when Andreas said he had to go to the office "just for an hour or so." She said she'd call her mother and they'd spend the afternoon doing "baby things." Still, somehow he felt he'd screwed up. Big time.

Dimitri had dropped off the computer and disks as promised, together with a handwritten note:

I have no idea what's on this and don't want to know. Promise. D.

A likely story, thought Andreas. Maggie had left Dimitri's note on his desk together with a typed one of her own:

OUT FOR A BIT. THE COMPUTER GURU IS LOOKING AT EVERYTHING. WHEN YOU WANT HIM, CALL HIM. YIANNI CALLED TO CHECK IN. I TOLD HIM ABOUT THE COMPUTER AND THAT YOU SAID, "STAY ON HOLIDAY, THAT'S AN ORDER."

There was a tiny word at the very end of the note he couldn't make out.

Andreas shook his head and talked to himself as he rummaged through his middle desk drawer looking for a magnifying glass. "I didn't tell her that, but yes, that's what I would have said. Still, she can't go around doing that sort of thing without checking with me first. I'll have to speak to her. I run this office, not Maggie. Great, now I'll have the other woman in my life pissed at me." He found the glass and stared at Maggie's note. The word was "Over." He read the other side of the note.

HE DIDN'T BELIEVE ME. SAID YOU'D NEVER BE THAT CONSIDERATE AND YOU SHOULD CALL HIM IF YOU WANT HIM TO COME BACK.

Andreas laughed. He picked up the phone, called the computer guru, and told him to come up and show him what he'd found so far. Then he hung up and laughed some more.

He looked again at Dimitri's note. A phrase caught his eye: "and don't want to know." He ran the thought through his mind. Maybe he really meant that. Curiosity can be a curse, and there's a certain comfort in ignorance of facts you do not need to know in order to live out your life in peace. Especially those facts almost impossible for you to change, like the number of people in the world who die each year in freak accidents. Or whatever can of worms might be on Vassilis' computer.

The intercom buzzed. "Hi, I'm back. Ilias is here."

"Who's Ilias?"

Maggie whispered, "The computer guru."

He paused for an instant. "Send him in." I'm too damn curious for my own good.

◇◇◇

Ilias said there was a lot of information on Vassilis' computer, even more on the disks stolen from the monk's room, but without knowing exactly what Andreas was interested in, it was "needle in a haystack time." Still, he'd narrowed things down, or at least hoped he had by focusing on what Vassilis was working on in the thirty days before his death. "I'm not sure if what I've come up with helps, since I don't know what you're looking for."

"Any luck on finding sources for the images used to doctor the photograph we took off the USB drive?"

"All but one."

"Which one?"

"The carpet. The faces were lifted from group photographs stored on the computer's hard drive, the painting was a recent download from a museum site on the Internet, so was the photo used for the empty chairs, but the carpet…" He shook his head. "I found the image of the carpet on the hard drive, but no idea of its source. It could be buried on one of the disks or lifted from something online. Can you give me some help?"

"Like what?"

"Keywords. I can use them to search the files."

"Revelation."

Ilias keyed it in. "Looks like a zillion hits."

Of course, thought Andreas. He's a scholar monk living on Patmos. "Can you limit it just to file names?"

"Sure," and with a few keystrokes Ilias brought up a hundred entries.

Andreas read the list. Nothing recent, and nothing interesting. "Try Russia, but only recent entries."

That brought up a lot of newspaper articles, but nothing earth-shattering. He told him to try Mount Athos. That got him what he expected, more newspaper articles but nothing more than what everyone already knew.

Andreas kept suggesting keywords, but none led to anything helpful. "Okay, I've about had it." He paused. "Try Zacharias."

Ilias typed in the word. "Nothing."

"Nothing? How can there be nothing? Try searching for more than just file names."

"I did, there's no 'Zacharias' anywhere in the computer." Ilias paused. "But it's a biblical name. Someone would have had to intentionally purge every mention of it."

Like some do 666, thought Andreas. "Let's check out the disks."

There were about fifty. Not a hit anywhere.

"It's almost like someone's trying to call attention to the name by its absence," said Ilias.

Andreas had been leaning over Ilias' back reading off the screen. He patted him on the shoulder. "Sure does." He walked over to the window and stared up at the sky. Neither man said a word for about a minute. "Try 'time is at hand' as a file name." Andreas spoke without taking his eyes off the sky.

A few seconds later Ilias said, "Nothing."

Andreas shook his head. "Damn, I was sure there'd be something." He turned away from the window. "I have another idea, but for luck I'll type it in myself." He walked over to the laptop, typed four words, and hit ENTER.

The computer came up with a single hit, a file titled, "Thief in the night."

"*Bingo*," Andreas shouted and slapped Ilias on the back so hard the whiz kid almost fell off his chair. "Sorry, I'm used to slapping my partner."

"Lucky him," said Ilias, rubbing away at his back.

"So, what do we have?"

Ilias opened the file. It was a folder containing a dozen different documents, including three lists. One was a list of monks at Zacharias' monastery, but Zacharias' name wasn't on it. Another was a list of newspaper articles, arranged by journalist, accusing the Russians of a hand in the scandal at Mount Athos, and the third listed TV journalists known for sharing those same views on the Mount Athos scandal. Of the remaining documents, all but one were newspaper articles published more than a decade ago, and not in Greek. The last document was a photograph of a monk in his cell, probably from a magazine.

"*Maggie*, come in here."

The door swung open. "I wondered when you'd invite me."

Andreas pointed to the two lists of journalists on the screen. "What do these names mean to you?"

She read the lists and smiled. "Officially or unofficially?"

"Maggie!"

"Okay, they're the best money can buy. If you want a story and are willing to pay for it, you get it. Facts are secondary to these guys."

Andreas let out a long breath. Just like the ones who brought down my father, he thought. He pointed to the newspaper articles. "Any idea what these are about?"

Maggie looked and gestured no. "They're foreign, not my area of expertise."

"Uh, Chief."

"Yes."

Ilias pointed to one. "This one's in German, the others I believe are in Serbian."

"Can you read them?"

"Not the Serbian, but I think I can make out the German." He studied the article for a couple of minutes. "It's German, but from a Swiss paper. It's about an escaped war criminal who burned to death in a car crash in Switzerland."

"How was the body identified?"

"From documents on the scene."

How convenient they didn't burn, Andreas thought. "Anything else?"

"You'll need a professional translation for details. My German isn't that good, and my Serbian is practically nonexistent. But," Ilias pointed to the articles in Serbian, "one thing I can make out is that all the newspapers mention the guy who died in Switzerland."

Andreas nodded. "What about the photograph of the monk in his cell?"

"I have an idea." Ilias tore through the disks until he found a particular one and popped it into the laptop. It was from a CD collection giving a virtual tour of Mount Athos monasteries. "Here." He pointed to a photograph. It was the one of the monk in his cell. "I thought I saw it before. It's from that monastery you're interested in."

"Damn, you're good."

Ilias jerked forward as if anticipating another congratulatory whack.

Andreas laughed and high-fived him as they bent to the screen.

"Wait a minute," said Andreas. "What's that over there?" He pointed to a photograph next to the one of the monk's cell.

"It's of the library in the same monastery," said Ilias.

"Can you make this part bigger?" Andreas pointed to an area of the floor, and watched the photograph grow.

"My God," said Ilias. "It's the carpet."

Andreas gave no back slaps, no high-fives, no shouts; he just stared at the screen in silence. When he spoke, he first cleared his throat. "Thanks, Ilias, good job. Please print out copies of everything. I sincerely appreciate your help."

Ilias nodded and left with the computer. Maggie was right behind him. "Maggie, please stay."

"I was afraid you'd say that."

Andreas didn't speak immediately. "Are you sure we can trust him?"

"Trust who?"

"Ilias."

Maggie smiled. "I'm sure. His mother used to work here and always complained to me about her 'ungrateful son' who knew 'all these secret things' but never gave her any gossip."

Andreas nodded. "So, we have a list of corruptible journalists accusing the Russians of nastiness around Mount Athos, old newspaper stories about a war criminal apparently incinerated in Switzerland—where Zacharias' passport was issued—a photograph of a monk in a cell in Zacharias' monastery, and the mysterious Satan-bearing carpet from the doctored photograph on Vassilis' flash drive turning up in the same monastery. What do you think Vassilis was trying to tell us?"

She shrugged.

"Like, 'Hello, if you want to know where to find Satan, take a look at this.'"

"That's somewhat flippant, don't you think?"

"Frankly, I think the proper way to describe it is 'goddamn frightening.'"

She sighed. "Should I call Yianni?"

"No reason to, at least not yet. Let me speak to the Protos first. I want to hear what he has to say about all this."

"He may be hard to reach. After all, it's Holy Thursday."

"Even to learn the whereabouts of Satan?"

Maggie's face was serious. "Especially so." She picked up and waved Dimitri's note. "Sometimes, not knowing *is* better."

Chapter Fifteen

For a little less than three more days Zacharias must remain a faceless monk, locked away among more of the same, droning on in endless prayer within the walls of an undistinguished monastery. It would seem the perfect place to lurk unnoticed by the world. But this wasn't Zacharias' style. He hated being one of a flock. His preferred form of anonymity involved standing in the shadows of power, silently appreciated by everyone who mattered for his behind-the-scenes contributions to their successes.

How far things had come. Some would say it was luck, but he knew better. It was ordained. Nothing else could explain his escape from that prison camp, safe passage to Switzerland, and good fortune at finding a new identity easily matched by modest plastic surgery. It was ordained, even if his new features did require the death of the original bearer. But the man got to die in a splash of publicity, albeit anonymously: "Escaped war criminal dies in fiery crash."

Now, all of that was old news, lost as a footnote to history and of no interest to anyone. No one knew of his true past, not even the three collaborators he'd dispatched to Patmos who shared a similar history. His mind wandered from the three men to thoughts of what might have happened on that Holy Island.

Zacharias kept reassuring himself that even if something went wrong, he was covered. Everyone who counted owed him, and not just those living on this Holy Mountain, because all men seeking higher position in the church at one time or another passed through Mount Athos. Powerful men, like that fast-rising abbot on Patmos who called him "my true friend." Still, that wasn't what kept him safe. Owed favors only went so far. Indeed, today was the day for remembering the ultimate betrayal.

No, he had a far greater hold on all those he'd helped. They'd bought into him, vouched for him, called him brother and meant it. And they knew enough about his past that if the full truth ever came to light they'd never convince a soul they hadn't known it all from the beginning. It would bring every one of them down with him, and a crippling scandal to Mount Athos and the church. Yes, they would protect him. They *will* protect him, because they must protect themselves.

◇◇◇

Andreas left two messages for the Protos. The first was, "Please call me as soon as you can." Thirty minutes later he placed a second call saying, "It's urgent." He was about to call again when Maggie came into his office.

"I think you're going to be interested in this."

Andreas looked up.

"I did the follow-up you suggested on that war criminal. Swiss authorities took no dental or DNA records, and what was left of the body was cremated at the request of family."

"How convenient. So much for a simple way of proving someone else fried in that car. By the way, what's the part that's going to interest me?"

"We're not the only one asking questions."

"What are you talking about?"

"A few weeks ago, someone else wanted to know if there was some way to identify the body 'for certain.'"

"You're putting me on."

"The caller said it was an inquiry 'in connection with a church matter.'"

"Did they tell him?"

"They saw no reason not to, but called him back just to make sure he was on the level."

"Please tell me they kept the number."

Maggie smiled. "Their file note read, 'Monastery of Saint John the Divine, ask for Kalogeros Vassilis.'" She emphasized his name with her fingers.

"Yes!" Andreas pumped his fist in the air. "I just love Swiss efficiency."

"Yeah, but it takes a Greek to improvise."

"Meaning?"

"If you can't find a dead body, find a live one."

"And do what with it?"

Maggie stuck out her tongue. "Wiseass, if Zacharias is the war criminal, then whose identity did he assume in conning the abbot into admitting him into the monastery? I found the full name and details Zacharias used when obtaining his Greek citizenship papers and ran that past the Swiss. Their records have a man with that name leaving Switzerland for parts unknown."

"Let me guess, right after the war criminal died."

Maggie nodded.

"Any family?"

"No record of any."

"Damn, another dead end."

"But, guess what, once more we're the second one making the same inquiry."

"Vassilis?"

"Yes, and less than a week before he died."

"Sounds like he'd connected the dots."

"But how could he prove anything? All roads lead to dead ends."

Andreas leaned his elbows on his desk and held his head in his hands. "Did the war criminal leave family?"

"Yes, according to the translations I had done—we Greeks also can be efficient—he had several brothers and sisters."

"Then there's a superhighway leading to an answer. If we can get a sample of Zacharias' DNA and match it against his blood relatives…" Andreas spread his arms wide. "We've got the bastard," and slammed his hands together in a loud clap.

"But how can we get him to cooperate? Mount Athos is an independent state."

Andreas nodded. "Probably the same way Vassilis intended to do it, by telling the Protos what he knew and getting him to force Zacharias to cooperate. I'd bet my badge that was the real reason Vassilis insisted on the Protos coming to Patmos. To confront his old friend with the evidence and urge him to expose Zacharias for who he really is."

"But why wasn't that proof on the USB drive in the cross Vassilis was bringing to his meeting with the Protos?"

"My guess is…caution. Sort of the same reason for keeping the component parts of an explosive chemical reaction far away from each other, to avoid a bomb going off—in this case at the heart of the church. The flash drive only held clues to a silent *coup d'état* underway on Mount Athos. Without the information on Vassilis' computer, there was no way to determine who was behind it. The photographs on the USB were no more than a list of names. The catalyst that would make everything go *BOOM* was what Vassilis had come up with on Zacharias, and there was no reason to put that on the drive. Once Vassilis told the Protos his suspicions, everything could be verified from newspaper articles and public records."

Andreas paused, then shook his head. "Or maybe Vassilis didn't completely trust the Protos."

"You don't really think that, do you?" said Maggie.

"I don't know what to think anymore." He shook his head again. "If only the poor man hadn't been carrying copies of the photographs. The killers recognized the faces in the doctored photograph and took that to mean Vassilis knew of Zacharias' plan. They killed him to protect the plan—not the man. They may not even know about Zacharias' past."

Andreas picked up Vassilis' list of monks from Zacharias' monastery. "The reason Zacharias' name doesn't appear on this list is because Zacharias is not his real name. Here is his real name." Andreas pointed at the name of a war criminal supposed to have died long ago in a car crash in Switzerland. "Buried in the middle of a list of monks!"

Andreas smacked his desk. "I think it's time to call the Protos again, and this time he'd better take my call."

He dialed and waited for the answering machine to pick up.

"Hello, office of the *protos*."

Andreas was surprised to hear a live voice. "Hello, is the Protos available? It's Chief Inspector Kaldis."

"Chief Inspector, as I'm sure you understand, the Protos is terribly busy this week. I've put you at the top of his list and I'm certain he will call you back as soon as he has time. And I can assure you that your repeated calls insisting he call you back immediately will not get you a faster reply. *Kalo Paska.* Goodbye."

Andreas held a dead phone up to Maggie. "He didn't even wait for me to say goodbye. Just gave me Easter wishes and hung up. Arrogant son of a bitch."

"You should be used to that by now. Everybody's available to you when they need you and don't want to know you once you've fixed their problem. You remind them of what went wrong."

"Well, if he thought that was a problem, wait until he sees this." Andreas wrote something out in longhand across Vassilis' list of monks. "Here, fax this to the Protos. And mark it personal so that everyone who touches it reads it." If the Protos wanted to dodge Andreas' phone calls that was his privilege, but to Andreas' way of thinking the Protos did so at his peril. There was no danger posed by the Russians; they weren't involved in these intrigues. The Protos' problems were in his own backyard, so if he wouldn't take Andreas' calls he damn well better pray no Judas had access to his fax machine.

Maggie took the paper from Andreas and read it out loud. "'Your Holiness, I obtained this list from our mutual friend. It's supposed to name all the monks serving in one of your monasteries. Please check the list to make sure no one is missing and call me. Thank you. Respectfully, Andreas Kaldis.'"

Maggie looked at Andreas. "I like it. Simple, courteous, innocuous, just the sort of friendly note you'd expect if someone were trying to tell you, 'Do you happen to know that a notorious, long-thought-dead war criminal is living in your midst?'"

Andreas smiled. "Let's see what this gets us."

Fifteen minutes later Maggie buzzed Andreas on the intercom. "It's the minister."

"Hello, Kaldis here."

"Andreas! How are you?" The voice was all joy and light.

"Fine, Minister, and you?"

"Great, really great. I've been meaning to call you, to thank you for your assistance on that Patmos monk thing."

Andreas wondered how this guy could so easily believe his own PR. "Glad to have been of help."

"I really can't thank you enough for closing this case so quickly."

Something's coming. "No need to thank me, Minister, it's my job. Besides, it's not closed. There's a major new development."

"*Yes, it is closed!*" The tone was that of a mercurial temper tantrum by an insecure bureaucrat.

Andreas was used to that. He also was used to pushing back. "Sorry, Minister, it's not over."

There was a decided pause on the other end of the line. Andreas assumed it was so the minister could give thought to all the threats he wanted to make but knew better than to voice. The bottom line was he needed Andreas more than Andreas needed him. And both men knew it.

"Andreas, let's be reasonable. You caught the killers. Everyone, and I mean everyone, is overjoyed at your triumph. You're even getting a raise. The prime minister himself just called to tell me how much he appreciated your work. There is no reason to go on."

"Did he tell you about the fax?"

Pause. "Andreas, sometimes you can be a real pain in the ass."

"Thank you."

"Yes, he did. Look, no one is going to help you on this. *Absolutely no one.* You will get no help from the ministry, the press, the church—certainly none from the church. You are shut down on this, officially and unofficially." He paused. "The church will deal with this problem in its own way. This cannot come out. It benefits no one and destroys many good people who were deceived by this…well, you know what I'm talking about."

"Yes, I do." Andreas was fuming; he'd heard this sort of honey-coated cover-up crap many times before. "Let's cut to the chase, Spiro. Is there anything I can say to change your mind?"

"I'm sorry, Andreas, no. It's really out of our hands. Let us just accept it. Consider it the internal problem of another country, and none of our concern."

"But it's our church."

"And we must protect it."

"From whom?"

"Andreas, this is going nowhere. We both know it."

Andreas let out a deep breath. "Get some balls" was what he wanted to say. The minister wasn't really a bad guy, just an ass-kisser forever afraid of losing status in the eyes of his social crowd. In other words, he did as he was told to keep his job. But, to be fair, in this instance it was pretty clear to Andreas that it wouldn't matter if a huge pair of steel *arhidia* magically appeared. Someone above him would cut them off for sure. Andreas said goodbye and hung up.

"It's out of our hands." That was the phrase the minister used. Poor bastard doesn't even realize the irony of what he'd said. It's not "out of our hands." It is, as Vassilis wrote in the two-line note he carried to his death: Prepare, for the time is in *their* hands.

Chapter Sixteen

Greece's Cycladic Aegean island of Mykonos was only twenty-five minutes by plane from Athens. About one and one half times the size of Manhattan, Mykonos had more than three times the population of Patmos and the reputation for an in-season, 24/7 party lifestyle unmatched in the world. In other words, Mykonos was about the last place you'd go to find a monk. Which was exactly why Kouros chose to spend his unexpected Easter holiday there. He still had buddies on the island from his rookie cop days, and that meant places to stay for free.

In winter Mykonos was a sleepy island village with virtually no tourists, no business, few open bars, fewer restaurants, and no clubs. But come Easter Week everything changed. The old town came to life, like the red and yellow springtime poppies bursting out all over Mykonos hillsides. It seemed that every world-class partier in the know and every Greek who could find a place to stay was on Mykonos from Thursday through Monday of Easter Week. But this taste of the coming mid-summer craziness was short lived. If you didn't catch the action that weekend come back in June, because the island was back in hibernation come Tuesday.

It was a particularly warm weekend for April and that meant time on the beach; maybe not in the water quite yet, but definitely on the beach. Kouros was face down on a towel, thinking of nothing but the naked bodies lying not too far away when he heard his phone.

"Let me guess, it's my dream come true."

"I sure as hell hope not for your sake."

"What's up, Chief?"

"Honestly, nothing. I mean nothing we can do anything about. I'm just calling because you're the only one I can bitch to."

"I guess that means Maggie won't listen."

"Her exact words were, 'I told you so.'"

"Oh boy."

"Let me share with you my most recent example of why police work is so fulfilling."

"Uh, Chief, are you sure you want to do this over a cell phone?"

"I think the appropriate line is found in a famous American movie. 'Frankly, my dear, I don't give a damn.'"

"Thank you too, dear, but still, don't you think—"

"Yianni, unless we're going back to the days of runners carrying messages from lips to ears—and that Marathon sucker Pheidippides died anyway—we'll just have to risk it at times. Besides, if what I'm about to tell you gets out, it won't matter anyway. I've been told no one will pursue it."

Kouros turned his head away from the naked. He concentrated on the rocky hills, bright blue sky, and his chief's anger. By the time Andreas finished, Kouros was sitting up, shaking his fist, and yelling, "Miserable bastards, I'd like to show them what I'd do to that cocksucker Zacharias if he were in *my* hands."

Kouros watched a nearby couple grab their clothes and hurry away from him. "I understand why you're angry, Chief, but what can we do about it?"

"Wish I knew. Well, think about it, and if anything comes to you let me know."

"Why don't you run it past our friend?" Kouros paused. "Mr. T."

"Mr. T?"

Kouros heard a laugh.

"I get it. I see we're back to Marathon-style communication. Okay, will do. Enjoy the rest of your holiday. Bye."

Kouros let out a deep breath and looked around. The sun was almost down. He'd better get back to the apartment and take a nap. Tonight would be a late one. He intended to get plastered. Miserable bureaucrats, they're everywhere.

"You just missed your mother." Lila was sitting next to the window in her study looking out toward the Acropolis.

Andreas stood in the doorway, staring at her: a Madonna at the window, framed in an illuminated Parthenon against a jet-black sky. "How is she?" Andreas blew her a kiss.

She did not turn. "Still as lovely a person as I've ever known."

"She feels the same about you."

"I know." She looked at him. "She's all excited about the baby."

He nodded. "How's the little bugger doing?"

Lila stroked her belly. "Fine." She looked back out the window.

Andreas grabbed a chair, pulled it up next to her, and sat down. He reached for her hand. She let him take it. "Everything okay?"

"Perfect. Just perfect."

In Andreas' experience with women, that generally meant just the opposite. "Are you nervous?"

"No."

"Sad?"

Lila gestured no.

"Then what is it, *kukla*? I know something is bothering you."

She turned her eyes toward him; tears were welling up. "Disappointed."

He felt the knife.

"Why don't you love me enough to want to marry me?" Her lower lip was quivering.

He felt the twist. He shook his head. "Not now, please. This isn't the time. You're not thinking clearly."

"I'm not thinking clearly? Andreas Kaldis, even your mother knows how fucked-up your thinking is on this."

That was not the sort of language he was used to hearing from Lila. And to have his mother brought into this—

"You just don't get it, do you?"

"Maybe I'm just too hung up on this Patmos monk's murder."

Lila shook her head violently. "No, no, no. There will always be something, some reason, some excuse to fall back on. You, my love, are afraid. Purely and simply afraid."

"Of what?"

"You tell me."

Andreas paused. "Okay." He paused again. "We've too little in common. You know that. It could never work out. You'd be miserable if you had to live your life with me as your husband."

Lila smiled. "Great, you finally said it."

"That makes you happy?"

She squeezed his hand. "Yes, because until you are willing to talk about it, we can't work it out."

"We can't 'work it out.' It is what it is."

"No, this is the only thing that 'is what it is.'" Lila pointed to her belly. "The rest is illusion."

"Be realistic. Our backgrounds, everything about us is different. What kind of a life could we have together? It would frustrate you to no end."

Lila smiled again. "Owning things, attending gala events, receiving honors, or solving big cases is not life. Those are just landmarks along the way. A life is made up of everyday, simple moments. Like making love in the morning in a bed filled with crumbs from your sloppy toast-eating habits, laughing together at the pigeons in the park who pounced on your souvlaki after you put it down to tie my shoelace when I couldn't bend over." She paused. "Your being there when I needed you most, night after night, holding my hand, not knowing if I'd ever come out of my coma." She squeezed his hand and placed it on her belly. "And sharing moments like this. That's what a life is. The hard part is finding someone to share those moments with who loves and cares for you as much as I do you."

He turned away.

"Andreas. It's okay to cry."

"Haven't in years."

"I know, your mother told me." She paused. "Don't worry, we don't have to talk about this now. I just wanted you to know how I felt."

Andreas swallowed. *Amazing, and I thought she'd be the one who couldn't handle this conversation now. I guess imminent motherhood toughens you. I have a lot to learn.*

Lila stood up and kissed him on the cheek. "You have a lot to learn, my love."

◇◇◇

Kouros ate dinner at his favorite place on Mykonos, a little taverna on Megali Ammos beach within walking distance of the old town. Great people, great food, a terrific view, and perhaps the best prices on Mykonos—a particularly important consideration for a cop treating his buddy to dinner for letting him crash at his apartment.

Now it was many hours and what seemed a thousand bars later. His buddy had gone home, leaving Kouros alone at what he called the "hottest" spot on Mykonos. The place was around the corner from Mykonos' town hall, thirty feet from the edge of the sea, and faced the nearby island of Tinos. Kouros was on a barstool a few feet away from a pair of open French doors, relying on a breeze off the sea to keep him from falling asleep on the spot. The bartender was a nice guy. Kept pouring him water every time he asked for vodka. It wasn't a ripoff, because he knew Kouros was a cop and wouldn't take his money anyway. It was an act of kindness that preserved Kouros' *macho* image at the same time as it protected his liver.

The guy next to him started to talk. "This place stays open in the winter, gets a mostly Mykonian crowd. Now it's mixed, part Mykonian, part tourist. Later in the season it's mixed in a different way. Gays and straights, mainly gays in August."

Why is he telling me all this? Kouros took another sip of his drink and swung around on his stool to look across the bay toward Tinos.

"Delos is beautiful, isn't it? So spiritual. You can catch a boat for it over there." He pointed off to the right. "In the morning."

Obviously, the guy had no idea who Kouros was or that the Holy Island of Delos wasn't where he was looking. Kouros gave the guy a "please stop bothering me" stare. He was afraid if he said something it would be "Fuck off." No reason to start something.

The guy didn't take the hint. "You know, I come to Mykonos to get away from all the pressures of my life as a Greek living high in London." He launched into a story about his business, his corrupt partners, what he'd done for revenge, and a host of other things he probably wouldn't even think of telling his pillow. But now he was drunk at four-thirty in the morning in a bar on Mykonos. If Kouros were interested, he probably could get the guy to confess his deepest, most secret fears. That's just the way it was here; everything seemed so unreal that people talked as if their words held no consequences.

But Kouros wasn't interested, so he tuned the guy out, stared off into the distance, and tried to concentrate on how to nail Zacharias.

"So, what do you do my friend?" The guy smiled and put his hand on Kouros' thigh. In the not-too-distant past, that move would have resulted in a certain loss of fingers.

Kouros returned the smile, reached into his shirt for his ID, stuck it in the man's face, and said, "I'm a cop charged with investigating special crimes that come to my attention."

The guy's eyes turned to headlights and he was off the stool and out the door before Kouros could say another word.

Kouros shook his head and grinned. The chief would be proud of me, he thought. Damn, I'm starting to sober up. Guess it's time to head home. He thanked the bartender and swung off the stool—right into a stunningly well-built blonde trying to slide onto the barstool next to his.

"Easy there, big fella." There was a dazzling smile behind the words. "What's your hurry? I'm just getting off work. The evening's still young."

Kouros slid back onto his barstool thinking, I just love it here.

◇◇◇

It's an unstated law on Mykonos that no one disturbs a partier before two in the afternoon. When the banging began on Kouros' door it was just before one.

"Jesus, Mario, how could you forget your key?" Kouros stumbled out of bed and kept yelling to his buddy, "Mario, cool it already, I'm coming." He yanked open the door. It wasn't Mario.

"Morning, Yianni. Nice shorts."

"Tassos? What are you doing here?"

Tassos stepped inside without asking permission. "Andreas told me you were here for the weekend. I didn't want you being alone for Easter. My cousin's family lives here and you're invited to everything, just like one of the family."

"Thanks, Tassos, but—"

"Honey, who is it?" The voice came from the bedroom.

"Just an old friend."

"Thank God it's not a wife. They make such scenes."

Kouros looked at his feet.

Tassos smiled. "I think I should come back later."

A flash of blond raced into the room headed toward the front door. "No need to, old friend. I have to get to work. Kisses." Another dazzling quick smile, a single blown kiss, and gone.

"What was that?"

"Four-thirty in the morning on Mykonos."

"I think I arrived just in time." Tassos laughed again.

Kouros yawned and walked into the kitchen. "Coffee?"

"Sure. Tough break about the minister shutting you down."

Kouros shrugged. "I'm past that. With all the juice involved in this case, we're lucky they let us catch the bastards who cut the monk's throat. No chance of getting to Zacharias; he's too wired into the right people."

"Christ, Yianni, you're too young to be as cynical as I am."

Kouros shrugged. "So prove me wrong."

"Wish I could. As I said to Andreas, 'The only ones I see likely wanting to hang his ass are the Russians.'"

"Have any Russian friends we can talk to?"

"None who'd believe us. We're just cops, claiming everybody but us is involved in a coverup. No way the Russians are going to take our word for it without checking everything out first. And that means whatever we say gets back to someone involved in keeping things quiet, and bye-bye pension for me."

"And a career change for me. Directing traffic if I'm lucky."

"In the middle of the National Highway."

"So, like I said, 'Prove me wrong.'"

Tassos shrugged. "I'm sure the Russians know all about the bad press they're getting here, and the rumors that they're behind everything that's gone wrong on Mount Athos. But Russians are a naturally suspicious sort, born and bred on intrigue. So, for working-level Greek cops to appear on their doorstep out of nowhere with a story about some war criminal Mount Athos monk being behind it all smells just too much of setup. They know damn well how much the Greek Church would love to link them to a church politics plot involving Mount Athos. It would make every smoke and mirrors press story and rumor instantly fact."

Kouros picked up two cups of coffee, handed one to Tassos, and started drinking from the other.

"Thanks, Yianni, but there's no way the Russians will believe us. People just don't confide such serious stuff to total strangers out of the blue without a motive. Unless, of course, they're insane."

Kouros paused in mid-sip. "I have an idea. Let's call Andreas." He put down the coffee, picked up the landline phone, and dialed.

"What kind of idea?"

"A good one, I hope." He waited for someone to answer.

"Hello, Vardi residence."

"Chief Kaldis please, it's Yianni Kouros."

"One moment please."

Kouros looked at Tassos. "I think this has a speaker on it." He pressed a button on the handset and a few seconds later both men heard, "Yianni, what's up?"

"Chief, I'm here with Tassos and he filled me in on your conversation about the Russians."

"You're on holiday, Yianni, forget about it. It's dead and buried."

"I have an idea. What if we get the Russians to think they figured out on their own who Zacharias was and what he was up to? And that it was something we didn't want them to know."

Andreas did not sound impressed. "I think you're forgetting something. We're the good guys. Not vigilantes. Nor are we supposed to be helping foreign powers."

Kouros sounded offended. "Who's talking about helping a foreign power? We're talking about a known war criminal behind the assassination of a Greek monk. His interest in screwing the Russians is incidental, but it's a convenient hook to use to hang the bastard."

Tassos said, "Look, I'm not a big fan of the Russians, but I see Yianni's point, and if he has an idea that works, it might be our only hook."

They could hear Andreas letting out a breath. "So what's your idea?"

"You remember Mario. He's now a sergeant here. I'm staying with him, and he told me that there are a hell of a lot of private jets in for the weekend, including a huge beauty belonging to one of the richest men in Russia."

"I know him," said Tassos. "He has a house on Mykonos, and a friend of mine takes care of things for him here."

"Well, he has a reputation as a pretty wild partier, always with an English-speaking entourage, and if we somehow can break into his crowd for a few hours, there just might be someone in there we could tempt with the story."

There was a noticeable pause on Andreas' end of the line. "Yianni, what sort of shit have you been taking?"

"No, listen, Chief, if we can get the right guy interested—"

Andreas cut him off. "Why on God's earth would one of the richest men in the world give a rat's ass about what a monk in Greece is doing to embarrass the Russian Church?"

Tassos answered. "As a matter of fact, that might be the only part of what sounds like a wild-ass plan that's a sure thing. If the rich guy bites, I'm sure it will get back to the right person."

"Are you two sharing the same bong?"

Tassos laughed. "No, asshole, listen. After the fall of the Soviet Union, some young Russians made a lot of money in highly questionable ways and left Russia to live big capitalist lives elsewhere. A lot of old, ex-socialist types who remained in power back home were jealous of what they called the 'oligarchs' and came up with a plan. They offered those newly rich a choice. Share your wealth with us, or Mother Russia will bring you home to stand trial over how you stole from her to make your fortunes. A few examples were made through all-expenses-paid, long-term vacations to the gulag life, and *voilà*, the others started paying. But the oligarchs still are deeply resented, and there's always someone else wanting a piece of them.

"Exposing such a serious assault on the Russian Orthodox Church could buy our Mykonian oligarch a hell of a lot of good will. Remember, many of Russia's current leaders are deeply religious and no strangers to the Russian monastery on Mount Athos. They know what's at stake there."

"Damn you both," said Andreas. "I'm supposed to be at Lila's parents' this evening."

Kouros spoke. "Look, Chief, maybe you're right and we should forget about it. It's really just a farfetched idea, anyway. Not even a plan. We'd have to get you some sort of introduction to the oligarch, find some way to get him to want to hang out with you, and then—"

"Whoa, what's with all this 'you' crap?" said Andreas.

"You're in charge of the investigation. You're the only one with enough credibility to be believed. You both speak English, and you're also the only one of us who fits in with the look of his crowd."

"I beg your pardon," said Tassos with a smile.

"What else were you going to say?" said Andreas. He sounded testy.

"You have to convince him you're drunk enough to be honestly confiding secrets to a total stranger at five in the morning in a Mykonos party bar."

"Damn, damn, damn. And I bet the plan has to start today."

"Don't see a choice," said Kouros. "He's probably here only for one night, then off to wherever for Easter."

"Ah, Eastertime on Mykonos," said Tassos. "A perfect example of spiritual and temporal coexistence. All of the island's Good Friday church rituals strictly observed during the day, followed by its nearly as hallowed party traditions through the night."

"What time would I have to be there?"

"Not before two," said Yianni.

"It's almost two now."

"I mean in the morning. These guys don't come out until two at the earliest."

"Great, I can't wait to tell Lila I'll be spending Good Friday and Saturday on Mykonos hanging out in bars, getting drunk with wildly partying Russians. Let me talk to her first. Not sure I want to wreck my life here anymore than I already have over what sounds about as crazy a plan as any I've ever heard."

"Thank you," said Kouros.

"I'll see what I can do about arranging an introduction through my mutual friend," said Tassos.

"Not yet, I have to speak to Lila."

"Don't worry, it won't be a problem. Besides, she would love to see you."

"Who's 'she'?"

"The lawyer for the oligarch on Mykonos. You remember Katerina. She always asks about you."

Andreas hadn't seen Katerina since his promotion to Athens from Mykonos. She always had a thing for him, but he'd somehow managed to avoid her, not an easy thing to do once she'd set her mind on a man. She was a bigger player than most guys, and better at it. "Are you smiling?" asked Andreas.

"Yes," said Tassos.

"Bastard. Okay, see what you can do and let's talk later."

They hung up.

"What do you think of our chances?" asked Yianni.

"About the same as Andreas does. But at least it'll keep you out of that sort of trouble for a night." Tassos pointed toward the bedroom and grinned.

"Like the Chief said, 'bastard.'" He picked up his coffee.

Tassos patted him on the shoulder. "It's a really good idea, Yianni. But I think we're all concerned about the same thing."

"Losing our jobs?"

"No, setting something in motion over which we have absolutely no control."

"Like pouring gasoline on a campfire in the middle of a tinder box forest?"

"Something like that, but let's not forget who we're playing with. If these guys get pissed they don't need gasoline. They're Russians, they have nukes."

Kouros swallowed. "Maybe I'll go to church."

"Good idea. I think I'll join you."

Chapter Seventeen

Zacharias' monastery was in full mourning mode, readying itself for the funeral of Christ. At Good Friday morning services, the body of Christ was brought down from the cross and the symbolic shroud of his earthly form placed upon his bier, the *epitaphios.* Across Greece this was the day of Christ's wake, a time for paying respects, practicing traditions like passing three times beneath the *epitaphios* for good luck and blessings, and prayer.

Zacharias remembered other funerals and other bodies. Mainly bodies: the unburied, the buried together. The times had demanded it. One must do what must be done on earth as it is in heaven, he thought. There was no choice then, and there was less choice now. Time was running out. The Ecumenical Patriarch would not live forever.

I must make sure that the new Ecumenical Patriarch's home is here, he thought. The Russians would isolate him from outside influences more than did the Turks. My plans need his ear. The Russians must be vilified. And not just by petty, bribed journalists whose reach rarely exceeded Greece's borders and few believed anyway. He must validate their words with an unequivocal act of proof.

That would come Sunday, after the three men returned. The tragic passing of the abbot of the Russian monastery would be mourned deeply. But once the new abbot publicly denounced his predecessor's death as a brutal assassination—from the same source and uncommon poison as the victim's native Russia stood accused before the world of using in a botched, but horribly disfiguring, attempt to silence the Ukraine's president—all that was written before would become fact. The Russians would never recover from the impact of those words coming from its own abbot. Only one more death, and the world shall be on a better path to life.

"So how long do you think we'll have to stay at your parents?" Andreas had been standing in the doorway to Lila's dressing room for ten minutes, talking to her as she sat at her vanity table putting on makeup.

Lila put down the mascara brush and swung around on her chair. "Enough already. You're like a little kid dancing around something he's afraid to talk about with his mother. What's on your mind?"

He shrugged. "Guilty as charged."

"You'd make a lousy crook, I can read you like a book."

"You better be the only one who can. Otherwise, I'll be in a hell of a mess by morning."

Her eyes narrowed. "Why do I think you're about to tell me you're taking off again?"

"Well, only if you say it's okay. That's what I told Yianni and Tassos."

Lila shook her head. "As if I have a choice. If I don't agree, you'd never forgive me."

Andreas pulled up a chair and sat next to her. "That's not true at all. What they have in mind is crazy anyway. And it's not worth jeopardizing us."

Lila smiled. "That's nice to hear." She looked at her watch and sighed. "We're late anyway. So, what's going on?" She pointed at her belly. "Don't worry, I'm in no condition to do any more stupid things like I did before."

"Promise?"

"Promise."

Andreas told her everything: from the very first phone call ordering him to Patmos up through his conversation with Tassos and Kouros thirty minutes ago.

When he finished Lila stared at him, not saying a word for a full minute. "We're bringing a baby into this world."

He looked down. "I know. Don't worry, I'll stay."

"No. You don't understand. We're bringing a baby into this world. We must do whatever we can to make it a better place."

"I'm not sure that trying to get the Russians to take care of a Greek problem will make the world a better place."

"But I'm sure doing nothing will make it worse."

Andreas smiled. "You're tough."

Lila let out a breath. "But if you're going to try to pull this off, there's only one way to get and keep that Russian's attention beyond a perfunctory 'Hello, how are you, nice to meet you.' I know him, and if you want him to include you in his partying…" She waved her hand in the air. "No doubt what you'll need."

"And what would that be?"

She smiled. "To put it in the common vernacular, 'the hottest piece of ass on the planet.'"

Deadpan, Andreas said, "But you have to be at your parents."

Lila pointed at him. "Very good answer." Then laughed. "So we'll have to find you the second hottest. And only one, because if you show up with more than one he'll get insecure, think you're trying to compete with him. If it's just you and a woman he'll bring you into his crowd, like the spider offering its web to the fly. It's a game these guys play to prove they're men. They'll keep you occupied by making you feel important, while hustling the woman away with promises of whatever she wants to hear."

"How do you know so much about this?"

"Remember, I'm the hottest." She smiled. "Dickless types like that have tried it all on me. But you're the only smooth-talking stud who…uhh…scored."

"Ms. Vardi, what language."

Lila smiled. "I wish I could offer you more, but at the moment I'm afraid I can't."

"But I can't risk using a hooker, and even the hottest female on the force is out of the question. It would look like a setup if the Russian ever found out. And once he hears what I have to say, he'll try to verify everything. How am I going to find someone by tonight?"

"I know the perfect person. She's already on Mykonos, and utterly believable."

"What do mean 'utterly believable'?"

"Barbara."

"She's your best friend!" She also was one of the most unpredictable people on the planet, although Lila and her friends preferred characterizing Barbara's behavior as "spontaneous." Andreas attributed their charitable attitude to the fact that Barbara was rich, young, and gorgeous. It was much the same way that people called an old, rich nut-job "eccentric," rather than the more fitting "raving lunatic."

"That's what makes it so believable," Lila said. "It's the ultimate male fantasy, right?" She smiled.

Andreas didn't know if he should laugh or protest. He decided doing neither was the best choice.

"Don't worry, she can handle any man. Only one promise."

"Which is?" As if he hadn't guessed.

"I want her returned 'unused.'"

"I promise."

"Let me see your fingers, they're not crossed, are they? After all, we want to make sure 'doing the best friend' stays just a fantasy."

Andreas smiled and waved his fingers in her face. "You need not worry, my mind is on other things."

"Yeah, right. Now you're starting to worry me. Just promise you'll sleep on the couch. I'll settle for that."

"What couch?"

"Where do think you'll be staying? It has to be at Barbara's house. How do you think the Russians are going to believe you if you're not..." Lila stopped, as if there were another word she'd decided not to add.

He wondered if she was having second thoughts.

"Just promise."

"I promise." He leaned over and kissed her cheek. "I love you."

He smiled. "Me, you too."

"Okay, time to get you laid." Lila laughed.

Andreas tried to.

◇◇◇

Evening services on Good Friday on Mykonos started at seven in the old town's central churches of Kiriake, Metropolis, and Panachra. At precisely nine, each church's clergy and worshipers left their church in separate processions carrying their church's *epitaphios* along a prearranged route, winding past the other two churches before ending up back at their own. It represented the funeral of Christ, and Mykonians and visitors lined the route, some standing on freshly painted balconies sprinkling the participants below with a mixture of rose water and perfumes, the *rodhonoro* used on Christ's body when taken down from the cross.

Tassos and Kouros went to services at Kiriake, the church closest to the old harbor, and were walking through town somewhere in the middle of its procession.

"Haven't been to one of these in a long time," said Tassos. "I like it."

"I guess that's what keeps it a tradition—people like it."

They were about to turn onto Matogianni Street, Mykonos' compact version of New York City's Fifth Avenue. It started just ahead and ran down to Kiriake. For now, though, they were standing in a rare, much broader bit of lane amid the coffee shops and bars comprising the heart of Mykonos' late-night café society scene. It was barely thirty yards long. Everyone who wanted to see or be seen made an appearance here at some point in the evening, generally between midnight and four a.m.

"What time is Andreas supposed to get here?" Tassos looked at his watch.

"He said his plane gets in around midnight. He's lost his helicopter privileges."

"The first of many such experiences, I'm sure, if any of this wacky plan of yours ever gets back to the minister." Tassos nodded to someone waving to him from a tiny table in front of one of the bars. "And what did you do this afternoon, Mister Big Idea Man?"

"Slept. I was exhausted."

"I bet." Tassos grinned.

Kouros leaned over and whispered in Tassos' ear, "Asshole."

Tassos laughed.

"What's the story with Katerina?"

"She said she'd call me once she knows when and where her client will be in town. Not before one, at the earliest."

"Can you trust her?"

"Absolutely. Not." Tassos smiled. "That's the beauty of it. I know everything I tell her in confidence will get back to the Russian. She runs with the one who pays her bills."

"Sounds like a lawyer."

"God bless them. At least they're predictable."

"What exactly did you tell her?"

"That the chief of GADA's special crimes unit wanted to talk to her oligarch of a client about an investigation that has absolutely nothing to do with him, and that we would be eternally grateful if she could arrange an 'accidental' meeting. I impressed on her how important it was that her client not know the purpose of the inquiry, because this was to be a strictly backchannel, off-the-record conversation about a very serious issue."

"You've got to be kidding me."

"Andreas agreed that was the way to go. They'd find out everything anyway. It's called priming the pump." He smiled.

"And how did Mykonos' number-one lawyer react?"

"She wasn't too hot about the idea until I reminded her that the chief was Andreas. She said 'yes' and hung up so fast when I said his name that I had the image of a sprinter exploding off the blocks at the sound of a starter's pistol, except this one was racing for a beauty parlor."

Kouros laughed. "Should be an interesting night for the chief. I just don't like the idea of him flying solo. He's right, though, everyone here knows we're cops. They'd get suspicious if they saw us hanging around."

"Don't worry, cops like to play, too. I've got a few youngsters on the force from Syros, regulars on the Mykonos party scene, to keep an eye on him. He'll be covered. Besides, we get to share a night together in disguise in one of Mykonos' lovely mini-hauler garbage trucks, trailing them about town recording their every word."

"With all the noise in those places, we'd be lucky to hear a bomb go off."

Tassos shrugged. "At least we get to spend some quality time together."

"Yeah, like blind mice sitting together in a garbage truck."

"It could be worse. If this goes bad we could end up in the back."

"There better be room for three."

Tassos nodded. "Yeah, three blind mice. See how they run…"

Andreas was in a window seat on the plane, staring at the moonlight reflecting off the sea. He smiled as he remembered once thinking that being transferred from Mykonos probably was the only thing that kept him out of Katerina's clutches. She was one of a kind. With her wild red hair and impressively augmented five-foot-five figure, she could not be missed. And if by some chance an object of her attention did overlook her, she'd grab him with a roaring voice and thrust of mesmerizing cleavage. Hard to imagine she was over fifty, even harder imagining anyone with balls enough to suggest anything close to that aloud.

That's when it hit him. "Jesus Christ."

Andreas said it loud enough for the grandmotherly woman next to him to ask, "Are you okay?"

"Yeah, sure, sorry, just remembered something I forgot in Athens." Damn sure did. How could I forget what she's like? The second Katerina sees Barbara it'll be all claws and teeth. He put his elbow on the armrest next to the window, dropped his head into his hand, and sighed. That's all we need to make tonight the biggest clusterfuck of all time, a mega-catfight.

The old woman patted his arm. "Don't worry my son, it is God's will."

◇◇◇

The SMS message on Tassos' phone was simple: SEE YOU AT VENGERA AT TWO. Vengera was the name Mykonian locals used to describe the café society area at the top of Matogianni Street. Vengera was a legendary bar that gave the location its original panache. But it was long gone, replaced by a jewelry store, as were many places from Mykonos' more innocent times. All that remained was the memory and a name.

"We have a go. Start your engine, Mr. Kaldis, and good luck." Tassos raised his cup of coffee.

"How much time do we have?"

"About thirty minutes. No need to rush, I'm sure they'll be late. It's only five minutes from here." They were in an out-of-the-way coffee shop off behind Kiriake church.

"I wish I'd had the chance to speak to Barbara, warn her about Katerina."

"Didn't you drop your bag off at her house?" said Kouros.

"Yes, but only the maid was there to let me in, and she took off the minute I got there. It seemed everybody had some place to be after midnight tonight. Barbara left me a note." He handed it to Tassos.

Tassos read it aloud. "'Hi, Andreas. Looking forward to a fun night. I'm having dinner with friends out of town. My phone will be off, but I'll call you when I'm done so you can tell me where to meet up. Kisses. B.'"

"She doesn't seem to be taking this very seriously," said Kouros.

"The affectionate word to describe her state is 'relaxed.' She's not the type that gets anxious easily. All she knows is that she's my wife's best friend hanging out with me for the night with instructions to look and act as hot as she can so that I can get close to some super-rich Russian. That's a drill she has down pat. I just wish she'd call me. I can't get the damn show started until she's with me."

Kouros said, "Did you say—"

Tassos kicked him under the table. "Then it's probably better you didn't say anything to her. It might pump her up for a fight. These society types are pretty good at handling aggressive bitches trying to bring them down. And frankly, if she's as hot as you say, she probably runs into that sort every day."

Andreas stared at him. "You're just trying to make me feel better."

"Yep, Katerina will tear her a new asshole." Tassos laughed.

Andreas shot him a one-finger salute. "And yes, Yianni, I said 'wife.' No reason for the world to think otherwise. What with the baby on the way."

Kouros nodded. "No problem here, Chief, just checking to see if I had to buy more than a baby gift."

Andreas smiled. "I wouldn't worry about it."

Tassos shook his head. "This is not the time to say it, but sometimes you're a real asshole, my friend."

"Funny, Lila said sort of the same thing."

"I bet. Let's go, Yianni. We've got to find someplace to put our limo so we don't miss a word of tonight's performance by Mister Sensitive here." Tassos flicked the back of his hand in Andreas' direction.

"We can park on the street behind Vengera, by Panachra church. With the monster of a mess from tonight's processions, everyone expects to see a garbage truck there."

Andreas said, "Gentlemen, let's just hope we don't make a bigger one."

The three cops stood up, raised their right hands, and slapped high fives. Tassos and Kouros left, and Andreas sat back down. He looked at his watch. It was almost two and still no word from Barbara.

Time for a change of plans.

Chapter Eighteen

If the amount of bullshit men threw at women visiting Mykonos that actually was believed could be spread across that arid island, within a week it would be as green as picture-postcard English countryside. Why they believed what they heard no one knew. Perhaps they came looking for a fantasized Mister Right on an idyllic Greek island, or maybe just wanted to hear something, anything, to justify behavior unthinkable back home. No matter, whatever the reason, men sensed it and took advantage. For them it was a fantasy of a different sort, power over another being, something missing in virtually every other aspect of their lives that counted.

Unless, of course, you were Vladimir Brusko: for him, no rules applied, nothing was unattainable. His vast Russian-made fortune bought it all, anywhere and anytime he wanted. He came to Mykonos not so much to play, although he surely did, as to validate his choice of lifestyle. Surrounded by so many from so much of the world, struggling so hard to get just a taste of what came to him so easily, was what made his Mykonos holidays a joy. He was a voyeur here, admiring himself endlessly in everyone else's mirror.

At the moment, he was sitting at a tiny café table by Vengera, staring at cleavage, listening to a pitch from its possessor. Why do all these peasants I employ to do local tasks for me think they can draw upon my time at will?

"Like I said, Vladimir, he is very important with the police in Athens, and he said it's urgent he speak with you. Urgent. But you aren't supposed to know any of this."

She really thinks I need to know these low-level police? I know their bosses. I can get whatever I need with a phone call. "I do not wish to get involved."

"It doesn't involve you. If you don't like what he has to say, ignore him. It's all up to you."

No reason to offend this woman. I'll just say hello, let him make his little pitch and be done with it. He smiled and leaned over to her. "How could I ever refuse my Katerina?" Then kissed her on the cheek.

Katerina glowed. "Thank you, Vladimir."

"No need to," *because I shall give him nothing.*

Andreas began his stroll along Matogianni at precisely two a.m. With all the necessary hellos it would take fifteen minutes to make it to Vengera. Ex-police chiefs must listen to old and new gripes. Generally he didn't mind, though tonight he had little patience for other than "*Yiasou* Manos, kisses Irini, hello Theo." He must focus. This was far too important for more serious distractions. There was Katerina, dead ahead. *It's show time.*

"Andreas, Andreas." The voice came from a woman in a Greek fisherman's hat sitting to his left in front of a jewelry store. She was surrounded by colorful paintings of traditional Mykonian life. "I've missed you, *kukla*, how are you? Please, come and sit with me."

"I can't, Cee, I have to hurry." Everyone called her Cee. She was the dean of Mykonos artists, thought by many to be more symbolic of Mykonos than its pet pelicans. Her paintings brought Mykonos to the world, one tourist at a time.

"I see, now you're too important even for old friends. Just like everyone else who goes off to Athens."

He let out a breath, turned away from his path to Katerina, and walked over to her. "For you there's always time." He leaned down and kissed her on both cheeks. "But not now, Cee."

"Okay, but don't forget me."

"Never."

"Andreas, *over here*."

It was from a voice Andreas knew, and with an intensity that made you think he was the mayor handing out tax breaks. "Katerina *mou*, what a pleasant surprise."

She was the only woman sitting amid a group of men gathered around a small table. Some were on chairs, some sat on cushions on a low, smooth, white concrete wall, others stood. Three of the men wore black combat fatigues. Andreas wasn't sure if dressing bodyguards like that helped achieve their intended purpose, unless of course attracting attention was what you wanted.

"Come here, please, I want you to meet a very good friend of mine." She'd switched to English and was nodding toward a man on her right.

Andreas smiled. The man was about Andreas' age, looked fit, with sandy hair, brown eyes, and a "why are you bothering me" look. Andreas stepped up to the table, extended his hand, smiled, and said in English, "Hi, Andreas Kaldis."

The man did not stand, just reached up, gave a perfunctory handshake, and said in clearly Russian accented English, "Nice to meet you, Vladimir Brusko."

Andreas nodded, then leaned down to Katerina, kissed her on both cheeks, and said in English, "Katerina, my love, you look as fantastic as ever," making sure to sneak an obvious peek at her breasts.

"I've missed you, there is so much to catch up on." She slid along the cushion on the wall to make room for Andreas to sit between her and the Russian.

"Thank you. I'd love to, but I'm meeting someone and can't stay. Maybe we'll bump into each other later. Kisses." He patted Vladimir on the shoulder. "Nice meeting you, bye." And off he went, quickly lost in the Vengera crowds.

Andreas' phone rang almost immediately.

"What the hell was that?" It was Tassos.

"I had no choice, no bait to fish with. Until I hear from Barbara it's a waste of time. That guy's about as interested in talking to me as you are in going on a diet."

"Kiss my ass. When do you think you'll hear from her?"

"Wish I knew. Just have one of your boys keep a loose eye on him so we know where they are when she calls. I'm sure she will, just not sure when her spaceship will land on this planet. But tell them to be careful, he probably has bodyguards under-cover keeping an eye out for anyone watching him. Guys with camo-cops usually do."

"I cannot tell you how pissed Katerina must be at this moment," said Tassos.

"Serves her right. Only reason for her being pissed is if she told him all sorts of things she shouldn't have."

"Yeah, makes sense, but I'll let you explain that to her."

"Got to go, must find Barbara." Andreas hung up and dialed Lila.

She answered on the first ring. "Hello, daddy-to-be. Miss me, or are you just calling to verify your instructions?"

"Why aren't you sleeping?"

"Hard to sleep, what with my imagination running wild at what might be going on. Besides, you knew I'd be awake. That's why you called."

Andreas wasn't in the mood for banter. "Yes, I miss you, but it looks like you have nothing to worry about. Barbara is a no-show."

"You're kidding me." Her tone was serious.

"Wish I were. She was out when I got to her house a little past midnight. She left a note that she'd be out to dinner, her phone would be off, and she would call me later. It's now way past later and the whole plan is about to crash."

There was a long silence before Lila spoke. "At times she's a real airhead, with the attention span of a gnat. Let me try to find her." Her voice now was angry. "I'll get her to call you, or let you know if I can't find her. But I will. Love you." She hung up.

Andreas was standing between two churches, really three, just beyond the Nautical Museum. Time to say a prayer and light a candle. Make that three candles.

"Your friend seemed really excited at meeting me." The sarcasm was clear.

Katerina's nervousness was obvious. "Vladimir, I don't understand. He said it was important. Honest." That bastard Tassos, wait until I get my hands on him.

"Don't worry about it." He patted her bare knee. "He's just a *poseur*, and not a very good one at that. 'I'm meeting someone and can't stay.' I just bet he is, some fuck-me-for-a-drink mindless little tourist slut. Now he's just one less nobody looking to waste my time."

Vladimir gestured for a bodyguard to pour them more champagne, then raised his glass and stared into Katerina's eyes.

Her face lit up in a smile.

He leaned over and whispered in her ear, "To no more urgent meetings. *Ever.*"

Katerina's smile vanished.

◇◇◇

Lila called a dozen people before she found one who knew where to find Barbara: she was sitting across from him, naked in a hot tub. Lila thought, thank God he's gay, because no straight man in that position would ever have answered the phone. Staring at arguably the world's most perfect set of tits would be far too much of a distraction.

"Christo, let me speak to her." Christo was the most sought-after and prominent hairdresser in Athens.

"Not sure she's in any condition to talk, *kukla*. Thank God I was there to save her."

"*Christo, let me speak to her.*" It was a nonnegotiable tone.

Lila heard a muffled few words followed by "Hellllo."

"Barbara, what the hell are you doing?"

"Lila, darling, I'm here with the most gorgeous, blond-haired, blue-eyed, naked man…are you here? I mean I miss you. I—"

"Barbara, get out of that hot tub, get yourself dressed and get into town. You're supposed to be meeting Andreas."

"But it's still early."

"It's almost three o'clock in the morning."

"Oh. I lost track of time. There were so many people, we were having such fun, Christo said, 'why leave,' and you know how convincing he can be, and—"

"Let me speak to Christo."

She heard the phone drop.

"Hi, *kukla*, thank God she missed the water."

"Listen carefully. I want you to get her dressed, made up to look perfect, and into town, now."

"But—"

"*No buts!* No buts at all. Do you hear me? Barbara was supposed to meet Andreas over an hour ago. I'm hours away from giving birth, and you do not want to imagine how crazy I can be if you don't do me this simple favor and get her ass in town in the next twenty minutes!"

As independent and important as Christo liked to think he was, they both knew his business depended upon staying in the good graces of powerful Athenian women, and Lila was at the very top of that list. She hoped her tone would sober him up enough to do the same for Barbara.

"Will do. Sorry. Didn't know how important this was."

"Twenty minutes. Call me when she's on her way."

Lila hung up. She kept shaking her head. *I can't believe Barbara did this to me. What can I tell Andreas? I wish I could have a drink.* She let out a deep breath. *I'll just tell him she'll be in town in a half hour and ask where should she meet him. No reason to tell him the rest. It only would upset him. Besides a tipsy beauty might be more appealing to the Russian. Na zdarovye.*

Andreas kept looking at his watch. It was nearly four and still no Barbara. Lila said she'd be here by now. What a rat-fuck this was turning out to be. Come Sunday morning, when Zacharias finds out what happened to his three boys, either he vanishes to another part of the planet or presses the right political buttons and shuts us down cold. Either way, he gets away with murder, and all because some airhead doesn't know how to stop party-ing long enough to do what she promised. The devil must be laughing.

◇◇◇

"So, what do you think the Chief's doing?"

Tassos shrugged. "Same thing we are, killing time."

"At least he doesn't have to do it in a garbage truck."

"You really don't get it, do you? He isn't meeting any Russian, we're not waiting for some hot woman to show up, this all was set up as an opportunity for you to receive life lessons from a master."

Kouros looked at his watch. "I feel more like I'm cooped up in a phone booth with a parrot who can't keep its beak shut for thirty seconds."

Tassos shook his head. "Gratitude is the rarest gem to find."

Kouros watched two young girls walk by, stare at the two men squeezed together in the front seat of a garbage truck on a dark Mykonos back street, and giggle. God knows what they must be thinking, he thought.

"What you need to straighten out your life is the right girl," said Tassos.

"Whoa, now you're cutting in on my mother's turf. Only she gets to nag me on that subject."

"Sorry. I always respect union rules."

"And, besides, what's with you? You hook up with Maggie after a zillion years of bachelorhood and now you want all of us to go down with you? Power to the unattached, let freedom ring."

"Bolshevik."

"Royalist."

Tassos stared out the window. "If we sit here much longer we'll be playing rock, paper, scissors."

Kouros let out a breath. "Not much else to do until that lightweight Barbara shows up. Chief's been holed up in that piano bar in Little Venice for over an hour. If I have to listen in on this earpiece to one more bartender story from the two guys who own that place I'll scream."

"It's one of the few place he's not likely to bump into the Russian before we're ready for him. Guys like that avoid gay crowds, afraid it might cast doubts on their manhood."

"Besides, the chief likes the singer."

"The sexy broad?" said Tassos.

"We don't call them 'broads' these days."

"Whatever, she turns me on."

Kouros grinned.

"Screw you, I saw what turns you on."

Kouros smiled. "Now, now, you're getting back into my mother's bailiwick."

Tassos sighed. "I'm so bored."

Kouros grabbed his arm. "Not for long." He pointed out the window. Two men had stopped the girls who'd just passed the garbage truck. Two other men were coming up on the girls from behind. What bothered Kouros was that the men behind the girls were gesturing to the two men in front and pointing to a building. "That building is empty, it's under construction."

"Honk the horn, scare them off, they're drunk," said Tassos.

"But they'll just go after someone else."

"Just deal with the problem at hand."

The men now surrounded the girls. "I'm getting out," said Kouros.

"We're on a stakeout."

"They need help."

Tassos leaned over and pressed the horn. The men jumped. He hit the horn again and flashed the lights. The men left. "Now they don't."

Kouros stared at Tassos. "A life lesson?"

"Lesson number one. Beat evil when you must, but only when you must. There's an inexhaustible supply in this world to keep you busy every second of your life. Put differently, there's too much crap in this world to shovel it all. If we try, we end up buried in it. Lesson two. Protect and treasure all the good that comes your way, whenever and wherever you're lucky enough find it." He smiled. "Especially if it's the right girl."

Kouros pressed his hand against his earpiece. "Sounds like the chief found his. Hot chick number one is now in town and on the move. It's a go."

"Let the games begin."

◇◇◇

Starz was Vladimir's hangout on the island. Only two hundred yards down the busy lane leading from Vengera, its open, garden-like front was strategically set off from a continuing parade of the curious by an array of closely-grouped potted greenery. Starz was where everyone wanted to be seen late at night. Inside the music was deafening, outside the chatter nonstop. Everywhere nothing but beautiful people—and those who could afford to pay for them.

Vladimir would sit until dawn at his favorite table next to the front door, a few steps above the masses squeezed into tables in the garden below, and study those lucky enough to pass through the velvet rope guarded by lovely women. From there he'd watch them for hours, indulging in his favorite pastime: fantasizing how much everyone envied his life. It gave him more pleasure than sex, sometimes.

Tonight he felt particularly confident. Perhaps because he'd been to church, something he rarely did anymore. He stared at the tall, white wall enclosing the far side of the courtyard. Above the garden, and slightly in from each end, the wall sloped sharply up to form a triangle jutting into the sky. It reminded him that a kindred spirit shared this space. Few, maybe none, realized the other was here. But all anyone needed do was look up, for at the top of the triangle stood the sign of His presence: a simple, white stone cross atop the church bounding the garden courtyard.

Vladimir stared at the cross and smiled. "Don't worry, you take care of the hereafter and leave the here and now to me." He'd spoken his thoughts aloud.

"What was that?" Katerina asked.

He kept staring at the cross. "Just a private conversation with God."

Katerina nodded. It was after four and she'd been sitting next to him the entire night. Vladimir knew she'd love for him to show interest in her, but not a chance—even if she were twenty years younger. Make that thirty. There was just too much available without complications. He'd come to the conclusion that it was best to use hooker types. Not to pay them for sex, but to pay them to leave.

Vladimir looked down from the cross. A fat, sixty-year-old man at a table across from him was groping two twenty-year-olds in strapless cocktail dresses. From the bags at the women's feet and similarity in their dresses, it was obvious they were wearing the fat man's purchases. Vladimir watched the man take the hand of one girl and press it to his crotch. She rubbed, as the other kissed him on the lips. Vladimir couldn't help but laugh. Just who did he think he was impressing?

"Disgusting, that old man over there with those two young girls."

Obviously, Katerina had caught the subject of his interest. "Jealous are we, my love?"

"Not of them. They're classless, and," she gave what must have been her most coquettish, cleavage-emphasizing smile, "I'm sure lousy in bed."

He smiled, and squeezed her thigh. "I'm sure."

Suddenly, faces began turning and several people headed toward the velvet rope, led by the owner. Paparazzi started flashing away.

Vladimir gestured for the attention of one of his bodyguards. "Find out what's going on."

Katerina put her hand on Vladimir's. "I like it when you touch me like that."

He smiled and held her hand.

The bodyguard was back. "Nothing to worry about, sir. It's just a pretty woman everyone seems to know."

"Really, I think she should meet me."

"I don't think it will be a problem, sir."

"Why's that?"

He turned and pointed to a couple the owner was leading toward the VIP table across from them, as two members of the club's staff hurriedly relocated the obnoxious fat guy and his two ladies to a place on the terrace.

Vladimir stared at the woman: ice-blue eyes, long auburn hair, almost as tall as he, and more gorgeous than a dream. He pulled his hand away from Katerina's, waved to the couple, and said in English. "Andreas, my friend, how nice to see you again. Please, come join us."

He turned to Katerina. "Please, move over to make room for your friends."

Katerina's anger was obvious. "She is not a friend of mine."

"Too bad, then perhaps you should leave." It was time for him to reassert control over the here and now and all its beings.

The gorgeous woman smiled at him, said in perfect English, "Thank you very much, but we're expecting friends," turned away, and sat down in the power seat at the next table. "Darling," she said, waving to Andreas and still speaking English, "Come sit here," patting the seat next to her. People started flocking to her table.

Andreas shrugged and said to Vladimir and Katerina, "What can I do, but please, won't the two of you join us? I'd love for you to meet Barbara."

Vladimir paused and drew in a breath. He was the one who gave audiences. He stared at Andreas, then glanced up at the cross, and brought his eyes down so that they lingered on that gorgeous woman. He willed her to catch his eyes, but she never looked his way. Vladimir swallowed and smiled. "It would be our pleasure."

Chapter Nineteen

Big dogs ruled. So when Vladimir moved over to Barbara's table everyone made room for him to sit beside her, on the other side from Andreas. Katerina pushed herself in next to Vladimir, but she might as well have been in Siberia for all the attention he paid her. He kept trying to start a conversation with Barbara but she treated him as if he were a waiter pressing for her order, and kept leaning forward to speak to her friends around the table in Greek.

Andreas kept a sideways watch on the Russian's eyes. They hadn't moved from Barbara since he sat down. Every time she leaned forward he stared at her face, every time she sat back to laugh or sip her wine he closed them as if inhaling the scent of her hair. Rarely did his eyes stray down to her backless, turquoise sundress. A feat Andreas admired, considering his own inability to resist peeking at her virtually exposed breasts far more than he'd like Lila to know.

Barbara had deflected Vladimir's overtures enough times to make him look frustrated, but hopefully not enough to make him decide to give up and leave. Andreas put his hand on Barbara's bare back and gently nudged her forward. Then waved to Vladimir to lean in, over her back. His face was there in an instant.

Andreas shrugged and said in English, "I'm sorry that everyone is speaking Greek."

"Don't worry, it's no problem."

Andreas knew he wasn't serious. Men like Vladimir never expected to be left out of any conversation. "Still, I'm sure you'd be more gracious in your country."

Vladimir smiled, sat up, and said something in Russian to one of his bodyguards hovering nearby. In seconds three bottles of ice-cold vodka appeared, shots were poured, and lifted in a toast. "To Greece," Vladimir said.

"To Russia," added Andreas.

The two men smiled at each other, clinked glasses, did the same with Barbara, and downed their shots. That became their ritual over the next hour and a half. Vodka shots separated by animated conversation in English over Barbara's naked back, with both men gesturing and touching her in the process. She didn't seem to mind; it was as if she didn't even notice.

It now was five thirty in the morning and the place was jammed. Vladimir's head was halfway across Barbara's back, his hand down about her waist, just resting there, until needed for a gesture. Both men clearly were feeling the vodka.

"So my friend, what was it you wanted to ask me?"

Andreas smiled. "I see Katerina can keep a secret."

Vladimir laughed. "Yes, so I've noticed." They slapped high fives and Vladimir let his hand slide along Barbara's back to its resting place below. "No, really, if I can help you, it would be my honor."

Andreas shook his head. "No reason to get you involved. The investigation has been shut down. No one wants to touch it."

"Sounds interesting."

"Too interesting I'm afraid. But once I caught the three Serbian bastards who killed the monk, no one wanted to go further with it. Case closed."

"Was that why you wanted to talk to me, about the Serbs?" He gestured with his head to one of his men to pour another round. His hand never moved from Barbara's back.

"No, I was more interested in another guy."

"What guy?"

"I don't know, the dead monk had some press clippings on him in Serbian about a war criminal who died years ago in Switzerland. I thought you might know somebody who could tell us about the guy in the clippings."

"Why would you care about a dead war criminal?"

"The question is, 'Why would an old monk care about a dead war criminal?'"

They lifted their shots, clinked, and drank. Thankfully, thought Andreas, Barbara had stopped doing shots a half hour ago.

Andreas leaned in closer over Barbara's back. "Frankly, Vladimir, I wanted your help in getting some of your boys back home to take a look at what we found on the dead monk's computer. He was trying to prove Russians were behind all of the Greek Church's troubles on Mount Athos." Andreas sat back up. "But what the hell, I left the stuff at Barbara's. Doesn't matter anymore anyway." He poured himself another shot. "No one wants to find out if all this 'blame the Russians' talk is for real." He chugged the drink. "Or who might be behind it."

Vladimir stared at Andreas, and slowly stroked Barbara's back.

Andreas said nothing more. Anything else would be overkill. He knew Vladimir was sober enough to comprehend everything he'd said, for the Russian's mind was set on getting Andreas drunk enough to get a shot at Barbara's panties. Good luck to him.

Vladimir said something in Russian to one of his bodyguards, then poured another round for everyone at the table. "To us, the night is young."

◇◇◇

It was nearly eight in the morning when they got back to Barbara's house. Barbara resisted Vladimir's last-minute effort to get the two of them wasted enough to "watch the sunrise from one of my balconies," by dumping a string of "goodbye shots" on the floor, a sleight-of-hand technique she'd obviously mastered long ago. Andreas, on the other hand, was, as they say in French, "shit-faced." Barbara also resisted Vladimir's offer of a ride home, steering Andreas into a taxi instead.

As soon as they were out of the taxi she said, "No way I wanted him pushing himself into my house for a nightcap."

Andreas took that to mean she was afraid he might have assaulted her. "Don't worry, Barbara, drunk or not, if he'd tried anything—"

She was fumbling for her key in her bag. "It wasn't Vladimir I was worried about."

"Me?"

She opened the door and pushed him inside. "No, silly, me."

He stared at her.

She shrugged. "My late night started out naked in a hot tub with an absolutely gorgeous gay man, and I've had two utterly handsome men running their hands up and down my bare back for the rest of the evening. Darling, I'm horny as hell."

Andreas knew his next word, even gesture, would get him laid for sure right on the spot. He just stared and gave a silly grin.

She laughed. "Yeah, you really love her." Barbara turned and walked toward the bedroom. "Come on lover boy, we've got to keep up appearances."

He did as she said, but as soon as he saw the bed, he fell on it face down and was out in seconds.

Andreas had no idea how long he'd slept, but when he woke he was on his back, stark naked, and Barbara was beside him, just as naked but asleep on her belly. She must have undressed him and turned him over. No way he did anything. He definitely would have remembered that ass. And those tits, he could see them from the side. The thought had him erect. All he had to do was roll over slightly and he'd be inside her.

She might not even notice at first, and certainly wouldn't mind. It would be all so simple…easy…quick…and delicious. I could just slip right inside her, then move back and forth slowly, she'd start to moan and we'd be off to the races. Damn, I want her. He was so hard at the thought that he felt the sort of throb he'd get near the verge of coming.

He shook himself, rolled off the bed, and headed into the bathroom. Thank God I'm sober, he thought. Just a little bit drunk, no way I wouldn't be pounding into her this very second. He reached down and touched himself, thinking it might not be a bad idea to masturbate. He stroked himself twice, then stopped. He froze, felt some more, then turned and walked back into the bedroom and over to the table on Barbara's side of the bed. He picked up a purple-capped, clear plastic bottle: "Astroglide™ Personal lubricant and moisturizer."

He stared at the bottle and touched himself again.

"You were terrific, darling. Can only imagine how great you must be when you're awake." Barbara was talking with her head in the pillow. "Consider it payment in full for driving me crazy all night." She rolled onto her back, pulled her knees up toward her hips, and said, "But in case you can't remember what it feels like to be inside me…bare." She spread open her arms and smiled. Andreas stared at her, holding personal lubricant in his one hand and a very hard dick in the other.

"I think I'll take a shower."

"Lucky woman." Barbara rolled back onto her belly.

The conversation was so awkward for Andreas that he didn't know what to do next. He showered for twenty minutes, trying to think of something to say. By the time he came out of the bathroom, Barbara was gone. A note was on her pillow. He picked it up.

Ran off to town. Regards to Lila. Thanks. B.

Who the hell is ever going to believe this? He called Tassos.

"And how are we this morning, my little party animal?"

"Do not ask."

"That bad?"

"Worse. So, what happened?"

"I think we picked most of it up on tape. Good idea you had to talk over the woman's back all night. She muffled out a lot of the background noise. Surprised she didn't mind. A real trooper."

Andreas didn't dare respond. Tassos had been a cop too long; a tone of voice would tell all.

"They took the bait. Right after you told him about the stuff at Barbara's, Vladimir said something to one of his guys in Russian. It had to be to find and search her house. My Syros boys tailed them there. They were real efficient, in and out in less than ten minutes. Bet you didn't notice they ever were there."

"In my condition I wouldn't have noticed a herd of elephants camped out in the living room. Did your boys check to see if they planted any bugs in the house?"

"Yes. It's clean."

Andreas walked into the living room and looked at his briefcase. "Did your guys touch my briefcase?" He rarely carried one but did for this trip.

"I told them if they even breathed on it they'd be singing *castrato* at Easter services."

The briefcase was sitting on a patterned chair exactly where Andreas had set it down…almost. Just one half a flower too far back on the seat cushion. "Yeah, these guys were good, not perfect, but good." He opened the case. Again, everything almost where it should be. The flash drive was not exactly at the same spot on the newspaper as he'd placed it before going out, nor was the folder with copies of the articles and photographs exactly where he'd left it.

"Looks like they got to everything, and took care I wouldn't notice."

"Any chance they missed it?" asked Tassos.

"If they were blind and dumb."

"Not those guys. So now what?"

"Don't know about you, but for once I'll be spending my holiday at home. Let the other guys do the work."

"*Kalo Paska.*"

Andreas paused. "How do you say 'Happy Easter' in Russian?"

"Why?"

"Well, that guy Vladimir wasn't so bad. The fact he wanted to screw Barbara only made him human. I thought I'd call and say thanks. He did pick up the check."

"Probably not a good idea. The only reason he'd want to talk to you—unless you can get him laid—is to make sure this whole thing wasn't a setup. If I were you, I'd avoid him."

Andreas nodded at the phone. "Good advice. I'm off to the airport."

"I wonder what they're going to do with what they took?"

"My guess is, start off by ruining a lot of people's holiday."

"As long as it's not ours."

"Amen to that, my friend."

◇◇◇

The area of Costa Ilios was not far from the center of town, but trying to get a taxi from there to the airport at six in the afternoon on the Saturday before Easter required a bit of a miracle. In Andreas' case, it took a call from the current Mykonos police chief. Andreas hoped to get a seat on the 7:30 flight. It was the first one to Athens since he'd gotten up. He was banking on everyone being where they intended to be by now, what with Saturday night being the main event of Greek Easter.

Andreas was in the midst of a heated argument with a particularly belligerent ticket agent who kept insisting that despite a virtually deserted departures area there were no seats available on the flight, even for a GADA chief inspector.

"Chief Kaldis."

The voice was behind him. Andreas turned. "Yes?"

"Mr. Brusko would like you to join him for coffee." The accent was Russian but the man was not someone he recognized from last night. He was stocky, five-foot-ten, around sixty, and dressed like a college professor on holiday.

Andreas looked around. "I don't see him."

"He's at his home."

Andreas nodded. "I see. Well, please thank him, but I have a plane to catch." He looked at his watch. "In thirty minutes."

"It is very important."

"So is getting home in time for Easter."

"He can arrange to fly you there."

"I'm sure he can, but my family is expecting me on this plane. Please thank him, especially for last night, but I must respectfully decline."

The man studied him for a moment. "It's about Zacharias."

Andreas shrugged.

The man smiled. "Very good."

"'Very good' what? I don't know any 'Zacharias.'" Andreas looked at his watch and turned back to the ticket agent. The agent looked right past him as if expecting a sign from Vladimir's man. Andreas leaned in. "Bad move, numbnuts. If I don't have a ticket in my hand in fifteen seconds, I'm coming behind this counter and kicking the fucking shit out of you. And just try getting a cop to help you."

The guy started to stammer.

"Eleven…ten…no talk…just a ticket…seven—"

The agent frantically punched away at his keyboard, yanked out a ticket from the printer, and handed it to Andreas.

Andreas turned and faced the Russian man behind him. "Your turn. Just how long a holiday would you like to spend in Greece? Ever see *Midnight Express*? Would you like to experience the Greek version? Consider your next move carefully." Andreas stepped toward him.

The man stepped aside.

Andreas leaned over and whispered in his ear, "Smart move. And tell your boss sitting in the Hummer outside not to be so conspicuous next time."

Andreas walked to the check-in counter at the north end of the room. By the time he'd checked in and turned around, Vladimir was standing by the door to the departure gates.

Andreas walked straight toward him. "I see you missed my company."

Vladimir nodded. "Yes, but this is far more serious than drinks at a bar and playing with a woman's back."

"Maybe for you, but for me it's a hell of a lot less exciting."

Vladimir smiled. "May we talk outside?"

They went out and stood by the entrance to the parking area.

"What you told me last night could have severe implications."

"About what?"

"You know exactly what I'm talking about."

"Vladimir, you're a nice guy, and I know you want to bury your cock about as deep as it can go in Barbara, but aside from that I have no idea what you're talking about."

Vladimir smiled again. "You're right about point one, but I don't believe your second."

Andreas placed his arm over Vladimir's shoulder and locked eyes with him. "For the life of me Vladimir, I really want to help you out here, so if there is something on your mind just tell me directly, otherwise please stop with all this bullshit and let me catch my plane."

"If you don't confirm, nothing will happen."

Andreas dropped his arm from Vladimir's shoulder and shook his head. "I just bought the ticket, there is nothing to confirm."

Vladimir nodded. "Okay, have it your way. Your elaborate ruse of last night will have been a total waste of time."

Andreas patted him on the arm. "Obviously you've never slept with Barbara. Gotta run. Happy Easter." He never looked back. Just walked into the terminal, through the metal detector and out to the plane. He had no idea if he'd handled this test correctly but he'd gone with his instincts. What happened next was out of his hands anyway. And certainly not in God's.

Chapter Twenty

Vladimir and the other Russian sat in the back of the Hummer. It hadn't moved from in front of the terminal.

"What do you think?" Vladimir asked.

"He demonstrated the inborn, aggressive traits of an animal under stress. It's called the 'fight or flight response.'"

"Okay, Anatoly, I know you're a psychologist, but I'm asking for your KGB instincts. You dealt with these sorts all the time. Do you think he's for real, or is all this some sort of setup?"

"Does he have a motive for setting you up?"

"Who knows, a lot of people would like to see me fall. He could be working for any one of them."

"I know, even paranoids have enemies, Vladimir, but he reacted like someone who feared he'd told you something he shouldn't have. And the guy's a cop. He knew that the best way to deal with that sort of confrontation was with absolute, flat-out denials. Assuming of course there was no other way to prove he was lying. You get in trouble when you try building a story. An experienced examiner will tear you to shreds."

"Or he really didn't know what we were talking about."

Anatoly nodded. "Yes, but do you believe that?"

Vladimir shook his head no. "I heard him, I know what he said. I know what he planned on giving me."

"Then he's frightened."

"Could it be just another part of the con, a way of reinforcing what he said last night?"

"Anything's possible, but he didn't seek you out. He was trying to get on a plane and off the island. We stopped him."

Vladimir let out a breath. "This is all so risky. I'm tempted to just walk away. Did you mention Zacharias? That's not something he told me last night. We figured it out from the documents."

"Yes, but he never reacted."

Vladimir shook his head. "Damn it, if he really was as drunk as he appeared he probably doesn't remember what he told me. That would be consistent with your 'fear' scenario. Deny everything."

"Or he really doesn't know who Zacharias might be."

Vladimir shrugged. "Maybe."

"Perhaps I should ask some colleagues from the old days to check out this Zacharias monk, and if he turns out to be who we think he is, this could be a very serious matter indeed."

"Why do you think I had you flown here from Moscow?" Bringing in the former head of counterintelligence for the KGB's First Chief Directorate foreign intelligence service was not a decision he'd made lightly. It brought with it all the risks of petting an attack dog trained by another.

"The presumably dead man in the clippings was very clever, very ruthless, and very Machiavellian. His intrigues became Balkan legend. At the time of his death he was very angry with us. He claimed we weren't supportive enough against the Americans. Even blamed us for his capture. I can assure you we did not regret his passing."

"So, like I said, what should I do with everything that cop dumped in my lap?"

"Good question. You could ignore it, which is what I assume you'd prefer. If Zacharias is living out his days as a monk in some out of the way place, no one will care. Even if he is who I think he might be. But if he is the one behind these efforts to embarrass our country with the church, that is a very different story."

"A lot of people are trying to do the same thing to us with the whole world," said Vladimir.

"But no one like the man in the clippings. Few are as ruthless as he, thank God."

"Even if he's Attila the Hun reborn, what can some low-level monk in a mountain wilderness in northern Greece do to seriously harm Mother Russia? *What?*" Vladimir's frustration was showing.

Anatoly smiled. "I think your current status has you forgetting how the meek still can bring down the mighty. But to answer your question, if somehow this 'low-level monk' succeeds, and word ever gets out that you knew and didn't inform the proper authorities…" He shrugged. "The old ways are old, but not all forgotten."

Vladimir felt a shiver. He'd been thinking only in terms of how to turn this information to his advantage, use it to ingratiate himself to Russia's ultimate power. He never thought of the downside. And having brought this man into his tent, if anything should go wrong, Anatoly wouldn't hesitate to use it for the same ingratiating purpose or to blackmail him for the rest of his days. After all, you can take the man out of KGB, but you can't take… "Is there any other choice?"

"Prayer."

Vladimir unconsciously ran the fingers of his right hand through his hair. "Let's get everything we have to whoever you think should see it ASAP."

"It's the right decision. I'll transmit it as soon as I get to a computer."

Vladimir leaned forward, pressed a button and a laptop station descended from the back of the front seat. "So you don't waste time." And so Vladimir could verify the information actually was sent. The smart play for this guy was to compromise Vladimir by not sending it on, while allowing him to think that he had.

"Great, but I don't have the information with me."

Vladimir pulled a flash drive from his shirt pocket. "Everything's been transferred to this. All you need to do is the cover letter. Please, it's getting late, and I'm certain they'll want to get started on this right away."

Vladimir made no effort to conceal that he was reading every word Anatoly typed. It was his not-so-subtle way of reminding him who had the real power in that car, and that there would be no role reversal coming out of this affair. Once that e-mail was sent, Vladimir's hands were washed of this mess, and he was making damn sure there'd be no comebacks.

Anatoly finished typing. "Is this okay?"

Vladimir carefully read it, then smiled. "Perfect my friend, with one slight typo. The name in the e-mail address ends with an 'n,' not an 'm.'"

"Sorry about that."

"No problem, but we wouldn't want it going out like that, we might never know that it wasn't received." I certainly wouldn't know, because it wasn't my e-mail. Vladimir leaned over and made the correction, then reread the e-mail and verified that all the attachments were there.

Vladimir sat back, turned toward Anatoly and smiled in a manner reminiscent of a shark about to strike. "That would be a terrible tragedy." He stretched for the keyboard and hit SEND. "For everyone."

◇◇◇

Just one more sunrise until the monastery opened its gates. Zacharias was prepared for another long night of prayer. The *epitaphios* service had begun at one in the morning, the procession at four, and more prayer ran on past dawn. Now they were in the midst of celebrating the resurrection as was done in ancient times, with a vigil that began that afternoon and would not end until mid-morning, with only a cup of blessed wine, some bread, and dried fruit to give them strength. This was a period of intense fasting. Some had eaten nothing. It was as the abbot wished it to be, and so it was. It was a time to rejoice, he said.

But until his three monks returned, Zacharias could not rejoice. It wasn't that he cared for them, but they had arranged for the messenger, and the messenger was expecting to deliver the package to at least one of the three. It was not the sort of package one could just claim was being picked up on someone else's behalf. And he must have it before tomorrow evening. That was when he would be dining with the Russian abbot.

He shook his head. Another obstacle. He'd taken such care to isolate himself from this transaction, yet now he might have to step forward and not just claim but plead for the prize. But nothing in life was easy. He would do what must be done. This was too important. They had succeeded in obtaining the exact formulation of dioxin used on the Ukrainian. Even though there were far better and faster working poisons, nothing would change the world as quickly as this death by pure 2,3,7,8-TCDD.

Evening church services in Athens on Holy Saturday generally started at ten. Andreas knew Lila would use his late flight back from Mykonos as the excuse to her parents and his mother for why they'd probably not be there on time. As long as they made it to the church by midnight. That was the high point of the service, when church bells rang out across Greece and even total strangers exchanged the traditional *Christos Anesti* and *Alithos Anesti* greetings that Christ had risen, kissed each other, and lit each other's candles to share the light and joy of the occasion.

Andreas was not feeling, nor in the mood for, joy. He'd been biting away at his lower lip since boarding the plane, a long-dormant nervous habit from childhood. He didn't realize he was doing it until he saw his reflection in the plane's window. He shook his head. How could I have been so stupid? How could I have ruined everything? He stared out the window.

Should I tell Lila? How can I tell her now? She's about to give birth to our baby. The betrayal, and with her best friend, I can't tell her, I just can't. He tried to justify what happened, but instead kept coming back to what he did wrong. He got drunk, he agreed to follow Barbara into the bedroom after promising Lila he'd sleep on the couch. It was his fault. Even though he didn't remember a thing and refused when she offered herself again that morning. He was ashamed, and for one of the few times in his life utterly confused.

"Sir." It was the flight attendant.

"Yes."

"We've landed, you must get off, you're holding up the bus to the terminal."

Andreas mumbled, "I'm sorry," and hurried off the plane. He couldn't go home like this. Maybe he just shouldn't show up. Run away. Stay with Kouros for a few days. He couldn't bear to face Lila.

The bus stopped at the intra-European Union arrivals entrance to the terminal. He sat down on a railing just inside the terminal door. A cop walked over and told him no one was allowed to linger in that area. He showed his ID and the cop walked away. He wanted to disappear off the face of the earth. He took out his phone and dialed.

"Hello."

"Hi."

There was a long pause. "What's wrong?"

"I didn't know who else to call."

"Andreas, what's wrong?"

"I've done a terrible thing to Lila."

There was an audible swallow on the other end of the line. "Is she okay? The baby?"

"Yes, but she won't be after I tell her. And I have to tell her."

"Andreas, please, first tell me what happened."

"I'm so ashamed. I can't even say it."

The voice turned sharp. "Andreas, do not pull this Greek *macho* male bullshit on me. If you guys only had the balls to see psychiatrists you might actually be as perfect as you think you are."

He grinned. "Maggie, you are the best."

"Now, tell me!"

Andreas spent the next twenty minutes reciting every tormenting detail without a single interruption from Maggie.

"How can I face her?"

"I know how you feel." Maggie's voice was trembling.

"How could you?"

"I was raped by a friend once, too."

For an instant Andreas couldn't breathe.

"He got me drunk and…" her voice trailed off. "I still can't bring myself to talk about it. And it happened thirty years ago."

"I'm sorry."

"Don't be sorry, we're kindred spirits. Rape is rape. The fact you would have enjoyed it under different circumstances doesn't change things. That only makes you feel guiltier, giving you even more reason for blaming yourself. Believe me, you did nothing wrong. You were the victim. And, frankly, it may not seem politically correct advice, but I see no reason in the world to tell Lila any of this.

"If you were a woman raped by your husband's best friend, things would be different, especially if you thought he might try again. In your case, a repeat rape is out of the question. But you better confront the bitch and let her know in no uncertain terms the consequences if she even hints at what happened last night to *anyone*. Who knows what sort of fucked up thinking runs through the mind of a woman who'd rape her best friend's man? And when her friend is about to give birth to their child!

"Jealousy, competition, spite, maybe just some need to brag about her conquests—like men do endlessly—might cause her to say something to someone. She must be told that if she utters even a single word, it will be a decision she'll regret for whatever remains of the rest of her miserable life."

Andreas had never heard such passionate anger from Maggie. He was stunned into silence.

"Andreas, did you hear me?"

He nodded into the phone. "How can I threaten her like that?"

"You're right. You can't. I'll do it for you."

"Maggie—"

"Don't worry, I've done it before. Besides, it will be better coming from me—up close and personal."

Consciously, Andreas knew he should object, say no, not under any circumstances, but his gut said say nothing, let her do it her way, she knows best. He struggled with what to say next. "I can't tell you how much better you've made me feel. Thanks."

"You're welcome. That's what friends are for. I'll get to her as soon as she returns to Athens."

Andreas drew in and let out a deep breath. "I better head home." He looked at his watch. "And let you get to church."

"Don't worry about church. Helping friends in need is the true work of God."

"You're an amazing person, literally godliness on earth."

"Let's not get carried away here, but thank you."

"Do you mind if I ask?"

"Ask what?"

"What ever happened to the one who...uh—"

"He didn't take my advice." Maggie's tone was hard, the words said quickly.

"And?"

"He died. Suddenly, unexpectedly. As the random victim of a street mugging turned violent. *Kalo Paska*, bye."

The phone went dead before Andreas could speak. Perhaps because there was nothing left to say.

◇◇◇

The service was about to begin. For him, it was the holiest moment of the year, a time for personal rejoicing, embracing the very source of his faith. He needed the energy, the renewing power of this night, for difficult times were at hand. He prayed it was not *the time*; that his old friend was wrong. But he feared the worst. That was why he'd made the decision, the practical one now tormenting him. He saw it as the only path, but would God accept that what must be done in His name on earth could not always be as it is in Heaven? He only prayed no more innocents died at the hands of the evil one in their midst. He shut his eyes and bowed his head. "May you strike me down this very night if I have made a dreadful mistake in your name."

It was as genuine a prayer as the Protos ever uttered.

Chapter Twenty-one

The e-mail hit Yakov's computer screen just as he was about to leave for home. His wife would give him holy hell if they were late for midnight services. But the message was from his ex-director back in the days when Yakov was new to the foreign intelligence game. Anatoly had plucked him from the crowd and made him chief espionage analyst for southern Europe and the Balkans, better known then as Section V. He at least must take a quick look at it, if only for old times' sake.

Yakov began quickly scrolling through the message. The pace of his reading slowed, then slowed even more. He picked up the phone, pressed a speed dial button, and waited until the man now in charge of his old Section V duties in Russia's new foreign intelligence service answered. "Artur, come to my office immediately."

Yakov was reading the attachments when a man entered his office. "What is it, Director?"

"Artur, do you remember about a decade or so ago, the man we called 'the Balkan Butcher'?"

"How could I forget him. But didn't he die?"

"So we thought. I'm not sure any more. This just came in." Yakov pointed to the screen. "Read it."

Yakov kept talking as Artur read. "Even if this monk, Zacharias, is the Butcher, if all he's doing is running around creating political angst for the Greek Church, I'm not sure his past matters anymore. After all, we do believe in redemption, do we not?" He smiled.

Artur did not answer, just kept reading.

Yakov didn't mind, he was used to asking rhetorical questions and never expected them to be answered. "As for the symbolism of the photographs, I think it's an intriguing intellectual exercise, but I'm not sure of what interest it is to us. One could argue from the placement of the carpet and the superimposed face of Satan in the photograph that it was the Protos the murdered monk was linking to Satan. But let us assume this Zacharias is Satan's beast or even Satan himself, as I said before, does it matter? Yes, undoubtedly, the Butcher in his day qualified as the devil incarnate, but that was a long time ago. Now he's someone else's problem, and I see no reason to make him ours. And so what if this Zacharias is behind all of the bad publicity coming out of Greece? Would it not be better for us to bribe those same journalists to write retractions than risk being exposed as the eliminator of the source?"

"I'm not so sure about that, Director."

An actual answer to one of his questions caught Yakov off guard. "'Not so sure' of what?"

Artur kept reading through the attachments as he spoke. "We've received reports of someone attempting to locate the source of the dioxin used on the Ukrainian. At first we thought it was a journalist trying to wring yet another story out of the incident. Maybe even Yushchenko himself trying to find some way to revive his political fortunes with more emotional tales from the past.

"But then we learned that someone actually was trying to buy dioxin from that same source, and not just any dioxin, but the exact formulation found in Yushchenko. At that point we inserted our operatives into the transaction. We wanted to know who was so interested." Artur turned to face Yakov.

"We do not know who the buyers are. There have been no face-to-face communications, but we do know two things. One," he raised his right hand and popped out his index finger.

"The language used by the buyers was Serbian, and two," out came the middle finger. "Delivery is to take place in Greece. In Ouranoupolis."

Yakov's pulse was racing but his voice was flat. "The gateway to Mount Athos. This changes everything." He drummed his forehead with the fingers of his left hand. "Forget about looking for signs of the devil. This intrigue is a sign of the Butcher. Calculating, ruthless, deadly. Any idea of the target?"

Artur shook his head. "None."

"If Zacharias is the Butcher, whatever is planned will strike directly at our heart. We cannot permit that. When is delivery to take place?"

"There's no exact time, a messenger with the package is to wait by a taverna in the port for contact to be made." He looked at his watch. "Between twelve and eighteen hours from now."

Yakov picked up the phone and dialed his wife. He and a lot of other people would be missing church tonight.

It was almost midnight. Saint Dionysios on Skoufa Street in Kolinaki was packed. Andreas hadn't been to this church before, or for that matter, to any church, in a very long time. He'd gone with Lila to a wedding in a small church on Stisichorou Street behind her apartment, and managed to miss a couple of baptisms there, but this was the first time he'd been to her parents' church. They had insisted the "entire family" be together tonight, and that included Andreas' mother and his sister's family.

Andreas wondered if they could tell, if his sin showed. He was lucky they weren't the kind to talk in church. He feared he might confess despite Maggie's warning. He was holding Lila's hand and looking at his mother sitting next to him on his left. She was beaming. He knew what she was thinking: my family, all together in church, and my son happy at last with the right woman, his...his friend. Yes, that was what she insisted on calling Lila. Andreas had told his mother she could call Lila his wife, that Lila wouldn't mind. "But I would," was his mother's response. Not until they were married in church would she call Lila her son's wife, no matter how much she wished it were so.

Andreas felt Lila squeeze his hand and he turned to face her.

She was smiling at him and patting her belly. "Baby's happy, too."

If he confessed, he'd destroy the lives of the two people he loved most in the world. He could never do that. He'd have to live with what he'd done, accept it, and try to become better for it. He felt no guilt at his decision. Quite the contrary: for the first time in a very long time Andreas was at peace.

The chanting and prayer had hit its peak, bells were ringing, rejoice, *Christos Anesti.*

But Zacharias saw no joy about him, only mindless, rote prayer without purpose. He needed to escape this. Next year would be different. He would move on. It was not unheard of to switch monasteries. He needed a more civilized base for his plans, somewhere he could flourish and never be incommunicado again. There was too much at stake, too many in need of his guidance. His flock was prey to wolves without its shepherd. No, this year he would move on. There were many monasteries here that would accept him with joy. All he needed was the consent of his abbot. No problem, if the old tyrant were fool enough to refuse, it would be he who moved on.

Yes, the time to emerge from these depths was at hand. He was certain of it.

Now was the fun part of Easter in Greece, at least for those skipping out of church at midnight, carrying candles lit by fire from the Holy Flame of Christ's nativity cave in Jerusalem into their homes or favorite restaurants. Andreas and the family chose the latter, a fairytale place in the National Gardens next to the breathtaking nineteenth century Zappeion Megaron, the first building constructed specifically for the purpose of reviving the Modern Olympic Games.

They had challenged each other with the customary smacking of dyed-red eggs for good luck to the winner, devoured the traditional *mayiritsa* soup to break the fast, left very little of the salads, and very little of the wine, leaving Lila the only fully sober one at the table, and not by choice.

"The baby's on the wagon," was Lila's excuse to every well-wisher passing by their table and offering a toast.

It was two thirty in the morning and Lila was text messaging furiously. Reading, writing, reading, writing.

"What's going on?" Andreas asked.

"It's Barbara. You can't believe what she's telling me."

His heart stopped. Deny, deny, deny. No, not this time. He thought to beat her to the punch. "Lila—"

She burst out laughing. "I don't believe her. She's one of a kind." Lila turned to Andreas, all smiles. "First of all, she said to send you her love and that you gave a 'tremendous performance.'"

I wonder if Maggie has talked to her yet, Andreas thought.

"I had invited her to join us for dinner, she should have been here hours ago."

Maggie better have, but if she had she'd have told me.

"But she can't make it."

Thank God.

"Because she's in Moscow."

You've got to be kidding me!

"She was at the airport waiting to catch the last plane back to Athens, and guess who she ran into?"

Good thing she didn't know more than that I needed an escort.

"Your Russian from last night. He convinced her it would be a lot more fun to celebrate Easter in Moscow than Athens. She said to tell you she decided to go. 'So it wouldn't be a total loss.' What does that mean?"

"Got me. She's a bit wacky."

"I'll say." Lila laughed again. "Barbara, Barbara, you never fail to amaze me."

I'll say.

◇◇◇

"Thanks for inviting me. You were right, Easter dinner alone on Mykonos would have been a downer."

Tassos patted Kouros on the arm. "Hey, you're family. Besides, I didn't have to cook. He did." Kouros pointed to a man hurrying toward them with plates stacked along his left arm from fingertips to elbow. He was the vision of a Greek leprechaun with a round, rosy-cheeked face, twinkling eyes, and a Greek fisherman's mustache.

"Steline," the leprechaun shouted, "hurry with the rest of the plates before this old bastard from Syros arrests me."

"I see he knows you."

Tassos smiled and nodded. "Yeah, we've spent many a night together here behind city hall, closing up his place and exchanging lies. It started out as a locals' place, now it's the most famous taverna on the island. Everybody comes here."

Kouros looked over Tassos' shoulder at someone aimed straight for their table. "Oh, boy. Were you ever right."

"What are you talking—"

"You miserable fucking piece of shit!" And thus began a thirty-second string of expletives delivered at disco club volume. Tourist heads jerked around to see who was about to be murdered. Locals just shrugged and continued on with Easter dinner; it was only Katerina doing her warpath thing.

Tassos braced himself, then came a smack to the back of his head.

Kouros smiled. "I see you've been through this before."

Tassos stayed braced. "She's not done yet."

Smack. She did it again, then another.

Tassos relaxed. "I think she's done."

"I heard that, asshole," and gave him another slap.

Tassos turned to face her. "*Christos Anesti*, Katerina *mou*. Please, join us."

She was shaking her fist in his face and stopped only long enough to say, "*Alithos Anesti*," before starting in on him again.

"How could you have done that to me? Set me up so badly."
Tassos pulled out a chair as she raged on. Katerina sat down
without missing a beat in her diatribe. "I have never been so
embarrassed in all my life."

"I assume you know all of my cousins." Tassos pointed to
the people around the table. "And, of course, Yianni Kouros."

Katerina nodded and smiled to all the cousins, then looked
at Kouros. "You're as bad as this one," pointing to Tassos.

Kouros decided to follow Tassos' lead. "*Christos Anesti.*"

"*Alithos Anesti.*" She turned back to Tassos and repeated,
"How could you have done that to me?"

Tassos sighed. "Katerina, what did I do to you?"

"You set me up. You knew I would tell Vladimir."

Tassos leaned over and kissed her on the cheek. "I love you,
really I do. You're one of a kind. Here, have a drink." He handed
her a glass of wine. "*Yamas.*"

Katerina, Tassos, and Kouros clinked glasses and drank.

"Miserable bastards," she said. Then she poured the three of
them more wine. "I feel almost as stupid as some of my dumb-ass
clients, the ones who think they're so smart and end up getting
conned. Like you did me!" She didn't smack this time, just shouted.

They sat together for about an hour, mostly letting Katerina
vent but having fun as well. She was terrific company.

"And that bitch who was making a play for Vladimir."

"What bitch?" said Tassos.

"Baarrrrbarrraaa." Katerina drew out the name as a child
would in a schoolyard taunt.

"She was hitting on him?" asked Kouros.

"Fellas, please. How blind and naïve are you men? Believe
me, I know how to hit on a man and I can tell you, that bitch
is a master."

"What are you talking about?" said Tassos.

"That's right, you weren't there to watch the show. No woman
would allow a man to stroke her back as she did if she weren't
interested. And then she'd make just enough of a subtle push

back against Vladimir's hand to let him know he had a shot at her. He was so hard I thought he'd come on the spot."

Neither cop bothered to ask how she knew that.

"But Andreas better be careful. Vladimir is no one to fuck around with. Don't forget where or how he made his money. It took a body count as well as brains to make what he made in Russia. People tend to die who get in his way. I never forget that, and Andreas better not either."

Tassos shrugged. "Thanks, but Andreas has nothing to worry about." He didn't bother to say there would be no competition for the woman.

Katerina poured more wine into their glasses. "Let's hope Vladimir sees it that way. For all our sakes."

◇◇◇

"Oh my God, oh my God, oh my God." As Barbara moaned she thrust her hips up to meet his, her legs wrapped around his back, squeezing and touching wherever she could.

I can't believe this woman, thought Vladimir. It's our third time since the plane landed. And that one time in the air. His mind was lost in her completely and without warning he was on the verge again. My God, how does she know how to do this? As if on cue, she touched him in just the right place at just the right moment, and from that instant on it was nothing but, "Barbara, Barbara, Barbaraaaahhhhhhhh." They came together. Again.

They lay together in the dark without moving. Then she gently stroked her fingers along his spine.

"Where have you been all my life?"

"Athens."

He laughed. "I hope you like Moscow."

"A nice place to visit."

"But you wouldn't want to live here?"

"Vladimir, are you proposing?"

He laughed. "You have too many boyfriends for me."

She patted him on the back. "Don't start getting jealous on me."

He cringed. She probably was right about that. "Well, I can't help remembering what that policeman said."

"Andreas?"

"Yes. I bumped into him the day after we met and he said, 'Obviously, you've never slept with Barbara.'"

"I have no idea how that subject ever came up, but one thing's for sure, we both know he'd be wrong now, darling."

"Yeah, but it still bothers me."

She grabbed his dick and squeezed it. Then pulled at it twice. "My love, that's the most Andreas ever got from me, and he was out cold when I did it. All I did was rub some lubricant on his dick so when he woke up he'd think he'd had me, and could have me again. I wanted to see if he was like every other man chasing after my girlfriend, Lila. He's not. Darling, he's my best friend's almost-husband, I'd never screw him. He just needed me for company for the night." She kissed his cheek. "There, that's the truth. So, now, do you feel better?"

It was dark in the room so Barbara couldn't see his face. It was not a look of joy. "Excuse me, my love, I must make a telephone call." Vladimir left the room.

"Anatoly, we have a problem."

"Vladimir, it's almost five o'clock in the morning."

"We've been set up."

"What are you talking about?"

"The cop used the woman to get next to me. It's been a hustle from the very beginning. He wanted to make me curious enough to break into the woman's house, copy the information, and pass it on—to make it seem real and legitimate. We have to stop it."

"We can't. It's too late."

"I was afraid of that. Then we must do whatever it takes to make it seem that the information did not come from me. I'm certain I'm being set up as the link to something intended to embarrass Mother Russia and get me sent off to a gulag."

Or worse, he thought but did not say. "I wonder which of my enemies is behind this."

"Vladimir, relax. We can come up with another source, one that covers both of us. But who else knows about your involvement in all this?"

"Only the cop, as far as I know."

"Then he must be eliminated."

"What about the woman?"

Vladimir paused. "I think not. She knows nothing more than that she was to be his companion for the evening."

"Are you sure?"

"Yes."

"This is going to cost a lot of money."

"That is not a problem."

"I didn't think it would be."

"Just do it. And leave no witnesses."

"It will take a couple of days to organize, but consider it done."

Vladimir hung up the phone. Too bad, he thought, I kind of liked that cop.

◇◇◇

Andreas knew he had no control over what he'd set in motion. Too many variables, too many different agendas involved. No telling what might happen. All he knew for certain was that this time he'd done the right thing. He just hoped no innocents suffered because of him if the Russians decided to act. Unlike the traditional Italian concept of a hit—assassinate just the offending one—Russians were prepared to blow up a room full of people as long as they took out their target.

That thinking led him to other thoughts and other concerns. For those who believed in heaven and hell there was always hope that good would prevail and bad would be punished. For those who didn't believe it was a tougher call, because bad guys didn't play by the rules, giving them a decided advantage. As Andreas saw it, a cop could be a believer in his heart, but damn well better think like a *Dirty Harry* nonbeliever on the job.

He decided to spend the rest of the week keeping an eye on Lila, just to be on the safe side. Besides, it was a good excuse for sharing what remained of their pre-baby era of life. He couldn't imagine being happier, no matter what the future brought.

But he also told Maggie to keep up on the news from Mount Athos, just in case.

Chapter Twenty-two

Free at last. Praise the Lord. It was noon, and the monastery's doors at last were open. Everyone was off to eat, then to sleep. Forty days of fasting without meat, fish, cheese, butter, or eggs had taken much of their energy. But Zacharias had no time for that. He had to hurry to catch the fast boat from the port of Daphni to Ouranoupolis and be back in time for supper at seven in the Russian abbot's monastery. A two-hour mountain road walk to the bus, a half-hour ride to the boat, a one-hour voyage aboard the *Little Saint Anna*, and a return voyage getting him back to Daphni before evening prayers at six was the plan. Thank God the Russian monastery wasn't far from Daphni. Still, it would be close.

As he hurried along the dirt path toward where the bus would be, he fiddled with his cell phone. He couldn't get it to work. Couldn't be the battery, he'd left it in the charger all week. Then it hit him. He'd also left the phone on, just in case a message somehow got through—and the abbot must have turned off all electricity into the monastery. The phone was dead. Damn, damn, damn.

He quickened his pace. No matter, he'd assume the worst, that none of them made it to Ouranoupolis and he'd have to do this alone. He could do it. He could do anything.

As he walked, Zacharias thought of other possibilities. What if they were caught? What if there were police waiting for him in Ouranoupolis? No, the three would never talk. They're afraid of the Lord and what would happen to their souls should they stray from the path they'd chosen to walk together with him—and to their families should they cross him. He had picked his men carefully, each with a past and a family to protect. Yes, they would never give him away.

The bus wound its way through timeless green beauty. He stared out the window; there seemed no human presence, man non-existent. This now was his place. This was where he belonged. He would make it worthy of his work. The boat was there. As if ordained to wait for him. Yes, it was ordained. It was part of the Lord's plan. The time was now.

It was almost four in the afternoon, and the man had been sitting in the same taverna chair for almost five hours. His ass was killing him. But his orders were clear and direct: "Petro, do not move under any circumstances until contact is made, and that means *any* circumstances." They were not instructions one could misinterpret. Especially considering their source. He'd been doing this sort of work for more years than he liked to remember, but this was the first time the director had given him his orders personally.

The jet, the parachute, the underwater approach were right out of one of those James Bond movies, but considering the last minute timing involved with this operation, there was no other real choice. You couldn't get even a donkey to move in Greece on Easter. Still, he was getting too old for this special ops craziness. He just hoped the boat was here to meet him. All he could do was wonder, because the plan didn't allow him to leave this goddamned chair to check.

Some plan. Once contact was made it was up to him to make the call: kill, grab, or walk away. The choices had been conveyed in their reverse order of preference. "We'd prefer no more dead Greek monks on public streets during Easter Week, and if he seems no threat, let him take the package and go—the dioxin is phony anyway," were the director's exact words.

"Where the hell is that monk?" Petro muttered under his breath in Russian. The *Little Saint Anna* had docked twenty minutes ago.

"May I have a light?" someone said in Greek. It was a man who looked to be in his late thirties, early forties, sitting at a nearby table. He could be older, but his full beard was black and neatly trimmed. He was wearing jeans, a plaid work shirt, a fisherman's hat, and construction boots, drinking coffee, reading a Greek newspaper, and holding a cat on his lap.

"Here you are." Petro responded in Greek, handing him a lighter.

"Thank you very much, that is very kind of you," said the man with the cat. "So, where's the package?" He now spoke Russian with a Serbian accent.

"Package? What package?" Petro responded in Greek.

The man with the cat continued in Russian. "Since you understood what I said, there is no reason for you to continue straining to speak in Greek. I'm very comfortable in your mother tongue." He smiled in a way suggestive of twinkling eyes, but his remained dark and focused.

"So I see," Petro said, switching to Russian, "but I still don't understand what you're talking about."

The man stroked the cat and spoke as if talking to himself. "Of course you don't. And if I gave you 75,000 reasons you still wouldn't know, would you?"

That was the amount the director told him would be paid for the dioxin. "That's a lot of reasons."

The cat man smiled, staring off toward the sea. "Yes, I know. And I also know that you were expecting someone else to give them to you."

Petro nodded. "Yes, one of two possible persons as a matter of fact, and you do not fit the descriptions they provided."

Cat man smiled again, still staring off to sea. "You mean three."

Petro nodded again. "Yes, three. So why isn't one of them here?"

"They had commitments elsewhere and asked me to come in their place."

"Highly unusual for this sort of transaction."

Cat man nodded. "I accept that."

"Well, I can't."

The man dropped the cat to the street and looked directly at Petro. "I am not with the authorities, although I do not expect you to believe me. But I am the one who is providing the money."

"You're right, I don't believe you."

"How can I change your mind?" His tone was conciliatory, solicitous.

Petro shrugged. "I have a job to do, to deliver whatever's in that package to one of three people and pick up the payment. If I deliver it to the wrong party my ass is on the line."

Cat man shrugged. "It's going to be a lot more on the line if you don't show up with the money."

"Maybe, but then again, why take the risk? I get paid the same whether I deliver or I walk. But unless I get a specific ID confirmation on the party I'm supposed to meet, my instructions are to walk."

Cat man nodded. "Okay, now that we understand each other, what do I have to do to make you comfortable enough to take the risk? Shall I present you with the 'ID' you were to be given or descriptions of the three you were expecting to meet?"

He shook his head. "No need to, I'm sure you know the three. I just don't know you."

"Okay, then let me put it simply. How much?"

Petro smiled. "Forty thousand."

"Ten."

"Thirty."

"Fifteen."

"Twenty-five."

"No."

"'No?' Why 'no'?"

"Fifteen thousand additional euros for no additional risk. Take it or leave it."

Petro hesitated. "Okay, but I want to see the money now."

Cat man looked around the taverna, leaned toward Petro, and opened his shirt to show a money belt strapped about his waist. It was more like a bellyband for a bad back, but with pockets filled with euros.

"I see you've done this sort of thing before."

Cat man smiled. "A long, long time ago. So, where's the package?"

"It's in a boat at the pier on the other end of the harbor."

"Go get it."

"Not a chance. For all I know your missing three guys are waiting out there to rip me off."

"We have a standoff."

"Not really. We go to the pier, you wait at the entrance, I go to the boat, and come back to you. We make the exchange there. Assuming you put the money in something other than your shirt."

"Don't worry about that." For the first time cat man seemed nervous, as if deciding whether or not to continue. "Okay, but you stay in front of me the entire way."

"We walk side-by-side until the pier."

Cat man paused, then nodded. "Okay, but give me a minute." He walked over and said something to the waiter, then gave him ten euros and picked up a beat-up plastic fishing bucket next to the kitchen door. "Let's go."

"What's that for?" asked the man.

"For your fucking money."

Zacharias wanted to say, "For the bait that hooked you." But that would have given away his ruse, and besides, he enjoyed being able to swear in public for a change.

He thought his idea of wearing workingman's clothes was brilliant. No one would expect a monk to be dressed like that. Amazing how easy it was to convince that *Little Saint Anna* seaman to let him borrow some clothes so Zacharias the monk "could see what it was like to walk about this hard world in your shoes, my son." Everyone believed him, it was his gift.

Zacharias had picked up on the Russian within minutes of walking into the taverna, but it was as if he were invisible to the Russian. Zacharias smiled to himself. It was the stray cat touch that did it.

He knew the Russian ultimately would turn over the package for money, probably his own mother if the price were right. He was paying a lot more than he thought necessary, but there was no time to play out the negotiation game longer. He had to get the package and be back on the boat before it left for Daphni. He also didn't like leaving the busy end of the harbor, but then again, he understood the man's point. Each had to be wary of the other. It was the way of the jungle in which they lived.

The walk along the cobblestone road took less than ten minutes. No one seemed to be around. Of course not, it was Easter Sunday, everyone was home cooking and eating lamb. He stood where he could see anyone approach from any direction. "I'll wait here," said Zacharias.

"No problem," said the Russian, as he turned and slowly walked toward a military-style inflatable tied to the far end of the pier. Zacharias watched him jump into the boat, take something out from beneath the captain's seat, and step back onto the pier. Zacharias didn't see anyone else on the boat.

Good, he thought. No tricks. Zacharias opened his shirt and looked around to see if anyone was watching. Nobody. He pulled off the money belt and carefully arranged it in the bucket.

The Russian came back holding a canvas backpack. "It's in here." He unzipped the bag and pointed at a plastic canister.

"Open it," said Zacharias.

"Here?"

"Yes, here."

"Are you crazy?"

"No, just careful. You see, my friend, too many times in the past I've done the same thing."

The Russian smirked. "Do you think I'd not deliver what was promised?"

Zacharias smiled. "No, that's not my concern. If you were foolish enough to defraud me, I'd hunt you down and every member of your family. And destroy you all." He almost hissed the last words and his eyes seemed to glow. "But as I said, that's not my concern, that is yours. My only fear is that when I open the canister, there will be another surprise. One that will end my life. So, my friend, you open the canister."

"Fuck you."

Zacharias held out the bucket. "Don't you want this?"

"Yeah, and I'm going to take it."

Zacharias reached inside as the Russian grabbed for the bucket. The Russian came away with the bucket and Zacharias with the small pistol he'd hidden under the money belt. "Now, open the canister." Zacharias kept the gun trained on the center of the Russian's chest.

The Russian paused, then let go of the bucket, reached into the backpack, and pulled out the canister. "Fine, if you want the whole world to see, here." He twisted off the cap. Nothing happened, and he held the canister out in front of him. "Well, do you want to look or should I ask some cop to take it out for you?"

Zacharias kept his eye and the gun on the Russian, but leaned in to take a quick, sideways peek at what was in the canister. It was a package bearing all the markings of dioxin. Zacharias smiled. "Good, we have a deal." At that moment, Zacharias heard a *pop* and his world suddenly went very dark and quiet.

Chapter Twenty-three

"How much longer are you going to take? Your daddy and I have things to do. We can't keep waiting on you to show up. Come on out and see the world already." Lila was sitting in the passenger's seat, talking to her belly.

Andreas smiled and patted the object of Lila's conversation with his right hand, never taking his eyes off the road or his left hand off the steering wheel. "I like spending this time together."

"Try strapping a bowling ball to your belly and lugging it around 24/7 and see how much you like it."

Andreas laughed. "Hey, the doctor just told us everything is perfect, the baby should be here by the weekend, and not to worry. Besides, I'm sticking to you like glue until it's time."

Lila smiled. "I'm glad you are." She leaned over and kissed his cheek. "So, do you want to go dancing? I mean, it's only Thursday. We have at least a day or so."

He knew she was teasing. "Yeah, sure. But why don't we start out with lunch in Kolonaki? After all, it's the fashionable place to be in Athens, and who's more fashionable than my baby's mommy?"

"Oh you sweet-talking guy, if you hadn't already knocked me up I'd let you do it all over again."

"I think I still remember how."

"Glad one of us does."

He laughed. "Okay, where to?"

"Our usual hangout."

"Home?"

"Just not up for the social scene."

"No problem. I'll drop you off in front and park the car in the garage."

"Thanks, I'm not up for the walk."

Andreas patted her hand. He knew she wouldn't want to go out. They hadn't been out since Easter Sunday and probably wouldn't have gone out today if it weren't for her doctor's appointment. Lila described what they were doing as "nesting." Whatever it was, he liked it. And home also was the safest possible place for them to be. Their street running past the Presidential Palace was filled with police and military types protecting the powerful in and out of government who lived there. Their building itself was a modern-day fortress with automatic shut downs and security devices designed to foil even the most aggressive kidnappers, today's scourge of the wealthy.

The K-garage was only a few blocks from the apartment. It was where you parked when you couldn't find a place on the street. If Andreas were in a police car he'd park anywhere, but this was Lila's car and she kept it safely parked in the garage in a reserved space. He pulled up in front of the apartment building. It was on the left side of a one-way street, so he had to park with the driver's side at the curb. A black, American-made Chevrolet Suburban with deeply tinted windows was parked just beyond the building's entrance on the same side of the street.

"Wait until I come around before opening your door. Some idiot on a motorbike might run into it." Andreas jumped out and walked around the front of the car. He glanced into the Suburban. The light coming though the windshield allowed him to make out three men inside, two in front, one in the back. The engine was running.

Must be waiting for someone, he thought. Andreas smiled. Cop force of habit, stay alert, stay alive. Live in condition yellow. Green is in your mother's womb, red is in the heat of an all-out battle, and yellow is every other moment of a cop's life. He opened Lila's door and walked her to the curb. He heard a buzz. It was the sound you heard when someone opened a vehicle door with the motor running.

"I'll say goodbye here. See you upstairs." Andreas kissed her on the cheek, his peripheral vision on the Suburban.

"Is everything okay?" Lila asked.

"Perfect, I just want to put the car away and get back home to you. I don't like leaving you and junior alone."

"Don't worry, we'll be fine." She kissed him and walked toward the entrance.

He stood angled by the driver's door of the car so that he could see Lila and the Suburban. He waited until she was inside the building. Something wasn't right about the Suburban. Its warning buzzer still was blaring yet no one had stepped out.

Andreas got into the car, turned on the engine, and slowly pulled away from the curb. He inched up alongside the Suburban as if he were planning to stop beside the still partially open door. But just before reaching that door, Andreas floored the gas pedal and his car shot up the street toward the corner. In his rearview mirror he watched as the door yanked shut and the Suburban lurched away from the curb. Definitely not right. He reached for his phone and pressed the code for "officer needs assistance." Thank God for GPS.

The only question was, what to do until the cavalry arrived? Heading to the garage was a no-no. He'd be cornered there. Being stuck in traffic along the way wasn't a much better alternative. Only one thing to do. "Lila, please forgive me." He said the words aloud, as if to give himself courage, then slammed on the brakes, threw the car into reverse and sped backwards straight at the Suburban. The Suburban jerked to a stop. Andreas didn't. Thank God Lila's car was built to take a rear-end collision.

Andreas jumped out of the car with his gun drawn. The Suburban's driver door opened and a man in shirt and tie started yelling in heavily accented Greek, "Stop! Stop! Are you crazy?"

"Damn well fucking better believe I am. Face down, in the street *now*."

The driver hesitated and Andreas locked his elbows in the shooting position for a headshot. The man dropped to the pavement instantly. "You, in the passenger seat. Slide out this way, keep your hands where I can see them."

The man slid across the seat slowly, deliberately. Police cars were arriving from both directions, and military types from around the palace were racing toward them with M-16s at the ready. Andreas had pulled his police ID out of his shirt and was yelling loudly, "*I'M A COP.*" He did not want to go down in friendly fire. As the second man stepped onto the street, Andreas yelled at him to drop to the pavement.

Andreas stared. He knew this man. "Sergey?" Andreas did not lower his gun.

The rear door opened and out stepped a silver-haired man in an impeccably tailored Italian suit. "Need I drop to the pavement, too, my son?"

"Not sure yet. What are you doing here?"

By now, police were everywhere and the military was aiming at everyone.

"I don't think this is the appropriate environment for the conversation I've come to have with you."

Andreas realized he still had his gun pointed at the two on the ground. He said to one uniformed cop, "Search those two," and to another, "Check the vehicle." He gestured to one of the men with an M-16 to keep it locked on the two on the ground, then holstered his weapon.

He stared at the Protos. "I have a place to talk, but just you and me, not your boys."

"Chief, this one is carrying." The cop was pointing to Sergey.

Not surprised, thought Andreas. "What about the other one?"

"Clean."

"This is clean, too," said a cop getting out of the Suburban.

"Hold these two cuffed in a cruiser until the—" Andreas stopped himself. "Until this gentleman and I come back. Everybody else, thanks, and you can go now."

He turned to the Protos. "Why all this cloak and dagger, engine running, open the door but don't get out dramatics?"

The Protos shrugged. "Your office said you were on vacation, and your doorman said you were out but probably would be back sometime after lunch. I decided to wait for you here, and the driver kept the engine running for the air conditioner. You came back earlier than we expected and when we realized it was you, Sergey started to get out but I told him to wait until you were inside the building. I wanted our meeting to be private. I didn't want to start a conversation on the street, but you surprised me when you sent your wife inside alone and drove off."

Andreas shook his head. "All you had to do was return one of my calls. It would have saved me one hell of an explanation to my—" he paused again, "to Lila about why I rammed her car into yours."

The Protos smiled. "Your explanation actually may be more difficult to make than the one I've come to deliver to you. Come, my son, lead the way and I shall explain many things."

They were sitting in Lila's study, looking out toward the Acropolis. Andreas, the Protos, and Lila.

"My son, I'm not sure this is appropriate for a woman to hear."

"Your Holiness, in your house I respect your ways, in my home I must ask that you respect mine."

"As you wish." The Protos drew in and let out a deep breath. "I do not know where to begin. Not because I haven't thought of what I am about to tell you, but because I don't know where the beginning is." He nodded for a moment, just staring out the window. "Vassilis was my dearest friend, going back to our days in school. He tried to warn me about the scourge we faced." He turned to Andreas. "But you know all of that." He let out another breath.

"The scourge is gone, or so it seems. He left his monastery Sunday morning, the moment its doors opened, and took a boat to Ouranoupolis. He borrowed a seaman's clothes, left the man with all that linked him to life as a monk, and has not been seen since."

"I assume you're talking about Zacharias," said Andreas.

The Protos nodded.

"Has he fled or is he dead?"

The Protos shrugged. "I have no idea. As long as he does not return we are blessed."

"What about all those people he butchered in the Balkans?" It was Lila.

"His ultimate judgment is in the hands of God."

Andreas hoped Lila would let the subject drop. He knew she had strong feelings on the subject of war criminals. Lila looked down at her nails and said nothing.

"So, Your Holiness, what does all this have to do with me?"

The Protos nodded. "You were our savior."

Andreas looked at Lila, then back at the Protos. "That's a bit much, isn't it?"

The Protos shook his head. "No." He looked back out the window. "When I realized who was behind this—"

"Why can't you just say his real name, or at least call him Zacharias?" Lila sounded testy.

"Because, my child, that name was a monk's name and this was not a monk in spirit, heart, or soul. He does not deserve to be addressed or spoken of with the same words as revere the memory of a man such as Kalogeros Vassilis. I cannot say his name and never shall. He destroyed much and came close to destroying all."

"All?" Lila's tone hadn't changed.

"If who he was, and what he had done, became public, it would have inflicted irreparable wounds on the church."

"You mean on the church's current leaders." Lila wouldn't stop.

"I mean on the institution of the church. Its leaders did nothing wrong. We did not know his past, we saw a man gifted in bringing men together, working tirelessly without seeking glory, fame, or recognition for himself." He paused. "Our error was that we never saw the devil among us. Only Vassilis recognized the false prophet." His head sank to his chest. "And he died trying to warn us."

The Protos looked up at Andreas. "When I realized what he was I knew we were not equipped to deal with someone of such horrible, ruthless cunning without dooming ourselves openly before the world. He had created a network of followers across our Holy Mountain more loyal to him than to their abbots, and in some cases the abbots themselves had fallen to him. It was an infection we could not treat until rid of the source. That was when I reached a decision. You were the only one who could free us of this scourge, but only if you believed you were being forced to let him escape, that the power of the government—and the church—would allow him to go on, that there would be no justice for his crimes." He paused. "You have a thirst for vengeance and an ability to achieve it that I do not."

Lila's face was livid. "What you're saying is that you used your influence to shut down the investigation to make it seem nothing would be done to Zacharias, just so you could deceive my…my unborn child's father into risking his life to go after someone you wanted out of the way? Make him your own personal avenging angel? Or would you rather continue with your 'savior'…?" She was glaring, but let the sentence trail off.

The Protos stared at Lila. His face was sad. "I don't see it that way. I see your unborn child's father as slaying the dragon of Satan. Something no one without sin could have done."

Andreas wanted desperately to lighten the tone. "Now you're calling me a sinner. I preferred the other titles." He said it with a smile.

The Protos forced a smile. "You live in a world foreign to me, foreign to many both in and out of the church. We must rely upon others to protect us from the evil of that world, and to serve as judge when necessary—rendering the harshest of judgments at times, because it is the fair judgment and one that must be made. That is why I turned to you. To be our shield and our sword."

"Sounds like a speech to the Crusaders," Lila mumbled under her breath.

If the Protos heard her, he didn't react. "Please, believe me when I say I am not here to do anything more than thank you for saving our church from certain tragedy, and for bringing the killers of my close friend to justice. I live amid a world that many think is…," he seemed to be searching for a word, "*unsoiled.*"

Lila perked up, but did not interrupt.

"Whether or not I agree is not important, only that I realize no one from that world could have done what you did."

"That was an interesting and, I must say, unusual word choice, Your Holiness," said Lila.

The Protos smiled at her. "I'd thought you might grasp its meaning. You're a very smart woman."

"And a fan of anagrams."

He stood.

"Now, there is only one more thing left to do." The Protos reached into his jacket pocket and pulled out a cross. He waved it above their heads. "May the Lord bless you with long, healthy life and happy, healthy children. Make that 'many happy, healthy children.' Amen."

Andreas said, "Amen."

Lila nodded and said, "Thank you."

"This is yours by the way." The Protos handed Andreas the cross.

Andreas took it. "It's not mine."

"Yes, it is. It's the one Vassilis wore all his life. It came from his father's father. I know he would want you to have it, for you to pass on to the child of a new generation."

Andreas stared at it. "Thank you, Your Holiness. I will treasure it always."

"I know you will." The Protos patted Andreas on the shoulder. "By the way, in case you wonder how I came to have it, I asked a mutual friend on Patmos to pick it up for me from Abbot Christodoulos. Our friend said to say 'thank you' for convincing the abbot to let his building permit go through."

Andreas was puzzled. "I don't understand. I assume you're talking about Dimitri, but I never spoke to the abbot about his permit."

The Protos smiled. "I know, but we both know how much Dimitri likes to talk, and I'd rather have him publicly thanking you for that bit of meddling in another monastery's internal affairs than me. I'm sure you agree Dimitri was entitled to that modest reward for all his assistance?"

Andreas nodded. Guess that answers who Dimitri worked for.

The Protos' tone turned serious. "And that the abbot needed to be reminded that trusting the wrong sort, even innocently, has its consequences."

I like this guy's style, Andreas thought.

"Now, if you would please excuse me, I have a few things to explain to the Archbishop of Greece, who so kindly loaned me his driver and car for the day. And I think you have a few to explain as well." He was smiling again.

On second thought…

Lila said, "What is he talking about?"

"I'll tell you when I get back. I have to walk him out."

He looked at the Protos. "Thanks for that," then mouthed to him with a sarcastic look Lila could not see, "and I don't mean for the cross."

The Protos laughed. Probably for what must have been the first time in a very long time.

Chapter Twenty-four

"The operation was aborted."

"What do you mean, 'aborted'?" Vladimir's temper flared.

"Things changed."

Vladimir yelled into the phone. "Anatoly, I told you the cop must be eliminated. It was not a situation subject to change. How dare you make such a decision without consulting me?"

There was a long pause. "My old friend, I will permit you to speak to me that way this once, because I understand the pressure you are under. But do not forget what you asked me to do."

Vladimir swallowed. He'd asked him to kill a man. Something Anatoly had arranged many times before—and could do again, should Vladimir push him too far. "Yes, I am under pressure." It was as much of an apology as Vladimir was capable of giving.

"Good. Now let me tell you why the operation was terminated. Our man met Zacharias at Ouranoupolis."

Anatoly is calling him "our" man, thought Vladimir. Once KGB, always KGB.

"At first our man thought him not worthy of further attention and planned to let him walk away. He seemed to have lost his old edge, even allowed our man to bully him into paying a ridiculous bribe. Then, just as our man was about to turn over the package, the true Butcher showed himself. He threatened to wipe our man's seed off the earth and pulled a gun. But our man was prepared for the worst. The canister carrying the dioxin was equipped to flood a sixteen-square-foot area with an instantly debilitating gas at the press of a button. It took down both Zacharias and our man."

Vladimir wasn't interested in any of this. He wanted to know why the cop was still alive. But he dared not interrupt. He sensed Anatoly was dragging this out just to let him know that now he was in charge.

"Thankfully, comrades were hidden and watching from a nearby building. They carried both men to a waiting boat, administered the antidote to our man, and made rendezvous with a helicopter at sea. Zacharias awoke in Moscow."

"Did he say anything?"

"Not at first."

Vladimir didn't have to ask what that meant.

"Ultimately, he told us everything."

Vladimir couldn't control himself. "Anatoly, stop with this. What did he say? Is there a problem?"

"Not for you, my friend."

"Anatoly." Vladimir's frustration was patent.

"I just learned what happened myself. It took days to break him down. But, as I said, he broke."

Vladimir realized that the more anxiety he showed the more likely Anatoly was to drag this out. It was a torture technique. Old ways never changed. He decided to say nothing and let Vladimir ramble on until his point was made. He'd make it, no doubt he would. It was a trait common to all *apparatchiks*, an irresistible urge to reinforce their personal illusions of power by revealing information they alone possessed.

"He has made you a hero, my friend."

Vladimir held his tongue.

"The Butcher had followed the traditional route of many fleeing the world's attention. He found a perfect place to hide until memories faded enough for him to acquire a different, less isolated exile elsewhere. But the Butcher could not resist his basic nature. He came to believe that God had chosen him to change the world. Whether his thinking was the product of mad, messianic delusions or a fundamentally evil soul, I do not know, nor do I care. What I do know is that he planned on killing the abbot of our Russian monastery on Mount Athos. Our leader's favorite cleric."

"My God." Vladimir didn't even realize he'd spoken.

"Well put. Our leader thinks of him as God's emissary on earth today. He personally called to congratulate me for obtaining the information that saved his friend's life. Of course, I told him it was you who actually was responsible for saving the abbot's life."

Yeah, I bet, Vladimir thought. *I wonder if you even mentioned my name.*

"Under the circumstances I thought it would be unwise to kill the policeman who passed on the information that saved the abbot's life. Although Zacharias no longer is of concern to this world—the exact words of the order were, 'Send that bastard back to his maker in Hell'—passions still are running high on how close he came to killing our abbot. We wouldn't want someone thinking you were working with Zacharias as an accomplice and sought to murder the policeman and his family as revenge for exposing your friend and ally, the Balkan Butcher."

Vladimir's heart skipped three beats. Only two people on earth could validate that it was Vladimir who passed on the information. One was Anatoly, the other the Greek cop. He'd carefully kept all mention of his own name out of the original e-mail to Moscow. And his call to Anatoly ordering the immediate elimination of the cop—and the opening words of this conversation—were undoubtedly recorded by this snake, to be edited into who knows what form. Yes, Anatoly was telling him what could happen to him, and what would happen…unless—

"So, my dear friend, Vladimir, don't you think all of this wonderful news is deserving of a reward? And certainly one far greater than you offered me to eliminate the one who saved the life of our leader's spiritual guide?"

"How much?"

"How much is one of your many private jets or boats worth? Surely you do not need them all?"

Vladimir swallowed hard. "I will expect you personally to inform our leader in my presence that I am the one responsible for saving the abbot's life."

"Absolutely."

"Goodbye."

"Goodbye, my friend." There was a tinge of harshness to the words.

Vladimir hung up, drew in and let out a deep breath. He'd been blackmailed before and no doubt would be again. That was the price of success in Russia. He looked at his watch. He thought to call Barbara in Athens. No, she said she would be at the hospital with her friend, the cop's wife. The woman had just had a baby.

He shook his head as if tossing away all thoughts of what he'd planned to do to that family. I must send them a gift.

◇◇◇

"He's absolutely the most beautiful baby in the world."

"Thank you, Maggie." Lila was glowing.

"Frankly, I think he looks like Tassos," said Kouros.

Tassos smiled. "That's the blessing of having a Winston Churchill-like face. All babies look like you."

"When are you going home?" Maggie's eyes were glued on the baby snuggled next to Lila on the bed.

"Tomorrow morning."

"She wanted to go home tonight, but her parents insisted she stay the night. After all, the baby was only born this afternoon," said Andreas.

"Parents. Forever protecting their children." Lila stroked her baby's forehead. "Now I understand."

"Where are your parents?" asked Tassos.

"They left with my mother." Andreas answered for her.

Lila's eyes stayed on her baby. "They said they wanted to make room for our friends."

"Maybe I should leave," said Kouros.

"Don't worry, there's plenty of room. I'm only expecting one more. Barbara should be here any minute."

Andreas glanced at Maggie.

"Oh, Chief, in all the excitement I forgot I have a message for you." Maggie handed him a note.

THE PARTY FINALLY RETURNED TO ATHENS EARLY THIS MORNING AND SWEARS NOTHING EVER HAPPENED. YOU'VE BEEN HAD. OR RATHER, NOT.

Andreas stared at Maggie. "Is this for real?"

"Absolutely."

"Is what for real?" asked Lila.

"Us." Time to change the subject, thought Andreas. "I still don't know what to make of yesterday."

"Or what you made of my car."

Andreas shrugged. "Sorry."

Lila looked at the baby and smiled. "All is forgiven."

"Pick a name yet?" asked Maggie.

"Andreas' father's name," said Lila.

"Good choice." Tassos smiled.

"What was it?" asked Kouros.

"Tassos," said Maggie.

Kouros smiled. "Poor kid."

Tassos smacked Kouros lightly on the back of his head. "So what happened yesterday that has you wondering?"

Andreas gave a quick version of the Protos' visit. "All I know for sure is that this case is closed. Too many intrigues for my little cop mind to handle. Let the church sort out its own affairs."

"Do you think the Protos was telling the truth?" asked Tassos.

"Who knows? Not even sure if I care."

"Why would he lie?" asked Maggie.

Andreas shrugged. "If the Russians were embarrassed and the Ecumenical Patriarch relocated to Mount Athos, that would knock the position of *protos* off the top of the Holy Mountain. Can you imagine two popes sharing the same Vatican?"

Maggie gestured no. "But this *protos* wouldn't care."

"How can you say that?" said Andreas.

"Well, for one thing, the Protos never has to worry about an Ecumenical Patriarch moving to Mount Athos during his lifetime."

Andreas stared at Maggie. "You never fail to amaze me, but how can you possibly know that this Ecumenical Patriarch will outlive the Protos?"

"I don't, wise ass, but remember, I'm the one who checked out Vassilis' background. In addition to our current Ecumenical Patriarch, Vassilis was one of only two surviving graduates of the Halki School. That makes his schoolmate, the Protos, the only living person qualified under Turkish law to serve as the next Ecumenical Patriarch in Constantinople. To him it wouldn't matter whether the Russians were embarrassed or not, for he'd be the next Ecumenical Patriarch, if he wanted the position."

Andreas kept staring at her, then shook his head and let out a long sigh. "I give up. I'm not going to delude myself into thinking I'll ever figure this out. All I know is the bad guys have all gone bye-bye."

"Or so we hope," said Tassos.

Lila smiled at Andreas. "That reminds me of our conversation with the Protos."

"Let's not get into that again, please. I'm anxious enough at being a new father without worrying about being a pawn in church wars."

"No, I'm not talking about that part of the conversation. I'm talking about where he impressed me with his candor."

"I must have missed it."

"Well, it wasn't something he said directly and, besides, you had other things on your mind…like my car." Lila laughed. "It was when he was grasping for a word to describe something very important to him, one that explained why he needed your help. The word he chose seemed odd to me and when I hinted at what else he might have meant he changed the subject. I didn't pursue it out of respect."

Lila glanced down at the baby, smiled, and looked up at Andreas. "The Protos said, 'I live amidst a world that many think is *unsoiled*. Whether or not I agree is not important, only that I realize no one from that world could have done what you did.'"

"Yeah, I know, he was saying he needed a sinner to deal with sinners."

"No, he wasn't calling you a sinner. He was describing his world, one 'that many think is *unsoiled*.' Whether intended or not, 'unsoiled' is an anagram for another word." She paused to kiss the baby's forehead.

She did not look up when she said, "'I live amid a world that many think is…' *delusion*. 'Whether or not I agree is not important, only that I realize no one from that world could have done what you did.'"

The thought just hung there, as if no one wanted to touch it. Any vigil for the truth seemed further from an answer than when it began. Assuming there was any truth to be found.

Andreas cleared his throat. "Could you guys give us a few minutes?"

They left, leaving Lila and Andreas alone with their baby.

Andreas sat on the edge of the bed, the baby between them. He held Lila's hand. "I guess you were right about what you once said about us."

"And what was that?"

He drew a circle in the air around the three of them. "This is the only thing that 'is what it is.' Us. 'The rest is illusion.' I'm just beginning to realize that. It's why a parent will run into a burning house to save the children." He touched his son's fingers. "Or kill himself to spare them a life of shame."

Lila squeezed his hand. A tear ran down her cheek.

"There was something else in our conversation with the Protos that bothered me. I didn't like the way you both kept referring to me as the 'unborn child's father.'"

She scrunched up her face and sniffled. "Sorry, I just couldn't bring myself to lie about something like that to a holy man."

Andreas nodded. "I understand, I had the same problem. I think we have to come up with another way to describe me, one that's honest."

She shrugged. "Okay, what would you like to be called?"

Andreas paused. "Your husband."

Lila smiled. "Done."

To receive a free catalog of Poisoned Pen Press titles, please contact us in one of the following ways:

Phone: 1-800-421-3976
Facsimile: 1-480-949-1707
Email: info@poisonedpenpress.com
Website: www.poisonedpenpress.com

Poisoned Pen Press
6962 E. First Ave. Ste. 103
Scottsdale, AZ 85251